JUST WHAT I NEEDED

CARDINAL SPRINGS

LAUREN MORRILL

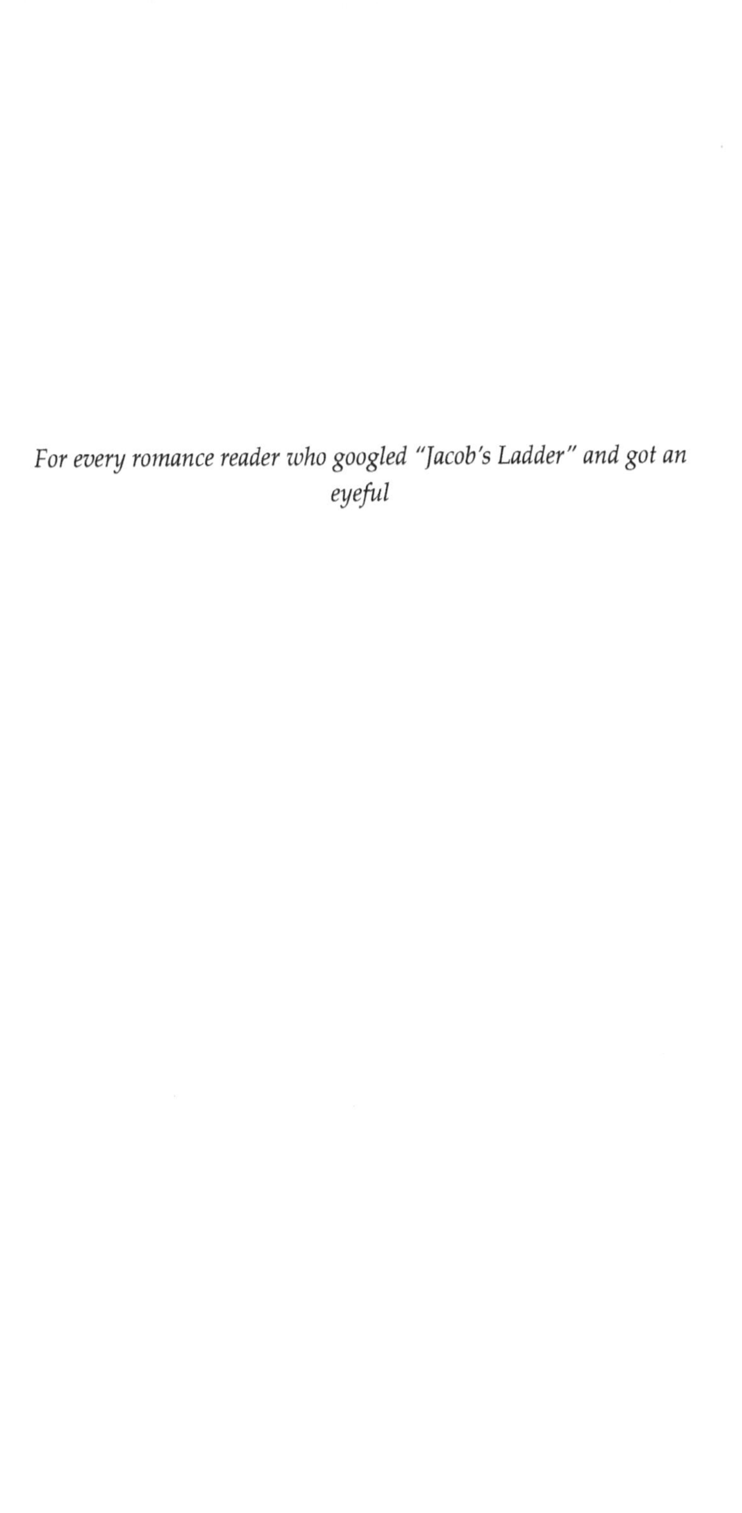

For every romance reader who googled "Jacob's Ladder" and got an eyeful

AUTHOR'S NOTE

Just What I Needed is a romantic comedy with plenty of spice and a touch of angst. This book does feature instances of body shaming (in the past), some instances of parental judgement and body shaming (on page), and brief mentions of diet culture (derogatory). Please take care if any of these are triggering for you.

CHAPTER 1

DAN

R ay-Ban aviators to shield my eyes from the summer sun: $244
iPhone...*fuck,* I don't know what number they're on—
whatever the newest one is: $1568

BMW M850, carbon black with a merino leather interior, purring to
life like a nepo baby's kitten: $115,855

Balance in my checking account: $0

Okay, that's not exactly true—it's actually $436.29, and yes, I know down to the penny at all times—but after what my bank account used to look like, it certainly feels like zero. And without a real job or the ability to get one, that number just keeps ticking closer and closer to nothing.

It's been two years since my life in New York began to fall apart. And it's only gotten worse.

I know I should sell the car. I kick my own ass about it every day. Selling the BMW, replacing it with some old Toyota beater, would give me more than enough padding to get through another year, maybe even two. If I'm smart (and I used to be), I could make that money last until this investigation wraps up and I'm (please, god) cleared.

But every time I think about handing over the keys and giving up this last vestige of my old life, the one where I was smart and successful and didn't have to crash on a series of couches and guest beds in the tiny hometown I couldn't wait to leave…well, I still have the car, so that should tell you how fucking weak I am.

As I turn onto Main Street, I spot Mrs. Eberle, my old high school English teacher, standing on the corner. She lowers her sunglasses and tracks my car as I make the turn. I instinctively sink lower in my seat, trying to avoid her gaze. I don't know what's worse, being investigated by the feds or living under the watchful eyes of your hometown's biggest gossip.

I think I prefer the feds.

The Bluetooth in my car connects to my iPhone, my Favorites tab lighting up the screen. My dad is at the top, then my siblings, descending in age: Archer, twins Felix and Owen, and then my little sister, Grace. The sixth name on the list is the only one that doesn't belong to family.

Marcel Lewis.

My attorney.

I tap his name and brace myself.

"Dan the man!" Marcel's deep voice booms through the high-end sound system. The speakers are so good it sounds like he's sitting in the passenger seat. "Tell me something good!"

If only…

"Change of address," I grunt. I press the accelerator at a stop sign, the car leaping forward with the grace of a prima ballerina. The two blocks that make up downtown Cardinal Springs blur by.

"Seriously? I thought you were done with the couch-surfing life. You were staying in that hockey player's apartment, right?"

Until this morning, that was certainly the case. But then I turned on the kitchen faucet to rinse the glass from my protein shake, and a creak, crash, and gush sounded from the bathroom. It took a shockingly short time for the burst pipe in the ceiling to flood the floor of the tiny bathroom, then start working on the bedroom.

Two hours, a call to the landlord, and an emergency plumber's visit later, my apartment—well, the apartment I've been borrowing from my sister's recently retired pro hockey player boyfriend, because I can't afford my own place on no income and a rapidly dwindling bank account—was damp as a bayou and had no running water.

Leaving me once again in need of a place to stay.

It took an hour and the entire McBride family phone tree to find someplace. Archer's house is being treated for termites, so he's bunking in our dad's only guest room, eliminating both of those options. Felix and Owen only have a couch available, which is barely long enough for my six-foot-two frame. And even if I wanted to destroy my back and shoulders by crashing there, Owen and his new girlfriend, Wyatt, are spending as many nights together as possible these days, and the walls in that house are too thin for my taste. Just last week Felix confessed to sleeping with earplugs *and* a white noise machine, and his bedroom is on the opposite end of the house.

I was seconds from demolishing what remained of my savings and booking a room at the Motel 6 out by the highway when Grace solved my problem.

Or created a whole new one—I'm still not entirely sure. I grit my teeth as I make a left toward the west side of town.

"Plumbing issue," I explain to my lawyer.

There's a long silence, and I know Marcel is hoping he'll goad me into saying more by leaving the space. But he should know better by now. I prefer silence to almost anything else.

"You being charged by the word?" he asks.

If I were, I'm pretty sure I wouldn't be able to afford any more.

Marcel's sigh reverberates through the speakers. "Okay. Where are you headed?"

"Eight-oh-five Henderson Road," I say, turning onto the street in question. It's lined with mature oak trees and nearly identical brick cracker box houses, all built in the fifties during central Indiana's postwar baby boom.

"Thanks for letting me know," Marcel says over the sound of typing. "You doing good?"

I shrug before I remember that Marcel can't see me. "Fine."

"Any reason for me to push you further on that?"

"Nope," I reply, popping the *p* for maximum effect. I'm very good at giving off social cues that say *I don't want to talk.* Unfortunately people aren't always very good at picking up on them.

Another sigh from Marcel. Why did I end up with the only lawyer in New York who thinks he's also a therapist? Well, because after the finance community declared me persona non grata, Marcel was the only attorney who'd return my calls. And that's probably only because he's married to Jameson Lewis (formerly Lander), my roommate at Princeton. So even though I'd rather stick my hand in a tiger's mouth than discuss my personal life, I have to share all manner of secrets with Marcel. That's what happens when you're part of a federal investigation. For example, the federal government likes to know where they can find you at all times.

Otherwise they might track you down at a child's first birthday party that you're forced to attend out of family obligation (entirely against my will, I might add—my family might be worse than the feds). That will quickly make you the center of attention, and as someone who prefers not to be perceived by anyone *ever*, that's basically all the levels of hell in one afternoon.

"Okay, well, thanks for the update. I'm hoping to finally get this deposition on the books soon. Do you want to schedule a Zoom so I can run you through the questions?"

"I'm good."

"That's what I figured you'd say. You're my one client who I never have to worry will say too much. Honestly, you should run a training course on how to keep your answers short," Marcel says, and when I don't reply, he chuckles. "I know you're totally focused on this case wrapping up, but please make sure to live your life while you're waiting."

"That a message from Jameson?" I ask.

"Of course," Marcel says. "He misses you at dinner."

"Tell him I said hi," I reply, because it's a better answer than *What life could I possibly be living in the middle of Indiana?*

"I will. Take care of yourself," Marcel says, and I end the call.

I pull over in front of the third house on the street, distinguishable from the others only by the red tulips blooming in the front garden and the shiny new pink paint on the front door. A bright blue older model Prius is parked in the short driveway, a sticker affixed to the back that says IF YOU CAN READ THIS, THANK A TEACHER.

I'll be crashing at Carson Webber's house—she's my little sister's childhood best friend—for however long it takes the elderly plumber working on the leak to finish the job. Burt has a flip phone, takes only checks, and moves with the urgency of an exhausted sloth, so I'm thinking it'll be a good long while.

I take a deep breath, steeling myself to exit the blessed silence of my car. Because I know that it will not be silent inside the house. I'm grateful Carson is taking me in. It's just that Carson is…well, I don't know what she is. She's like her pink front door or those happy little tulips in human form. She's always smiling, always talking, always wearing bright colors. Her cheeks are always flushed pink to match her pouty lips.

And I could deal with all that—I'm well practiced at existing in a world full of extroverts—but Carson drives me a different kind of crazy. Every time I'm around her, I feel like a fucking cartoon bunny, ready to sit at the feet of the singing princess and bask in her glow. The way I feel physically pulled into her orbit every time I'm around her is fucking wild. It takes the kind of focus I usually bring to work or the gym to keep myself from getting too close to her. She's like a pesky craving to tamp down, same as the kind I get when I pass a hot dog cart on the street in Manhattan. And I allow myself only one hot dog a year, on opening day from my season ticket seat on the Mets first base line.

But those tickets are long gone, and I missed opening day this year.

Still, as I end the call with Marcel and climb out of the car, dragging my duffel bag across the center console, I let myself linger on the image of my fingers sinking into the flesh of her soft, round hips. I imagine her pretty pink lips. I imagine twirling one of her thick blond curls around my finger.

I let my mind run wild as I take those few steps up to the door, and for a moment, my life isn't a total shit show. I'm able to imagine I haven't let down myself, my family, my friends. That I'm not dangerously close to an indictment, to prison.

For just a moment, I feel fucking amazing just thinking about her.

But by the time I'm face-to-face with that pink front door, I've shoved it all back down. Carson is bad for me, and I have plenty of experience resisting things that are bad for me.

And even if I did let myself indulge, let myself feast on her like the most decadent of cheat meals, *then* I'd have to confront the fact that as bad as she is for me, I'm way worse for her.

She may be a decadent chocolate tart, but *me*?

I'm poison.

And with that final firm reminder, I hoist my duffel over my shoulder and knock on the pink front door.

CHAPTER 2
CARSON

'm going to kill Grace.

No, I won't kill her. Instead I'll go through her bookshelf and tear every sex scene out of her romance novels. I'll mix her setting spray with blue food coloring. I'll replace all her bras with identical ones a size too small so she has to dig underwire out of her tits all day but can't figure out why.

And why would I do this to my best friend in the whole wide world, whom I've known since the day we were born?

Because thanks to her, the hottest man I've ever seen is standing in my living room, and I can't stop word-vomiting at him.

"Sorry for the weird mishmash of décor," I say, trying to make eye contact with the silent, hulking Dan McBride. Unfortunately, as soon as my eyes meet those blue-gray stunners, I feel a hot, patchy flush start to creep up my neck, and I immediately look away. "My parents gave me this house after they won the lottery and moved to Boca Raton to live near my aunt Frida, and I know it's been, like, six months, but exorcising the Midwest nineties décor hell that lives in every corner of every room has been a real journey. I mean, do you know how hard it is to get wallpaper borders off the wall? I did not! I spent a solid month picking at them while watching three seasons of *Law & Order*, and there's *still* residue." I point up near the ceiling, where a white film stuck to the burgundy paint job still haunts me.

I make another attempt to look at Dan, who is standing stock-still on the old beige carpet, his duffel slung over his shoulder. He's infuriatingly quiet, and as a kindergarten teacher, I'm used to trying to draw people out. With him, that usually involves way too much talking, but maybe I should try the sock puppet that worked so well on Jaxon Holmes last year.

Oh crap, I've been quiet too long. I've made things weird.

Dan flexes his jaw, which does hot, molten things to my insides, and I send my gaze back to the last vestiges of the wallpaper border.

This is why I'm going to kill Grace. Because I cannot be normal around Dan McBride, who is now my temporary roommate. He makes me nervous, with all that height and that jawline and those smoldering eyes that seem to see beneath the layers of me to some kind of truth even I don't know. He is absolutely the most beautiful human I've ever seen in real life, a real solid hunk of a man whose sculpted muscles are apparent even in a white dress shirt, untucked over a pair of khaki shorts with an inseam so short it borders on slutty. My eyes drop down to his tanned, muscular legs.

White tennis shoes with no socks?

Definitely slutty.

Whenever Dan is around, I have exactly two modes: panicked silence and panicked word vomit. There is no in-between. I simply cannot be normal around him.

And today, apparently, my nervous word vomit setting is turned up to eleven.

Fabulous.

"I'm really trying to make the house my own, but I don't want to make any rash decisions and wind up regretting them. I mean, it feels like minimalism was the thing three minutes ago, and now it's cottagecore cozy maximalism. And I want the place to feel like mine, you know? Not some Pinterest board come to life. Anyway, I'm working on it. But you probably don't care that the couch is mint green gingham and you can still see the stain from where I threw up white chocolate–covered Oreos on the middle cushion when I was nine. I was watching the Hannah Montana movie at the time, and I still feel nauseated when I hear 'The Climb.'"

My whole body cringes at the confession. Any attempt to keep my embarrassment from turning me the color of a summer strawberry is now completely futile. I would burn this whole house down around me if it meant I could escape this moment.

But all I get from Dan is a minuscule quirk of his left eyebrow.

Jesus Christ, tighten it up, Carson.

I squeeze my fists until I'm sure my nails have permanently branded little crescent moons into my palms, and then I try to smile.

"I'll show you to your room," I say, hoping I look pleasant and not, you know, feral.

I lead him down the little hallway past the kitchen, toward the three small bedrooms in the cramped house. At least now that I'm walking, my body seems too occupied to offer up any conversational embellishments.

Oh, wait, no. I feel more words coming a split second before they spill from my mouth.

"I'm actually on my way out, so you can get settled in peace. I have a date. With this guy I matched with on Hinge? We're going roller skating, which was his idea, and I'm taking that as a good sign, because I cannot meet one more man at one more brewery and drink one more extra-hoppy IPA. I don't even *like* beer, much less level-ten beer," I say as I lead him past my bedroom door, which I thankfully remembered to close. Not only does the room feature all the furniture I've had since I was nine—twin bed and teal chevron comforter included—but the entire contents of my closet is spread across the floor after trying to pick an outfit for said date.

I stop at the second door, the guest room that doubled as my mother's sewing room before she relocated to Florida. I step aside and let him step in.

"Feel free to make yourself at home. Move anything around, whatever. There's a closet and a dresser, and in the hall linen closet you'll find extra blankets and bath towels. The bathroom is across the hall. We'll share it."

And then I nearly fall over as a cascade of realizations hits me. Like that I'm going to get naked in the exact same shower where he's going to get naked—not at the same time, of course, but that doesn't mean the images that spring to mind are less vivid. Images of hot water sluicing over what I imagine to be an incredibly cut body.

Am I sweating? I think I might be sweating. I worry I'm about to start audibly sizzling when the honk of a car horn saves me.

"That's him!" I cry, my voice cracking. I swallow hard. Clear my throat. "My date," I croak.

For the first time, Dan's face betrays an actual emotion. Which one it is, I'm not sure. But his eyebrow is quirked *high*.

"He's picking you up?" he asks. It may be the longest string of words I've ever heard him say.

"Yeah. Carpooling." I gulp, trying to keep from gasping in a breath. "For the environment."

Oh my god, could I be any more of a goober?

Dan's face goes shadowed. Then he holds out his hand.

"Phone," he says, somehow conveying an entire paragraph, punctuation and all, in that one word.

I look down and realize I'm already holding my phone, flipping it over and over in my hand like a worry stone. Silent panic is setting in (and frankly, it's about dang time), so I unlock it and pass it to him. He taps the screen several times, then passes it back to me.

"My number," he says. "Call if you need to."

I would not have been more shocked if he'd asked for my phone to record a TikTok dance.

"Thanks," I say, or at least I think I say it. My ears are ringing too loudly to hear my own voice. How long will he be staying here? And can I avoid having a stroke for that amount of time? Will there come a point when I'll get used to him? When I can actually look him in the eye and talk to him like the grown woman I allegedly am? Because right now the answer feels like a resounding *heck no*.

My date—Gabe is his name—honks again. Dan sucks in a breath through his clenched teeth, the sound going directly into the black lace panties I picked out on the off chance that Gabe is cute and can put a few coherent sentences together. I cross my fingers for this as I turn and bolt away from Dan, because my *god* do I need to get laid.

CHAPTER 3
DAN

I wait until I hear the front door slam before I stalk back to the living room. I stand just to the side of the front window and watch Carson scurry around the front of a bright red lifted pickup truck with a grille kit that looks more suited to an African safari than a jaunt through rural Indiana.

Not only did that motherfucker sit his ass in his truck and honk for her to come out, he doesn't even get out of his car to open her door.

I try to put eyes on the guy through his tinted windows, but all I can see is a baseball cap and a pair of those stupid wraparound sunglasses that look like ski goggles.

Carson pulls the door open and climbs into the passenger seat, a big step up for such a short girl. As soon as her ass hits the seat, the truck starts chugging like a steam engine and pulls away from the curb.

I can't believe I'm going to be living in a house with this goddamn ray of sunshine, with those jeans that curve perfectly over her ass and the thick strawberry-blond curls that drape over her milky-white shoulders, the tips of them dipping into her cleavage.

And I can't believe I'm standing here, watching her drive

away with a strange guy who has a redneck truck and the manners of a teenage incel.

I shouldn't care this much.

I *hate* that I care this much.

Wanting her the way I do is deeply inconvenient.

I need Burt to fix that pipe fast, because my life is far too much of a disaster without being this distracted by Carson Webber.

CHAPTER 4
CARSON

I am roller skating alone to "The Thong Song."

One perk of my verbal breakdown in front of Dan was that by the time I climbed into the car with Gabe, my Hinge date/punishment from Satan himself, I wasn't the least bit nervous.

Which was great, because it left me free to notice every single red flag that Gabe pulled out of his pocket, unfurled, and waved around like a high school color guard champion.

First he took me to a burger place near the skating rink, where he ordered *for* me and picked the veggie burger and a side salad because—and this is a direct quote—"I know you're probably trying to stay in a calorie deficit."

Red flag.

He spent the entire meal telling me all about the customized features of his truck, including how much they'd cost.

Bright red flag.

He did not ask me a single question.

Red flag under a red spotlight.

He didn't even listen when I talked, and I know this because even though I told him I'd been roller skating many *many* times, he still said he'd "teach me the basics."

14

Red flag dripping with the blood of my enemies.

And you know what? He didn't even teach me. I could have played dumb for an hour and had a cute little lesson from him, maybe even one that ended with our hands all over each other before we raced out of the rink to tumble into his bed (I really *really* need to get laid).

But no. He couldn't even follow through on being condescending. When we got to the roller rink, he threw on his skates (which he'd brought from home, leaving me at the counter alone to rent my own) and immediately took off. He began to sprint around the rink, showing off his jam skating skills like he was nine and I was his mommy. I could tell all he wanted was for me to tell him how great he was.

Meanwhile, my knees are shaking and by back is screaming, because okay, yeah, I've roller-skated a lot, but not since Jenny Milford's birthday party in the fifth grade when I tried to do the limbo and split my pants.

But after a few laps, it starts to come back to me. I'm getting comfortable, and since I've been left to my own devices, I decide to focus on being good at this. Why not brush up on my skills? Get in a little exercise while I'm at it. Not because I need to lose weight, *Gabe*, but because moving your body is good for you. It's why I start every morning in my kindergarten classroom with a little dance party.

So despite the fact that this date absolutely will not be ending with me in Gabe's bed—which I'm sure is a twin mattress on the floor with a navy-blue fitted sheet and a single pillow, no case—I'm determined for the night not to be a total loss.

I'm just starting to attempt wobbly crossovers in the corner when I look up and realize Gabe has left the floor.

"Looking for your date?"

The voice comes from just over my shoulder, making me jump. I nearly go down in a heap as a five-year-old in Rollerblades whizzes by, but I right myself at the last second.

"Sorry about that. Didn't mean to scare you," the voice says.

Then the body connected to the voice appears in front of me, skating backward. It belongs to a tiny punk-rock pixie with a purple bob, a septum ring, and a black-and-white striped referee shirt hanging over a tattered black denim skirt. She's skating backward as easily as I might walk down the street. "Your date—he's on his phone over by the snack bar."

She points, and I spot Gabe right away, the neon NACHOS sign reflecting off the sunglasses he's got perched on the back of his neck. Sure enough, he's hunched over his glowing phone.

"Seems like a real dill hole," she says, doing backward crossovers as we enter the turn. "Tell me he's not your boyfriend."

"Hinge date," I tell her, embarrassed that I'm slightly out of breath.

She very impressively mimes vomiting into her cupped hands and throwing it in his direction, then glances down at my wheels. "Nice crossovers," she says with an approving nod, then executes a little jump spin and takes off after some teens who keep doing baseball slides in the skating lane.

I feel like one of my kindergarteners who's just been told what a good job they did finger painting. Her compliment fuels me.

I skate a few more laps. Once I decide to forget my date and focus on my skating, my skills improve. Feeling a little more comfortable, I try to channel the speed skaters I've seen on the Olympics when I hit the turns, my legs crossing over, my knees bent as I lean. I pick up more speed, managing to keep pace with a group of middle school boys. (Granted, they skate half their laps backwards, but I'm still calling it a win.) I'm starting to sweat a little with the effort, but I don't care. Gabe isn't going to be peeling these jeans off of me, so there's no point in worrying about my appearance anymore.

And then Gabe reappears, bobbing to the beat of 50 Cent as he skates, his phone still clutched in his fist.

"Not a big skater, huh?" he asks, doing a few little spins around me that put me off balance. He holds out a hand to steady me, but I decide in that moment that I'd rather fall face-first onto the wood floor than touch this man.

"Not since fifth gra—"

He nods like he's listening but then immediately cuts me off. "Hey, listen. So, I don't want to be a dick or anything, but, uh, I got a text from my ex? We've been on and off for, like, three years. We broke up in April because I spilled a Big Gulp on her laptop after eating a gummy and I, like, laughed? She was so mad. I probably love her, but I don't know." He pauses, like he's actually trying to figure it out. While on roller skates. On a date. With me. And apparently he doesn't, because he shrugs. "She wants to talk, so I'm going to run over to this bar down the road to meet up with her."

And then I do fall. Hard. My feet fly out from under me, and I land right on my butt.

"Holy shit!" Gabe says, slamming on his brakes and skating back to where I've collapsed in a heap. He reaches down a hand, but I ignore it and climb to my feet.

It's not until I'm upright that I manage to say anything. Unfortunately, it's not a hearty *eff you*, which is what he deserves. I make it a point not to swear much during the school year—it keeps me from slipping up in the classroom when a student inevitably drops an open jar of paint on the carpet or throws up onto my lap. But there usually comes a point during summer break when I start to get lazy, and out come the f-bombs.

Luckily for Gabe (and unfortunately for me), the school year ended only two weeks ago, so I haven't accessed my treasure trove of curse words yet.

So instead of dressing him down, I say, "You drove me here."

He scrubs at the back of his neck, having the sense to look at least a little sheepish about ditching his date to meet up with his ex.

"Yeah, you could, uh, Uber? Or, like, if you can't get one, just message me on Hinge when you're ready to go. I could, like, come back and get you."

My mouth drops open. "Oh, really? You'd do that? You'd leave a bar meetup with your ex-girlfriend to pick up the date you ditched and drive her home? Wow. *Wow.* You're, like, *such* a good guy."

Gabe's nose wrinkles. "I'm sensing a little sarcasm."

That loosens the lid on my personal swear jar just enough.

"Sense this, asshole," I say, and then shove him right in the chest with both hands as hard as I can. His feet fly up damn near over his head, and he lands flat on his back with a dull thud, a shockingly high-pitched *oof* escaping his lips.

Seeing him on his ass, small children leaping over his splayed legs, doesn't wipe about the fury I feel.

But it helps a little.

"Hey, we okay over here?" The skate referee comes skidding over, assessing Gabe, who is still flat on the floor.

"She pushed me!" he cries, sounding for all the world like a small child.

"I was talking to her, ya jackwagon," skate girl says, then turns to me. "Want me to eighty-six him?"

I glare down at Gabe, who looks like if they made Morgan Wallen-branded Zyn pouches. I try for a moment to find even a hint of the guy I matched with. I can barely remember what it was about his profile that made me swipe right. Maybe it was the dimples, or the fact that there were no fish in any of his photos. I remember that he messaged me using full sentences and punctuation, which seemed promising.

My god, the bar is in hell.

"He was just leaving anyway," I tell her.

"Oh good." She grins down at him like she wants to eat him for lunch. "I love when the trash takes itself out."

"Bitch," Gabe mutters as he climbs to his feet and skates toward the exit.

"Do you think he meant me or you? Oh, I hope he meant me. I collect pathetic men calling me a bitch like Pokémon cards." Skate girl grins and sticks out her hand. "I'm Violet, by the way."

"Carson," I say, then groan. "Crap. I've got to get an Uber."

"Nice to meet you, Carson. But why are you leaving?" She nods down at my rental skates. "You were just starting to get good."

"Well, my date peaced out to go on another date, so it seems like a good time to call it a night."

She scoffs. "Do not let that skid mark masquerading as a man ruin your evening. You're wearing roller skates on a Friday night, and you've got nobody to answer to but yourself. Be your own date."

And then, like a little punk-rock fairy godmother, she disappears.

Well, actually she races over to a kid who's about to skate onto the floor with a fountain soda, herding him back off the hardwood.

I nearly follow her, imagining thunking my skates onto the counter and sinking into the back seat of the nearest Uber.

But then "Call Me Maybe" comes blasting from the ancient sound system, a hint of static from the mounted speakers giving the song even more pep. My body reacts like I'm a deep cover spy and the song is my signal. I push off with my neon-orange wheels and pick up speed. I dig my feet into the floor to the beat, mouthing along with the words, my hips swaying on their own.

"Carly Rae Jepson works every time," Violet says, skating up beside me, and there's no judgment in her voice. She sings along with the chorus for a few bars. "I had the DJ throw that one on to keep you going. Have you ever thought about playing roller derby?"

I blink at her, my chest heaving with exertion. "What?"

"Roller derby," Violet says. "Roller skates, full contact, fun? You familiar?"

"I went to see it once in college," I tell her, recalling the outing with my sorority pledge class. I remember thinking it looked cool and also a little terrifying. I know I don't have nearly enough guts or tattoos to do it myself, to say nothing of my athletic ability.

"I coach the team here, and I think you should try out."

"Oh, I don't really do sports," I say.

Violet scoffs. "That sounds like a story you tell yourself because of public school gym class trauma, but I'm telling you, you've got natural form and an ass that could lay a bitch out."

I nearly look over my shoulder to see if she's talking about someone else. There's no way those words are meant for me. "I don't—"

Violet holds up a finger, and I notice her purple sparkly manicure, which matches her hair. "Keep doing laps. When you're done, I'll give you a flyer and you can think about it. Just...don't say no yet."

———

Two hours later, my legs are burning, there's sweat pooling in my bra, and I'm pretty sure I've got a monster blister beneath my big toe.

But I skated.

Fast.

And now I'm *very* drunk.

Oops.

I didn't mean to get this drunk, obviously. Or drunk at all. But over the last two hours, something strange happened to me. As I was whizzing across the floor, my hair flying out behind me, I suddenly felt...free. Light and fast and *free*. I haven't felt like this since that fifth-grade birthday party, before middle school started middle-schooling *hard* and I was suddenly behind. Not pretty enough or thin enough or cool enough not to care that I wasn't pretty or thin.

And I've felt like I was playing catch-up ever since. Through high school and college and even now, as a full-grown adult, still living in the house I grew up in (though now without my parents, fortunately). I still feel like there's a destination I haven't arrived at. A destination that I can't even seem to find on a map.

But tonight? Tonight I skated so fast that I almost felt like I saw something shimmering in the distance, some kind of oasis I might be able to reach. All I needed to get there were these skates and my own two legs.

And I did *not* need Gabe.

So I skated and skated and skated until the lights went up and the music stopped, the floor cleared, and I was the last one standing.

Well, except for Violet, who told me to hang around so she could give me that roller derby flyer and also offered to share her flask of tequila.

IPAs are not my friend, but tequila?

Tequila and I are *besties*.

"I didn't realize you were such a cheap date," Violet says as she strides over to the carpet-covered bench where I'm sitting, clutching my purse in one hand and her nearly empty flask in the other.

"I'm *sssssory*," I slur, then hiccup, which makes me laugh. It's been a while since I drank this much this fast on an empty stomach (the veggie burger I had with Gabe was *terrible*, and I barely had three bites...or maybe it was just the company that was unappetizing). I have to work to calm my wicked case of church giggles. "I need to get an Uber," I say after a deep breath, still laughing.

"Girl, I have listened to way too many true crime podcasts to put your drunk ass in an Uber alone."

"But my date *left me*," I remind her, and from the way she flinches, I fear I may have turned my personal volume knob up too high.

"I can drive you. Where do you live?"

"Cardinal Springs. How do I know *you're* not a murderer?"

"Because something like five percent of murderers are women, and you already cashed in your good odds on not having to go home and have disappointing sex with that jam skate ding-dong. But good job asking the question. You've got fight in you." Violet taps her phone. "Unfortunately, I promised to pick up my room-mate from work, and she doesn't get off for another forty-five minutes, so can you hang out until then? I won't make it to Cardinal Springs and back before she gets off."

I'm teetering right at the edge of the sleepy phase of drunken-ness, and the musty-smelling carpeted bench is looking like a lovely little spot for a catnap when all of a sudden, the memory of a strong pair of hands taking my phone pops into my brain. I remember that sharp jawline, the tawny color of his skin, like he spends hours every day in the sun and not in some bank office. Those deep blue-gray eyes that always look stormy, and the buzz cut. What is it about the buzz cut? I have never in my life been interested in a man who looked like he just got drafted, but Dan McBride? Hello, sailor.

I open my phone for the first time tonight, the screen filling with the brand-new contact information he entered.

Call if you need to.

My stomach flips, and with this much tequila swimming around in it, that could go either way. A mean little voice in my head starts in with *He didn't mean it, he doesn't want to hear from you,* but drunk Carson is somehow more rational than sober Carson. Drunk Carson thinks, *Dan McBride doesn't say anything he doesn't mean.* Because Dan McBride doesn't usually say much of anything at all. Not like Goober Gabe, who talks *a lot* and prob-ably never means a word of it.

I babble as I type. "I have a ride! I can call my best friend's brother! He's my new roommate and he said to call him and he gave me his number and I can call him! He has a car and everything!"

CHAPTER 5
DAN

had a feeling Carson was tipsy when I got her texts, but I am not prepared for the swaying, smiling woman, cheeks flushed and curls limp around her shoulders, slumped on the curb outside the roller rink.

I park my car, my headlights landing on her and the tiny woman with purple hair standing beside her.

"Who are you?" the tiny woman barks as soon as I'm out of the car.

"Dan," I tell her.

"And you're here for…" She arches an eyebrow like this is a test.

"Carson." I glance down at my sister's best friend. She's smiling up at me, her deep-blue eyes a little watery, and something in my chest goes watery too.

"It's okay, Violet. He's not a murderer," Carson slurs. She pushes herself up from the curb and nearly makes it to standing before pitching forward. I throw my arms out to catch her, but the tiny woman—Violet, apparently—beats me to it. She wraps an warm around Carson's waist to right her. Then she lifts her phone and snaps a photo of me, the flash lighting up the night, blinding me.

"If she's not home in forty-five minutes, I'm sending this photo to the cops."

I tower over this woman. Could probably do biceps curls with her. But something about her tone tells me she knows plenty of ways to hurt me that I'd never see coming.

I respect it.

For the first time since I got Carson's texts, filled with silly little typos and too many exclamation points, I let out a sigh of relief. The thought of her being drunk and at the mercy of that idiot asshole in a truck, in need of a ride in the middle of the night, had every muscle in my body tensed for a fight. A big part of me spent the drive here prepared to pull up and throw hands. I'm already in legal trouble, so what's a little more? Marcel would lose it, but I think it would be worth it. But it's clear that Carson found someone to look out for her until I could get here.

"Thanks for staying with me, Violent," Carson says, then reaches her arms high over her head, yawning and stretching like a cat in a sunbeam. "I mean, Violet."

"Hey, my derby name is Violet Rage, so it's all good. You were close," she says. She gently pulls her arm away and lets Carson test her drunk legs. "But seriously, text me when you get home. I put my number in your phone. And I'm serious about tryouts. I think you'd make a killer blocker."

The fact that this tiny fighter plays roller derby makes a lot of sense.

Carson snorts. "Sure thing." She takes two steps toward the passenger door and trips. Violet and I both lunge, but Carson catches herself. "Whoopsie," she giggles, then climbs headfirst into my car.

"Sorry, I gave her a sip from my flask to take the edge off. I didn't think she'd chug," Violet says after the door slams.

"Where's the leash kid who brought her here?"

Violet barks out a laugh. "Hey, I like you," she says, pointing a finger at me. "He ditched her. Apparently his ex came a-calling and he went a-running."

"Thank god," I mutter, though as happy as I am that Carson isn't ending her night with that asshole, I still want to rearrange his face for treating her like that. How did he not take one look at her and know what a lucky fucker he was to spend an evening with her? How did he listen to her voice and not know that he had a rare opportunity?

"She dodged a bullet with that one. He looked like the kind of guy who owns one towel that's never seen the inside of a washing machine." Violet rolls her eyes, then looks at Carson through the window. Her cheek is pressed up against the glass, her eyes fluttering shut like she's seconds from passing out. "Anyway, drive nice. I need her in one piece. I think she might be the secret to our season."

I hope Carson will remember what that's about in the morning, because I have no idea. And I don't want to waste time asking, because Carson is clearly walking that line between sleepy drunk and barfing drunk. And while I'll take care of her no matter what happens, I'd prefer it if my BMW didn't end up smelling like a frat house.

Violet gives me one last look that I think is meant to convey that she knows several places to hide a body, then heads over to a battered old Toyota parked at the end of the empty lot.

I start the car, but before I can pull out of the parking spot, Carson reaches over from the passenger seat and tugs at the collar of my T-shirt.

"Wait, do you have a tattoo?"

I was in bed when she texted, scrolling through old work files, and I threw on an old, worn Princeton shirt. The collar is loose, and it reveals the edge of the abacus I have tattooed below my collarbone. She swipes at the edge of the ink with her warm finger, raising goose bumps on my skin.

"A few," I tell her, clearing my throat and trying not to focus on the spot where she touched me.

"Any I can see?" she asks.

"No."

"Oh," she replies, and I silently kick myself for being so abrupt.

I expect Carson to quickly fall asleep to the purr of the engine, but we're barely to the highway when she starts talking. The words come fast, her drunken brain spitting out sentence fragments, and I only get part of the story.

"—tried to make me eat a veggie burger and, like, whatever, vegetarians, I can get down with a black bean burger but this was clearly fake meat and I'm so sorry to the Earth but fake meat is the *worst*, or at least this was, and he *sucked*, Dan. He, like, sucked out loud. So who cares that he left to meet another woman. I mean, I just feel sorry for *her* because I cannot imagine that Gabe has ever heard about the clitoris, not to mention knowing where to find it. And I'm *done* having sex where I don't come. I know I can! I've done it by myself so many times! But these, these *boys* are just hopeless."

My foot slips off the gas pedal.

And of course now she stops talking, and I worry it's my turn to talk. But I have no idea what to say to that. I mean, she's right —that guy *definitely* doesn't know where the clit is. And burgers made of fake meat *are* terrible. I should probably go with that. If I start talking about the clit with Carson, I'm going to have to pull this car over, because it will be unsafe for me to drive.

But before I can say anything, Carson sighs.

Then sucks in a deep breath.

Then shouts into the night, "I just wanna get *fucked*, you know?!"

Thank god there's no one on the road at this time of night, because I swerve clear into the other lane. Carson doesn't even seem to notice.

God bless tequila.

"Everyone around me is just so disgustingly in love. Grace and Decker, Wyatt and Owen. And I want that. I do. Love seems *great*. But that's not what I *need* right now. I don't need a great love. Great love will find me eventually. It's never too late. I'm not in a rush. But in the *meantime*, I just want to have great sex. And I never have! Not even close! My boyfriend in college, Kyle, was very sweet, but he seemed to think I was made of candy glass and he always called it 'making love,' which, like, gag, but also it was just boring in and out. I have yet to encounter a man on Hinge or even in the wild who can, like, really give it to me, you know? They're all trying too hard or not trying hard enough or chasing after their exes, and I'm so *tired* of these disappointing men and all their stupid large fish."

I'm not sure if *fish* is a euphemism for something or if she's somehow dated a string of disappointing fishermen, but I'm not going to ask. Couldn't even if I wanted to. My voice is trapped in my throat, and I need every ounce of my focus to keep this car on the road. Because while my mouth can't form words, my brain has plenty.

You could give her great sex. You could pull this car over right now and erase all those disappointing memories. The back seat is tight, but you could make it work. For her.

Absolutely the fuck not. Not with my little sister's best friend. Not while I'm living in her house. Not in my car on the side of a rural Indiana highway. Not when there's a semi-decent chance that if their lawyers are good enough and my lawyer is bad enough and a judge is annoyed enough, I could wind up spending some time in a federal prison.

Not when my life is probably over even if I escape conviction, even if this whole case goes away. I'll probably never work in finance again regardless.

But that doesn't stop me from spending a few miles of dark, empty highway imagining what it would be like to show Carson just what she deserves and how much I want her.

It was almost two years ago that I saw her, really *saw* her, for the first time since she was a kid. Everything in New York had just fallen apart. I'd lost my job, my friends, and I'd had to put my condo on the market. The legal implications were only just starting to become clear, and I'd already started draining my bank accounts trying to defend myself. All I knew then was that I needed to get out of the city, and with no money and nowhere else to go, I went to the last place I ever wanted to be.

I went home.

I walked into the Half Pint one warm summer day, and there she was, sitting at the bar with my sister, her golden hair shining in the dim light of the bar.

I didn't recognize her at first, not as the roly-poly little kid who used to spend the night in Grace's room, the two of them making up dance routines and giggling way too loudly. It had been a long time since I'd been home, nearly five years. And I hadn't seen Carson—or maybe I just hadn't noticed her—for years before that.

But there she was. Unmissable now, and a total knockout.

That was how I felt when I saw her: knocked the fuck out.

Over the last two years, as I've moved back and forth between Cardinal Springs and New York, trying to salvage my career and my life, trying to avoid prosecution or prison, I've tried to keep my distance. Tried to ignore the way I feel every time our paths cross in our tiny hometown. I've done what's always come naturally to me—kept quiet.

But now I'm living with her, this luminous woman who just told me she wants to get *fucked*. God, is she asking? Because if that's what she wants—not a great love, but great sex—I could be the perfect person for her. I'm not a permanent fixture here, and I'm sure as shit not the love of her life. I could give her what she needs and then disappear so she could find the great love she desires.

I could just…*fuck her.*

If that's what she wants.

But she has to ask. She has to want it. This can't be about what I want.

As if in answer, I hear the sound of light snoring from the passenger seat.

CHAPTER 6
CARSON

The light streaming in through my curtains feels like blunt pencils poking my eyeballs.

That's the first thing I notice.

The next is that I'm still wearing all my clothes from last night. And one of my shoes.

The third thing I notice is the full glass of water and the bottle of ibuprofen on my bedside table. And considering the fact that I was apparently too drunk to remove both of my shoes, that can only meant that the hangover toolkit was provided by—

I just wanna get fucked.

I groan, my stomach heaving, the night coming back to me in too-bright flashes. Gabe and his stupid truck. The veggie burger from hell. Violet and skating and shoving Gabe to the floor.

And Dan.

In his fancy-pants sports car.

Where I ran my mouth like a faulty water fountain. Where I told him I wanted to get *fucked.*

I groan again, this time praying for death.

When Grace proposed the idea of Dan staying here, my brain created all kinds of nightmare scenarios: having to sit across from him at the breakfast table or passing him in the hallway wrapped in a towel. But not even my anxious, catastrophizing brain could have come up with this.

I roll over, staring at the fifteen-year-old glow-in-the-dark stars that still cling to the popcorn ceiling with ancient sticky tack. Can I possibly stay in this room until Dan's pipes are fixed or he goes back to New York, whichever comes first?

I last approximately thirteen minutes before my bladder informs me that I cannot hide out in my bedroom for the rest of time, or even the rest of the day. I peek out of my bedroom and see Dan's blessedly closed door, so I creep across the hall to the bathroom.

An hour later, I've removed my remaining shoe and last night's clothes and showered off the roller rink smell, but not the throbbing shame of what I said in the car. It keeps playing over and over in my head, a torturous merry-go-round of embarrassment.

I just wanna get fucked I just wanna get fucked I just wanna get fucked.

I shuffle into the kitchen and grab a bowl and the family-size box of Lucky Charms I keep on top of the fridge. The only thing that interrupts my inner monologue is my mother's voice, lecturing me about sugary cereals. *The body needs protein and fiber to start the day, don't you know? And too much sugar leads to a crash.* The fact that there are Lucky Charms on top of this fridge and full-sugar Coke inside it are minor miracles that would've blown ten-year-old Carson's mind, having grown up with overprotective parents who lectured her on the perils of sugar (and basically everything else). My parents may be in Florida, but their words of warning have stayed put, as embedded in the walls of this house as the smell of my mother's favorite apple spice candles.

My parents were in their late forties when I was born, my father an insurance salesman and my mother the church secretary. They'd spent more than ten brutal years trying for a baby, and just when they gave up, I surprised them. They were great parents, and I love them dearly, but I'd be lying if I said I didn't grow up feeling pressured. They monitored everything I ate, everything I watched, everything I listened to, everything I read, and every person I hung out with. My parents knew how precious their one shot at parenthood was, and they were not going to blow it.

And I grew up knowing that I was all they'd get, so I couldn't disappoint them. I followed their rules. I worked hard. I went to church every Sunday, never skipped school, and never snuck out of the house.

It was exhausting.

When I finally left for college and was on my own for the first time, it was really hard to break the habits I'd had drilled into me since birth. I dated, had some sex, and drank some, but never got into too much trouble. And then I graduated, got a job teaching kindergarten in my hometown, and moved back home to save money as I paid off my student loans.

As my parents saw it, when I returned home, I suddenly became a little kid again. Despite the fact that I was twenty-two and gainfully employed with a grown-up job, they were still concerned with what I ate, who I hung out with, my church attendance, and—at least for my mother—my body.

When their ticket hit, we all won the lottery. My parents took their millions down to Boca Raton, where they bought a town house next to my Aunt Frida's and a boat and joined the country club.

And I got this house to live in alone for the first time in my life. And while most things haven't changed much in the eight months I've had it, there have been some small but significant improvements.

Like the Lucky Charms. And the Pop-Tarts. The Snickers ice cream bars and the Double-Stuf Oreos. This kitchen is one that doesn't know the difference between "good" and "bad" foods. This kitchen doesn't count calories or worry about carbs. This kitchen celebrates dessert.

My mother would die, but she has fourteen million dollars to fund whatever fad diet has her in its clutches these days, and for the first time in my life, I don't have to live with it.

It's a nice thought, but the moment I warm to it, the previous night comes roaring back.

I. Just. Wanna. Get. Fucked.

I drop into a chair at the breakfast table in the kitchen and pour myself an extra-large bowl of cereal.

But before I can even scoop up a mouthful, the front door creaks, then slams. The floor shakes from heavy footfalls.

Dan charges into the kitchen, then freezes, standing stock-still on the checkered linoleum.

We stare at each other silently for entirely too long. I can hear my parents' old grandfather clock ticking in the living room. I can hear the birds in the yard. I can practically hear my hair growing, it's so silent in this kitchen.

But I can't look away from him.

He's wearing another pair of slutty little shorts, these meant for the gym, and a long-sleeved athletic shirt. It stretches across his chest and molds to his arms and shoulders like oil paint on a canvas and makes me wonder about the other tattoos he alluded to last night. His legs are thick and muscled (no tattoos there), and the smell of him, sweaty and metallic, somehow doesn't turn my stomach.

I must still be drunk, because he smells so good that I want to lick him.

Lord, I don't need to *get* fucked, I *am* fucked.

"Thanks for the ride," I bark out, like saying the words will keep me from crawling across the floor on my hands and knees and rubbing against him like a cat. "In the car, I mean. The ride in the car. And the ibuprofen."

Dan just nods, dropping his gym bag on the floor and making his way to the sink to mix up a protein shake. I watch him run the faucet, measure out the powder, shake the cup. I brace for him to march silently out of the kitchen, never to speak to me again. I certainly deserve it after last night's little performance. Dan is a person who says virtually nothing, and I went and drunkenly said *everything*.

But he doesn't leave. Instead, he brings his protein shake over to the table, uses his foot to push back the chair beside mine, and drops down into it. The spicy, salty smell of him wafts over me, overpowering the sugary smell of the Lucky Charms.

His eyes drop to my cereal box.

"Do you want some? I can get you a bowl," I say, but he shakes his head.

He may be sitting, but he's not talking.

And suddenly I can't take it anymore. Everything that happened last night is starting to fizz inside me like the volcanos I make with my kindergarteners. All of it just bubbling and climbing and trying desperately to get out. And lord knows I've never been good at keeping things in.

So my mouth opens.

"I'm sorry about last night. About texting you for a ride. And being drunk. Oh my *god*, so drunk. And the talking," I say, then swallow hard. "The *talking*. Ugh, I'm so sorry. I never should have said…any of that. I should have just kept my mouth shut, though that certainly would have been a first. I should probably do that now too, in fact. And I will try hard to do it for as long as you're forced to say here."

I practically bite the tip of my tongue off to stop myself from babbling even more. I turn my gaze to my bowl of cereal, which is rapidly growing soggy, and spoon a bite into my mouth.

Dan clears his throat.

"First of all, you don't need to be sorry about the ride. I told you to call me if you needed me." He takes a long gulp of his protein shake, then sets the cup down on the table with such force that I feel the thud in my chest. His voice is low and steady with just a hint of a growl beneath it. If I weren't in the middle of some serious existential dread, I might find it sexy. "And as for everything else—"

I immediately drop my spoon, sending it splashing into the

milk, and wave him off like air traffic control trying to abort a landing. "Please, no. Let's not—"

"It's fine, Carson," he says. His voice races through my body like I'm sitting on a speaker, and the sound of him saying my name is freaking *delicious.* God, this is quickly becoming a five-alarm, Harry Styles–level teenage crush. I feel like I'm seconds away from doodling Dan's name in a notebook or hanging his photo on the inside of my closet door.

"I appreciate you saying that, but still," I say. "I'm deeply embarrassed by what I said last night."

He's quiet for a beat, and I wonder if he's already used up his daily allotment of words.

"Why?" he asks finally.

Oh man, I wish he *were* out of words, because how do I even answer that?

"Seriously?"

Dan shrugs.

Is this a dream? Surely it is. Because only in a dream would Dan McBride say this many words in a row to me. Only in a dream would his tone possibly, maybe, *potentially* be…inviting, as if my little exclamation in the car wasn't totally unwanted.

No. No *way.*

Still, I should check. So I try a little verbal pinch to see if I wake up.

"Well, first of all, the fact that I brought up my sex life—or lack thereof—to you at all makes me want to walk into the sea. The fact that I phrased it like I did? Even more embarrassing."

There's a beat of silence, and I let myself look at him, only to find him staring directly at me. I'm snared in his gaze. Couldn't look away if I wanted to. And I really, *really* don't want to.

"There's no shame in wanting what you want," he says.

This man's voice must be a defibrillator, because my heart jolts.

"I know that," I say. Then, because he's still looking right at me and I haven't woken up, I try something a little bit bolder. "I'm not ashamed to want it."

"Good," he says, his eyes still boring into me. I feel his gaze like it's a living thing, like it's caressing my skin, and I shiver. "Because you deserve it."

My blood turns to lava in my veins. This is either a dream, in which case dear god, let me never wake up, or it's a brand-new reality I never want to leave. Dan McBride, who never says *anything*, is talking to me, and he's saying that I deserve good sex.

"Thank you" is all I can say to that, and it comes out a little breathy, almost a whisper.

The tiniest grin tugs at his mouth, and then his teeth sink into his full bottom lip, suppressing the smile. "And if you don't mind me saying so, I don't think you're going to find it on Hinge."

As delicious as this conversation is, a sudden wave of indignation crashes over me, because buddy, I've been looking *everywhere*. "Well, where the heck am I going to find it, then?" I ask, then shovel another spoonful of Lucky Charms into my mouth.

Dan shrugs. "Hell if I know."

I bark out a laugh. "Well, thanks for the sage advice."

He takes a long swig of his gritty-looking protein shake. "Never said I was an expert."

"I'm sure you've got *some* expertise," I say before I can run that particular quip through my *make sure you're not sexually harassing your best friend's brother* filter.

My cheeks heat, but he doesn't glower or bolt. Instead, the corner of his full lips twitches again. But he bites back the grin a second time. Oh, I want inside that head so bad.

"I certainly do," he replies, his eyebrows lifting like a challenge.

Oh my god, is this really happening? Is this man actually *flirting* with me? The tension between us feels like a live electric current. My heart is pounding like a whole high school marching band drum line, and my breath comes in shallow little bursts.

Dan leans forward, pressing his elbows into the table as he

draws closer to me. I lean forward, closing the gap between us just a bit. I nearly stop breathing, so anxious am I to hear what he might say next. This moment feels big. Alive. And like I need to bring all my faculties to it, because whatever comes next is about to change everything.

He draws in a long, slow, deep breath, then looks up from beneath his impossibly long lashes. "Carson, if there's anything I can help you with—"

The sound of the doorbell interrupts us like a shriek.

If this were a dream, this would be the moment I wake up and sit bolt upright in bed. But I don't. Instead, I jump a mile, letting out an embarrassing little yelp. The spoon falls from my hand, clattering into my bowl again and sending a splatter of milk across the table. I gasp, sending a bit of marshmallow straight down my esophagus, and my eyes water as I try not to choke.

It's not a dream. I'm still sitting across from him. Staring at him. Dare I say…bantering with him?

Screw the doorbell. I'm not leaving this table. I want him to finish that sentence. What exactly is he offering, and how fast can I say yes?

"Carson! I want to hear about your date! I have muffins!"

Dan sighs, leaning back in his chair. Because that's my best friend at the door, his little sister.

Which means this conversation is over. For now, at least.

"I'm going to shower," Dan says, and before I can read his face, he's standing and reaching for his gym bag, then disappearing down the hall. A few seconds later, I hear the creaking of the old pipes as water rushes through them. Or maybe it's the sound of my own blood rushing through my body.

CHAPTER 7
CARSON

"He *what*?" Grace cries from the chair Dan formerly occupied. "Okay, that's it, no more app dates."

"I know, I couldn't believe it. It felt like I was experiencing one of those nightmare dates people write about on Reddit and you always wonder if it's fake. But this was *not* fake, my friend. This was so very real."

I've just finished telling the tale of my date with Gabe, all the way until up to the moment when he ditched me. I pick at the lemon blueberry muffin Grace brought, but can't bring myself to eat any of it. Between my hangover and whatever just happened with Dan, my stomach's not ready for it.

Grace, meanwhile, has peeled off nearly the entire streusel-covered top off her muffin, leaving her with only the stump. "So how did you get home?" she asks.

Now I reach for a chunk of muffin and shove it in my mouth. "Dan picked me up," I say around a mouthful of fluffy, sugary goodness.

Grace goes very still. "Dan? Like, my brother Dan?"

I nod, swallowing the muffin and willing it to stay in my stomach.

"How?"

"He gave me his number," I say, and when Grace furrows her brow, I add, "Since he's living here. We might need to get in contact. For roommate reasons."

My best friend's eyes—a brighter blue than her brother's—narrow like she's trying to solve a puzzle. Grace loves all her brothers fiercely, but she's always been a little suspicious of Dan, who rebelled against the tight-knit McBride clan simply by keeping his mouth shut. Until a little more than a year ago, he barely ever came home for holidays, always begging off for work. And when he did come home, he never had much to share. While the rest of the McBrides talked and teased, their lives open to one another because they shared a tiny town, Dan treated his life like a state secret.

When he showed back up this time, he'd mysteriously lost his job and his apartment, and he kept making runs back to the city to meet with a lawyer. Even when men in suits and badges tracked him down at a family gathering, he stubbornly continued to reveal nothing.

It's why the conversation we had at this kitchen table is so shocking. I've never known Dan McBride to say that much.

"Did he say anything?" Grace asks.

I try playing dumb. "Like what?"

Grace shrugs, but I've known her for twenty-five years. I can tell when she's digging.

"I don't know…anything?"

"You mean on the twenty-minute drive, during which I was drunk as a skunk, did he happen to explain why agents from the Securities and Exchange Commission showed up to Eden's first birthday party and led him away for questioning? Why he's back in Cardinal Springs for an extended stay, what happened to his job and his apartment in New York, and why the hell he's under federal investigation?"

Grace flushes. "Well, yeah."

"No, he didn't." And suddenly I realize that even if he had told me all that, I'm not sure if I'd tell her about it. Which is strange, since I've told Grace everything for the entirety of our lives. But Dan talking to me feels like an unspoken level of trust, and I get the sense that he doesn't have a whole lot of people in his life whom he trusts.

"Okay, well, how are things going with him living here?"

"Fine!" The word comes out a little too loud and enthusiastic, and I blush, reaching for another chunk of muffin.

Grace's eyes narrow again. She's back on the trail.

"You're not crushing on my brother, are you?"

I suck in a breath, a fluffy crumb shooting down my throat. I cough, my eyes bulging. "Are you serious?" I croak.

"I know you, Carson. You get this sort of starry-eyed look when you have a crush."

She's not wrong, but still, I resent the implication.

"I'm not!" I say, still half wheezing to get the muffin out of my lungs. God, these McBrides are trying to kill me, I swear. I take a deep breath. "And anyway, what does it matter? A crush is a totally victimless crime."

She sighs, giving me this look like I'm a puppy begging for a treat. "I just don't want you to waste your time."

The barb hits me, and I wince. I think of Dan, with his carved muscles and piercing blue eyes, radiating intensity at all times. And then I think of myself, with a closet full of craft supplies and four different methods for getting objects out of small children's noses. I own tutus in every color of the rainbow for when I teach kindergarteners about the color wheel. At least once a week, I find myself singing "Baby Beluga" to myself, and I'm usually not mad about it.

I hear Grace, and my rational brain knows what she means. That Dan is a guarded mystery, that he's just passing through, that nothing can happen between us, not because of me but because of *him*. But I still can't help but hear the voice that says, *The two of you don't match.*

Grace reaches across the table for my hands. "Hey, I didn't mean it like that. I just meant that you're in this incredible place right now." I know she's talking to that pesky voice, the one she knows talks shit to me sometimes. Nobody knows me better than Grace, and nobody is better at hyping me up. I love her for that. "After all those years of your parents hovering over your shoulder, telling you what to do and who to be, you finally get to live the life *you* want. The whole world is one big possibility for you, Carson. And Dan is just in a really different place. I don't even know what that place *is* because he won't talk to anyone."

He talks to me.

"Maybe cool it with the dating apps and focus on you for once," Grace says. "Spend the summer making the house yours. You've been putting off the redesign for months."

"That's because the school year was insane and I was so busy—"

Grace nods, but I can tell she's not buying it. "But it's summer now. You have two whole months to do whatever you want without your parents trying to rein you in."

She's right, of course. When my parents signed the deed to the house over to me, they left most of the furniture inside and instructed me to do whatever I wanted with it. I have endless Pinterest boards and stacks of design magazines. I really should make this place over into the cozy little bachelorette pad of my dreams. Make it match the front door that I painted pink the day my parents left. Finally get all that freaking wallpaper off the living room walls.

"Spend the next couple of months on *you*," Grace says, and I know she means the house.

But my mind is on the little flyer Violet shoved into my hand last night. And the ache in my muscles, the memory of the wind in my hair that I created with my own speed as I skated.

Grace's phone beeps, and she jumps out of her chair. "Okay, I've got to get to the bookstore. The last two Saturdays, I've had a line of strollers at the door for story time. Those moms don't mess around." She sweeps muffin crumbs into her palm and shakes them into the trash can. "I'm sorry about your date."

"It's fine," I say, and I mean it. I could not care less about Gabe and his rejection. Last night opened too many new doors in my brain. I have new rooms to explore.

"Let me know if you need any help with Project Carson, okay?"

I smile. "I will. Thanks, friend."

She winks. "Anytime."

As soon as Grace is gone, I make a beeline for my room, where I find my purse next to my bed, beside the one shoe I managed to take off last night. I dig through it and find the flyer crumpled at the bottom.

Have you always wanted to hit a bitch?
Are you looking for a badass girl gang?
Do you want to discover what you're capable of?
Then you should play…
ROLLER DERBY

Beneath that is a black-and-white photo of two women, both in roller skates, full pads, and helmets, crashing into each other, hip to hip and shoulder to shoulder. And it's not the short spandex shorts or the collage of tattoos on the girls that I can't stop staring it. It's the looks on their faces. Their eyes are narrow, their jaws tight, their focus fierce and determined as they each try to escape the collision first.

They look *tenacious.*

I've never been a sporty girl. I've always been a little soft, a little round. I preferred the library to the playground in elementary school. In middle school, I always made sure I got out early during dodgeball. In high school, I managed to avoid running the mile in gym class thanks to a well-timed sprained ankle. And by the time college rolled around, my exercise was mostly gossip walks with my sorority sisters. By the time I graduated, I figured my chance to participate in any kind of organized sports had passed, and that never seemed like much of a loss.

I stare at those two girls—*women*—and feel something I've never felt before. Suddenly I want that. To hit someone. To push myself. To be that determined about anything.

I pull out my phone and tap Violet's contact.

CARSON

tell me about tryouts

The reply is nearly instantaneous.

VIOLET

game ON!

CHAPTER 8
DAN

The summer sun has only started considering its rise on Monday morning when I pull into the parking lot of Gene's Gym on the edge of town. It's as far from the Soho Equinox as I can possibly get. The tin-roofed, cinder block box is musty and dank, the air conditioning a mere suggestion. The stereo system is crackly and plays only dad rock, and the water from the fountains has a distinct metallic taste.

I love it.

I stride across the floor beneath flickering fluorescent lights, taking in the usuals on a Monday morning. There's Carla and Dale, a middle-aged couple who spot each other through a full-body workout three times a week. There's a small group of meatheads who talk supplements between sets, unabashedly posing in front of the banks of mirrors. There's a trio of women who always do a little more talking than lifting, but they're quiet about it, so nobody minds. But the bulk of the crowd at this rural gym is a crew of silver-haired retirees who have been working out together for decades.

And the mayor of them all is Norm.

I drop my gym bag beside an open weight bench. "Need a spot?" I ask him.

Norm kicks a pair of fifty-pound dumbbells onto his shoulders. "Son, this is my warm-up set," he growls. "Mind your business."

He tips back onto the bench and presses the weights into the air as if they're made of marshmallows. A retired Marine turned retired high school football coach, Norm is in his seventies and in better shape than I've ever been in.

Despite Norm's grumbling, I step behind him when he progresses to the eighties, my hands hovering just below the man's elbows, ready to give him an extra rep or two. As far as I can tell, Norm's been doing the same workout for the last forty years, and everyone who comes to Gene's is familiar with his patterns and works around him. I like Norm because he commands a quiet respect. People always greet him, and he always gives the same stern nod in reply. They defer to him when he reaches for a set of weights or heads for a machine. He never offers training advice, never critiques another gym patron, just does his workout and minds his own business.

I recognize a kindred spirit in him, but Norm sees me as a project.

The old man hits failure on his chest press, drops the weights onto the rubber floor, and sits up.

"New girl at the desk," he says between heavy breaths. "Looks tough, like she could put up with your moody ass."

Norm is always trying to set me up with women: former students, great-nieces, any woman who happens to stumble into the gym at the same time as us. He usually makes a one-sentence pitch that I shut down, and he moves on. But still, he tries.

"I'm good, Norm," I tell him. It's what I always tell him, but he's still convinced that the root of my problems is that I'm lonely.

I've tried explaining to him that the root of my problems involves complex financial systems and the loopholes that allow for massive fraud, but he usually just rolls his eyes and tells me to ask out the next pretty woman I see.

Which of course sends my mind careening back to Carson. I

haven't even been living in her house for a week, and already I know that taking the room was a mistake. I've been avoiding her ever since our blessedly interrupted conversation at the breakfast table, when everything went from stilted nerves to what felt like playful banter, when I nearly offered to help her with her... problem.

I just want to get fucked.

I ditch my warm-up and head straight for the fifties. The thing I like best about a hard workout is that if you push yourself enough, your brain is too busy to torment you. Lifting my max weight usually silences whatever troubles or anxieties are rushing through my mind—and lately those have been plentiful. It's why I work out so much these days.

But today, even fifty-pound biceps curls aren't enough. My muscles scream as I lift the weights, but those words in her voice replay over and over again.

It's been a full week of those words in that voice looping through my head.

Carson, in the prime of her life, desperate to be treated with the care and passion she deserves.

I've always been a problem-solver. I was good at math and science in school, loved helping my dad fix things around the house, tinkering with electronics, and organizing shit. I tell myself that's why I want to help Carson. Because she's struggling, and I can fix things.

It's a lie.

"Take it easy before you snap your biceps," Norm barks, and I drop the weights, staring at my own red, sweaty face in the mirror. I run my hand over my buzzed head, still a little unused to the short cut, even though it's been more than two years since I visited the barber and had him take all my thick, dark hair off.

Thank god Grace interrupted us that morning last week. Because as hard as it's been to avoid Carson, to live in her house with her words bouncing around in my head like a pinball, it would have been even worse to drag her into my personal disaster.

My life didn't used to be like this. For a while, I had everything figured out. I graduated from Princeton and did my MBA at Harvard, where I was mentored by beloved business professor Ludwig Davies. From there, I landed an internship with Holt Capital, working under legendary investment banker Anders Holt. I worked like a Trojan, putting in eighty hours a week and soaking up every scrap of knowledge I could. Six months later, Anders recommended me for my dream job at ACR Bank. For the next five years, I climbed the ladder, building a multimillion-dollar investment portfolio. It was the perfect job for me—computers and numbers, but no interaction with clients. I had a condo on the Lower East Side and the car I'd always dreamed of. I worked too much to have relationships, but I never had trouble finding companionship when I wanted it. I fucked around like the world would always be at my feet.

And then I noticed the missing $250,000.

I personally maintained accounts for only a few clients: my brother, who had NHL money; my dad, with his modest retirement fund; and Ludwig Davies, my old business school mentor.

I remember thinking there'd been a simple clerical error in Juneau Davies's account. When Ludwig had started to succumb to Alzheimer's a year prior, Juneau had taken over the account. She'd trusted me with the money that would take care of Ludwig during his long decline and take care of her when he was gone. I'd been managing that account personally, and I'd taken care with every trade I'd made. That was why I'd invested a significant portion of it with Anders Holt—I'd worked under him at Holt Capital. I knew how good he was. I knew that investment would help Juneau care for Ludwig.

It had never occurred to me that Anders would do anything illegal.

That was my first mistake.

When I saw that the money was missing, I went straight to

Anders, riding the gilded elevator to his penthouse office, which looked out over lower Manhattan.

"We're going to look into this," my former boss told me, and I believed him.

It happened gradually at first. I began losing clients. I was taken off accounts. Soon my entire team at ACR Bank was reassigned, essentially demoting me to an entry-level position. Suddenly my name was nuclear, and since every friend I had worked in finance, they all disappeared too.

It had taken me five years to build my career, and it took only three months for it all to disappear.

By the time I went to the authorities with my suspicions—that the missing money wasn't an accounting error, that Holt Capital was skimming from the fund to pay off bad trades—it was too late.

Anders had gone to them first.

And he'd pointed the finger at me.

Now I've been exiled from the New York finance world and am scrambling to prove that the world-famous Anders Holt embezzled what turned out to be millions of dollars from his hedge fun. That I discovered it. That I blew the whistle on him, not the other way around.

And even though I have saved every scrap of paper and byte of data like a financial pack rat, even though I documented *everything*, it is still a very hard, very expensive battle to prove my innocence. It's Holt's lawyers versus me, with the US government playing referee. I have hope that the feds will believe me, but I just might break before we even get to court. Every day the investigation drags on is another day my name is dragged through the mud. It's another day I have to pay Marcel to take meetings and transfer documents, to ask and answer questions.

Which is why I'm lifting weights with senior citizens in central Indiana on a Monday in May.

Unemployed.

And crashing with my sister's best friend.

In the small town I vowed to get the fuck out of.

"I can see you thinking too hard," Norm says from the bench. He nods at the dumbbells I dropped on the floor. "Tell it to the iron."

Which is good advice, because curling the sixties burns so badly that the effort finally clears my mind.

Almost. Because even while counting reps, a small part of my mind is still wandering down dark hallways.

The ones that lead to Carson's bedroom.

———

I'm more than halfway through my workout when Archer finally shows up. My oldest brother is a former professional hockey player who became a high school history teacher and hockey coach after a career-ending injury. He likes to pretend that he's still a serious gym rat, but as soon as summer rolls around and he's faced with two months of freedom, that six a.m. gym time starts drifting later and later.

I love my brother, but I never mind when he's late. Because Archer? Archer is a talker.

He's not even done fucking around with his setup, adjusting the bench and placing dumbbells, before he starts his inquisition.

"Are you ever going to tell us what the hell is going on?"

I'm midway through a set of chest presses with eighty-pound dumbbells, so I decide to fuck with him.

"Yeah," I grunt through gritted teeth.

"When?"

I drop the weights with a thud. "When I'm sure you're not going to get called in to testify about our conversations."

Archer glares at me. "Dude, I would never sell you out."

"I know that. But do you know how much Manhattan lawyers charge per hour?"

"More than I make in a week," Archer says.

I glance at him between reps. "Try a month. You'd be looking at a year's worth of paychecks to get through a deposition."

He sighs. "I just hate that you're doing this alone."

Archer, ever the big brother.

"I'm not alone. I've got Marcel."

"Yeah, but he's your *lawyer*. He doesn't count."

"I'm going to tell him you said that."

Archer huffs. "Goddammit, Dan, could you be a little less of a sphinx for a second?"

"Leave the boy alone," Norm barks as he strides past the weight rack, arms wide to accommodate lats I could only dream of. "Let him focus so he won't drop those damn weights on his head."

Archer grits his teeth; shutting his mouth and getting out of my business requires far more effort than his workout. But that's the power of Norm. Even Archer's big brother energy is no match for the mayor of Gene's Gym.

But of course he can't let it lie. Two sets later, he's hunched over on a weight bench, elbows on his knees.

"Look, I get why you don't want to talk to us," he says, catching my eye in the mirror. "But you've got to talk to someone."

I roll my eyes. "Are you telling me to get a therapist?"

"I'm telling you to get a friend," my big brother snaps.

CHAPTER 9
DAN

The locker room at Gene's Gym is a petri dish that smells like Old Spice and mildew. The mint-green tile looks like it was last cleaned during the Clinton administration. But I can't risk running into Carson at her place, not until I figure out what I'm going to say to her after our little conversation. So the filthy gym shower it is.

I'm so pathetic.

As I tiptoe around public shower slime, Archer's advice keeps ringing in my ears.

I'm telling you to get a friend.

I think I'd rather get a therapist. Although a therapist would probably tell me to stop avoiding my problems, and I can't do that. Not when it's been working so well for me all these years.

Fortunately, I have one other way of avoiding Carson.

When everything went to shit back in New York, I cancelled my last appointment with Eamon, my tattoo artist in Brooklyn. I'd found him online, and we'd bonded over our shared Midwestern upbringing and the fact that we'd both found our place in New York. Eamon has done several of my tattoos, including the cardinal on a snowy branch on my ribs. It hurt like a mother-fucker, but it's gorgeous.

I've always been a doodler. As a kid, it helped calm my mind. As an adult, it helps focus it. Whenever I feel like the world is too loud or my mind is too cluttered, I pick up a pen and let the ink flow. I started drawing in margins of books and around my notes in school. But in college, Jameson got me a sketchbook for Christmas. At first I didn't know what to do with it. I wasn't an artist. I was a mathematician. A fucking business major. I felt like a phony holding the black leather–bound stack of crisp white paper. But Jameson started shoving it in my bag each morning, and one day, sitting alone in the dining hall, I took it out and flipped it open. I wasn't homesick, but I did feel unmoored, and so I took out a pencil and sketched a cornstalk.

Soon I was carrying the sketchbook with me everywhere I went, filling the pages between classes or when I needed study breaks. I learned that starting my day by drawing was like meditating, and soon I began every day that way. When I filled the pages of that first sketchbook, I bought another. And another. And another. Not only did a sketchbook serve as a distraction from my crowded thoughts, it had the added benefit of making me look busy. It kept most people from bothering me.

One day, I brought it with me to a tattoo appointment with Eamon. While he worked on a piece on the back of my shoulder, I hunched over the sketchbook, trying to distract myself from the sting of the needle. Eamon peered over at my doodles and asked if I'd ever considered tattooing.

I hadn't.

Eamon offered to show me around a tattoo machine, and I took to it quickly. He let me apprentice under him, and I was shocked to find that all it took to get licensed in New York was a twenty-six-dollar infectious disease prevention class, proof of a hepatitis B shot, and a hundred dollars for a permit.

I've been a licensed tattoo artist in the state of New York for the last three years.

Not that I've done it very much. I have a real job.

Or I did.

When I told Eamon that I was leaving the city to come back to Indiana, he connected me with Drake Douglas, the owner of Electric Sting, a tattoo shop in Bloomington. Drake had been his mentor back when Eamon was a seventeen-year-old little shit committing petty crimes.

I was glad Drake seemed to have no qualms about dealing with criminals, since the crimes I'd been accused of were far from petty.

He agreed to let me apprentice at Electric Sting, and I've been sneaking off to Bloomington to tattoo for months. As a relative newbie with a limited portfolio, I've mostly been relegated to tattooing infinity symbols and angel numbers on sorority girls, but I love it. I love the focus and concentration it requires, the precision. I love that whomever I'm tattooing is usually too focused on themself—their decision, their pain—to pay any attention to me.

It keeps me busy and out of the house, a real bonus after I nearly swallowed my foot while talking to Carson.

Electric Sting is located at the edge of downtown in a shabby little strip of commercial buildings. It looks like your typical tattoo shop: lots of black paint, walls decorated with sheets of colorful flash, and black-and-white checkerboard flooring that looks dingy but is actually clean enough to eat off of. Drake keeps the shop immaculate and sterile while still maintaining a trademark gutter punk look.

It's so different from the sleek glass high-rise of my former office, and I'd be lying if I said I didn't prefer it.

If only it paid as well as my old job.

I'd prefer to be here for a different reason, but all in all, I could be doing worse. I remember hearing about a whistleblower who ended up working at a call center in Delaware, fielding fraud reports for a consortium of credit unions after he got blacklisted from every bank in New York.

I think I'd sooner work a drive-through window.

Rosie, our front desk attendant, greets me like usual. And by that, I mean very unusually.

"Hey, Dan. I need to learn how to do a Jacob's ladder. Interested in being my guinea pig?" she asks as soon as I walk in the door.

I'm used to Rosie's bluntness. She's a little twenty-two-year-old pixie with green hair and a face full of metal studs. She's training to be a piercer. She's on the autism spectrum, which seems to make her particularly adept at it; she's methodical and works cleaner than anyone I've ever seen, and her blunt manner of speaking seems to put clients at ease. Turns out people like knowing exactly what to expect before needles are driven through their faces.

"Someone already beat you to it," I tell her. An aspiring piercer in Eamon's shop got to my dick three years ago. I made it to three barbells before I said no more. I like them now, but at the time I was not prepared for the experience of having a needle driven through my cock.

Zero stars. Would not recommend.

Rosie's eyebrows rise. "Seriously? Tall, dark, and grumpy is packing steel?"

"Rosie, that's an HR violation," Drake barks from his office just off the lobby. He leans out the door. "We talked about this."

"You also told me I need to learn," Rosie says. "How am I supposed to do that without a volunteer?"

"I've got a list of people willing to be guinea pigs in exchange for free body art. I'll send out an email. You'll get your chance. Stop harassing the staff," Drake says.

"Fine." Rosie turns back to me. "If you ever want to add an apadravya, I need to learn that too."

"Rose!" Drake barks, but I just laugh. Well, I laugh and wince, because the thought of a needle going through my entire cock, top to bottom, makes my knees feel weak. A Jacob's ladder is just the skin. The glans? Fuck no.

"It's okay," I tell Drake, then turn to Rosie. "But I'll pass on that."

"I don't blame you. Six months out of commission? No thank you," Drake says.

Rosie's brow furrows. "The book says eight to twelve months. You risk infection from an incomplete fistula."

"Some people heal fast," Drake says, but he's already bracing himself. Rosie's best quality as a body mod artist is her adherence to rules, but Drake has been doing this for so long that he tends to operate more on gut instinct.

"Drake, do you know what can happen if you get an infection in your penis? You could lose function, to say nothing of sepsis. You risk *death*."

"Losing function *is* death," Drake grumbles.

"First of all, you just agreed with me, so thank you. And secondly, that's incredibly gender essentialist of you."

Drake sighs. He's old, but I've been surprised by his willingness to learn from his younger staff. He takes getting called out like a champ. "Sorry, kid," he says.

Rosie shrugs. "Thanks for hearing me," she says. "Do *you* want an apadravya?"

"Fuck no," Drake replies, then rushes back into his office like he's scared Rosie might succeed at talking him into it. And knowing her, she might.

"You doing walk-ins?" Rosie asks me.

I nod.

"Excellent. You need anything?"

I'm telling you to get a friend.

"Rosie, are we friends?" I ask.

She looks at me for a long time, her brows furrowed.

"Not a trick question," I assure her. "I just...I think I need to take inventory."

She nods. "Do you like D&D?"

"I've never played, so I don't know."

"Hmmm...do you read manga?"

I shake my head.

"Watch horror movies?"

I wince. "I can do slashers, but paranormal shit keeps me up at night."

"It's not looking good for our friendship, Dan," Rosie says apologetically. "But we can be work friends. You can't be my work husband, because Andrew is already my work husband. But work friends. Work acquaintances at worst."

"Thanks," I say with a laugh. "I'll take work acquaintances. Maybe we can make our way up to work friends."

"If you let me give you an apadravya, I'll bump you all the way up to real friend," she says, eyebrows raised.

"Tempting," I say, laughing. "But no."

"Your loss," she says, going back to the manga open on the counter, and I'm not sure if she means the piercing or the friendship.

I head back to my booth, the one by the bathroom that everyone calls the loser stall, since nobody wants it. Every time someone flushes, it sounds like a tsunami in the walls, and it takes nerves of steel not to jump—a real problem when you're wielding a tattoo machine. I share this space with Natalie, another newbie tattoo artist who only works weekends. During the week, she tends bar at a fratty shithole where she makes bank.

I drop my gym bag and start by wiping the entire place down with antiseptic spray. I check the supplies in the drawers and restock what's low. I pull out my iPad and send a couple of new sketches to the printer to add to my bulletin board of flash. I've been doodling weeds a lot lately in response to all the florals people request, and I've had a few people ask for my dandelion and clover tattoos. It's not much, but at least my original art is on someone's body. I've only gotten to do it a handful of times, but every time feels a little bit sacred, like there are people out there in the world carrying around little parts of me.

While I wait for walk-ins, I turn to my iPad and start some new sketches of weeds. I begin with an attempt at Japanese knotweed, which has these branching white flowers. It can grow up through concrete, damaging the foundation of a house. I'm working on a little vine when Rosie pops her head into my booth.

"Walk-in?" I ask.

She shakes her head. "I was actually thinking that you can be my friend. You don't have to let me give you an apadravya."

"Oh. Well, thanks," I say. "What changed your mind?"

She shrugs. "You're really quiet. I like that."

I nod, smiling. "Then friends, I guess."

She nods. "Friends." Then she disappears.

Take that, Archer.

CHAPTER 10
CARSON

Violet's house is a shabby gingerbread Victorian with burnt-orange clapboard siding, green trim, and a wrap-around porch. It's nestled on a quiet street in Bloomington, surrounded by other shabby little rental houses.

Tonight is to be my introduction to the world of roller derby.

But before I climb the porch, I reopen the text I received earlier.

It's the first I've heard from him since that morning in my kitchen almost a week ago.

It's not that he's gone silent. It's that I haven't even seen him. He wakes up every morning before the sun and disappears. The only evidence that he's still staying in my house is the sound of my front door shutting every so often, followed quickly by the sound of his bedroom door shutting, leaving me to replay our last conversation over and over. The one where I thought that maybe, possibly, Dan McBride was *flirting* with me.

Maybe I imagined it. Or maybe he was flirting, but he regrets it, hence the disappearing act.

He never finished what he was saying, and it appears he doesn't feel the need to. His absence says everything.

Which sucks, because despite his very clear message that he's not interested, I cannot get the man out of my head. As I'm cruising the aisles at the grocery store, I imagine turning a corner in the meat department and finding him there. I stop at a red light and turn to the car next to me, hoping to see him behind the wheel of his BMW. I look for him in the stacks at the library, at the bar at the Half Pint, in the next booth at Pete's Diner.

He's everywhere in my head and nowhere in my reality.

So when Violet texted Thursday morning and invited me over to learn all about the wonderful world of roller derby, I happily accepted. With Grace enjoying Decker's retirement and Wyatt practically living with Owen, my summer break has been the biggest snooze on the planet. I was damn near ready to try Hinge again when I got the text from Violet.

"Carson!" The green front door flies open, and Violet waves me in like she's trying to direct a jet in for a landing. "Get in here!"

Violet's house is bursting with mismatched furniture, and the walls are adorned with a wild and vivid assortment of art. It's cramped and cluttered, walking the line between chic maximalism and hoarder. It's obviously a college town rental, and yet it feels more like a home than my own house. And I grew up there.

I love it immediately.

Violet leads me to a green couch printed with yellow cabbage roses. Her laptop is open on a dinged-up coffee table that screams *Someone found me on the side of the road!*

"You want a drink? We've got water, Coke Zero, and KO's kombucha."

A woman with a bright red wolf cut and a septum ring walks into the living room, a rainbow mug in her hand. "It's apple hibiscus," she says. "I made it myself. The mother is three years old!"

"This is Knockout, KO for short," Violet says. "I'd offer you alcohol, but KO is sober, so we don't drink in the house."

"I actually brought a water bottle," I say, holding up my ever-present Owala. "I'm still recovering from the flask."

Violet winces. "I'm so sorry about that. I'm usually such a mother hen when I'm drinking with friends. I hope the morning after wasn't too bad."

I'm mid-sip when I have a vivid flashback of the car ride home that night, which now takes up so much of my mental real estate that I've forgotten what it's like to think normal thoughts. The water shoots down my throat, and I launch into a coughing fit.

Violet gives me a wide grin. "Oh my god, *spill!*"

"What?" I gasp.

"There's clearly a story there. I mean, I saw that man. KO, you should have seen him. He looks like he's special forces, all tall and built with a buzz cut. And he was driving the fanciest BMW I've ever seen! I bet that thing cost more than my student loans, and I have *two* master's degrees. Is he military? CIA? He looks like he knows seven ways to kill a man and eight ways to dispose of the body."

"He works in finance," I say.

"Ugh, a capitalist," KO groans.

"We're all capitalists, KO," Violet says.

"Is he directly responsible for this nation's income inequality, or is he simply covering his eyes to prevent him from feeling guilt about the downfall of society?" KO deadpans.

"I think he does something with investment banking?"

Violet glares at KO, who is silent for a long beat before shrugging. "As long as it's not private equity. If you were in love with a guy in private equity, I definitely wouldn't share my kombucha with you."

"I'm not in love with him!" I cry.

"KO, leave her alone," Violet says, then narrows her eyes at me. "But you definitely have a crush, right? You're blushing like you're picturing him naked right now."

"I'm not!" I say, which was true until this very moment, though I am now absolutely picturing him naked. That corner of his tattoo lives rent-free in my mind. I keep hearing his gravelly voice rumble *a few* and then picturing all manner of ink beneath his clothes.

"Girl, you could start a fire with the heat in those cheeks. Tell the story!"

Oh god, what part of the story can I even tell? Certainly not all of it. Given how cagey Dan is with his family, I'm certainly not going to discuss his secrets with strangers. And I don't even know what the bigger secrets are.

"He's my best friend's older brother, and a pipe burst in his apartment, so he's crashing with me until it gets fixed," I say, the simplest version of the truth. Lies of omission abound, obviously, but this is not entirely my story to tell.

"And?" KO says.

"And that's all," I say firmly.

"Dubious," KO snorts.

"Doubtful for sure," Violet says, then shrugs. "But if you need to believe that fiction, we'll support you."

"Solidarity, sister," KO adds, raising a fist.

"But for the record, he's a smoke show. Treat yo' self," Violet says.

It feels good to be encouraged, which is easy for them to do because they don't really know me. Or him. There's no history or context.

I can't remember the last time I got to exist out of context. One of the many hazards of small towns, I guess.

"As fun as it is to grill you about your capitalist fuckboy, let's get down to business." Violet wakes up her laptop and taps a few buttons. The television screen fills with an image of skaters lined up on an oval concrete track. "Okay, here's the quick and dirty explanation. First of all, this is a real sport. It's not professional wrestling, it's not a soap opera, and there's no fighting. That's all male-gaze fantasy nonsense. This is a sport, and the players are athletes. Also there's no ball. For some reason, everyone thinks there's a ball, but there's no ball."

"Got it," I say, my eyes glued to the screen, where nothing is happening yet. But the women on skates in matching jerseys look fierce as hell. Intimidating. So very unlike me. But if Violet thinks I could be one of them, I'm willing to fake it.

"Four skaters from each team line up. They're blockers. They make up the pack. One skater from each team lines up behind them. They each have a helmet cover with a star on it. They're the jammers, and they are the point scorers. They get one point for every member of the opposite team who they pass—"

"While staying in bounds," KO adds.

Violet nods and points at the neon tape on the floor marking the track's boundaries. "Right. So the blockers are simultaneously trying to help their jammer through the pack and trying stop the opposing jammer from getting through."

"So blockers are playing offense and defense at the same time," KO says. "It's a very cerebral sport."

"Exactly," Violet says with a wolfish grin. "The jammers go round and round scoring points for up to two minutes. Then the ref blows the whistle, the lineups change, and a new jam begins. This happens over and over for two thirty-minute halves. Got it?"

Maybe? I nod anyway.

"There are tons of rules and penalties, which I'll explain as we watch. This is a recording of world champs from last season, so it's New York vs. Portland. It's *very* high-level derby, so don't be intimidated. I just think bouts like this are easier to use as teaching tools because the skaters are less sloppy and there are fewer penalties. Ask all the questions you want, but don't feel overwhelmed. Derby is one of those sports you really learn by doing."

Ah, yes, one of *those* sports. As opposed to all the other sports, which I've never learned by doing *or* watching. Even though I've spent my whole life in Indiana, the home of basketball, I couldn't tell you the basic rules of the game. Ball in hoop? Beyond that, I'm out.

My parents have always been more bookish, and they passed that nerdery down to me. And I certainly wasn't going to pick up an inclination toward sports on the street. Growing up, I didn't have the athletic look. My mother called me pudgy, but the kids at school called me fat. And nobody invites a fat kid to play sports. If you're a boy, you might get recruited to be a football player, but a fat girl? She's not getting pulled onto the soccer team or asked to play softball. Looking back, I can't tell if my lack of athletic ability was because I didn't want to join in or because no one ever encouraged me to.

But as I watch the video with Violet and KO, who chatter about penalties and strategy and player lore, I notice a buzzy feeling just beneath the surface of my skin. An itch to get out there. To try it. And when I see a blocker fly across the track like a sniper, connecting with a speeding jammer with enough force to send her flying into the trackside seating, I feel a little fear, yes, but also a glowing ember of excitement.

Suddenly I'm wondering if my inability to play sports was imposed on me—less nature, more nurture. Roller derby looks hard and scary and exhausting, but I want out there.

Because that blocker? The sniper?

She looks just like me.

———

It's closing in on midnight when I finally leave Violet and KO. I head out with an enormous green duffel covered in black marker doodles and a few patches. It's stuffed with a full set of gear for my first fresh meat practice on Saturday.

Because that's what I am.

Fresh meat.

"I like you, Carson, so I'm giving you first dibs on the community gear," Violet said as she pulled four large plastic storage bins out of the hall closet. "You're lucky, because some of this shit smells like a corpse. You don't want to get stuck with Betty Spaghetti's old wrist guards, trust me."

She loaned me her old skates, which are half a size too big, the toes held together with what I think used to be hot-pink duct tape but is scraped all to hell. Violet told me search eBay for a better secondhand pair, but these will get me through my first couple of practices. She shoved the skates, knee pads, elbow pads, wrist guards, and a helmet into an old army duffel, instructed me to pick up a mouth guard at the nearest sporting goods store, and sent me on my way.

The bag is unwieldy and bangs into my thigh as I walk, but already I love it.

I drive the forty minutes back to Cardinal Springs with the bag —which, despite promises that it contains gear that's on the newer side, smells musty—on my passenger seat like precious cargo.

I turn my music up loud, singing along and whizzing down the dark rural highway, imagining myself throwing my hips into skaters, sprinting with my head down and my heart pounding. When I pull into my driveway, I haul the bag out of the car and relish the feel of its weight on my shoulder. I'm half tempted to gear up right here on the front stoop and skate up and down my darkened street.

But just as I'm about to unzip the bag, a yawn overtakes me, and I remember that it's nearly one in the morning. It's only the beginning of summer, and my body is still hanging on to teacher time—bed by ten, up by six. Hopefully this late night will be the catalyst I need to break that cycle for the next couple of months so I can have a fun summer break.

I grip the bag and grin, my heart still fluttering with anticipation even as my body tries to remind me that it's time for bed. And when I unlock the front door, I use my hip to shove it open, imagining what it'll feel like when I'm on skates, hitting an actual body. Never in my life have I considered hitting another person, but suddenly it's all I can think about. That flyer Violet gave me asked if I was interested in hitting a bitch, and I'm shocked to find out that the answer is an unequivocal *yes*.

And I'll start with this damn front door.

CHAPTER 11
DAN

The soundtrack to my nights is the squeak of the screws in this ancient futon. Every time I roll over, it wails beneath me.

And I roll over a lot.

I've never been a very good sleeper. It started when I was a kid. One night when I was six, my mom left for the hospital, in labor with my baby sister, and she never came back. I said this to a therapist once while describing my sleep problems, and she gave me a look that said, *You see it, right?*

I never went back.

Some people can't sleep because their minds won't stop working or because their bodies hurt. I just...can't. Have never been able to. And it's never been too much of a problem for me. My body seems to function fine on what sleep I'm able to eke out, and I've always just used my late nights and early mornings to my advantage. All that studying got me the hell out of Cardinal Springs. It took me to Princeton, then to Harvard for my MBA. It took me to New York and some of the most prestigious investment banks in the world.

But now I'm stuck in this tiny room with floral wallpaper,

listening to squeaking furniture and screaming crickets, with nothing to distract me.

Nothing but the memories of Marcel prepping me for my deposition and my conversation with Archer telling me I need a friend.

My older brother telling me I need a friend…fuck, it makes me feel like I'm back in high school. And that didn't go so well for me the first time. The few guys I hung out with back then all did like me and got the hell out. The guys who are still here probably shoved me into a locker fifteen years ago.

But I can't totally blame Cardinal Springs. I haven't had real friends in who knows how long. Who has time for friends? When I still had a job and a life, my time was spent in the office and my social time was spent at happy hours and networking events, which I went to only because I needed to in order to succeed. I'm only still in touch with Jameson, my college roommate, because he takes a semper fi approach to friendship: leave no bro behind. At Princeton, he dragged me out to dinners and parties; when I was at Harvard, he texted regularly, asking for updates on my life; in New York, he forced me across the bridge to Brooklyn once a month for dinner with him and Marcel.

And thank god for that—if he hadn't, I don't know if I'd have a lawyer now. Hell, I'd probably already be in prison for something I didn't do if I hadn't let Jameson drag me out of my introvert hole.

I guess Archer's right. I do need a friend. And not one who's eight hundred miles away or involved in my defense or hoping to pierce my dick.

If only I knew where the fuck to find one.

The front door slams, followed by a heavy thud. I lie in bed, staring up at the ceiling, on the mattress that feels like it's made of gravel. I remember that therapist's face, begging me to connect the obvious dots.

I've been avoiding Carson ever since that morning in the kitchen when I damn near threw myself at her, as if what she needed was me. But every time I see her—every time I catch a glimpse of her in her little pajama shorts, her thick strawberry-blond hair piled up into a messy bun, the lines of her pillow still on her face—all I can think of is her talking about how badly she wants to be pleased.

And how much I want to please her.

But she doesn't need that from me. Nobody needs me, not in the state I'm in these days.

Maybe I need her, though.

I climb out of bed and pull on a pair of sweats, then pad down the hall. I find Carson leaning against the front door in a pair of cutoffs and a pink tank top, her eyes closed and a wild smile on her face. An enormous army-green duffel bag that looks like an emo teen attacked it with a Sharpie is resting at her feet.

There's something electric about her, something I've never seen before. She's standing up straight, a glow in her cheeks, like she could take on whatever might come through that door. Has she been out on a date? Has someone finally pleased her the way she deserves? The thought makes my blood hot. All at once, I discover a hole in my "stay away form her" plan—it means I have no idea where she's been or who she's been with. I can't decide which possibility I hate more: another asshole treating her poorly and stranding her somewhere, or a guy actually taking her to bed and making her smile like that.

I need to fix this.

And after a beat, I realize I'm standing here, staring at her like a fucking creep.

"Are you okay?" I ask.

Her eyes flutter open as she gasps, because of course I snuck up on her and scared her. She scans me, her gaze pausing at my waist, her pupils dilating. Then she gives herself a little shake.

"Yeah, why?" She's got a spark in her eyes that I haven't seen before. She looks sort of feisty, bordering on aggressive. It makes my breath hitch in my chest.

"I just heard a bang, and it's kind of late for you to be getting home," I say, and suddenly that spark in her eyes turns into a flame, her brows knitting together.

She glares.

"Look, despite all evidence to the contrary, I am a functioning adult and not a walking disaster," she says, then crosses her arms over her chest. It's meant to be a *so what* gesture—an attempt at intimidation, maybe—but all I can see is the way her breasts rise when she breathes, her cleavage spilling over the low neckline of her pink tank top.

Dammit, head in the game, McBride.

I try to steer the conversation back to solid ground. "I know, I was just—"

She holds up a hand to silence me. "I can date, and drink, and redecorate my house all on my own."

I blink, wondering what the décor has to do with this. I've clearly missed something.

"Right," I try again. "And I was—"

"I don't need a babysitter. Or a daddy."

Fuck, the way she says *daddy* makes my mind short-circuit, which does not help me make sense of what is turning out to be a very strange conversation. Why did I even come out here?

I'm telling you to get a friend.

Oh, right.

I try to meet her eye, but Carson is glaring at me, so I shift my gaze back to my toes. *Just talk to her. Just say what you mean.*

"I was hoping we could be friends," I try, then clear my throat. I search my mind for something to say that makes me sound less pathetic than I feel. "I think maybe, uh, you could use one?"

"I have friends!" she cries. "And yeah, they've both found the loves of their lives and are busy having mind-blowing sex all over town. But I'm *happy* for them and all they have going on, because that's what friends do."

This is going so much worse than I ever could have imagined. And then I go and make it even worse by letting the words "Are you drunk?" fall out of my mouth.

"No, I'm not drunk! I'm just full of kombucha, which I can't decide if I like, because it kind of tastes like cider and it kind of tastes like feet!"

Fuck. I didn't mean for this to happen. I meant to ask her to be my friend, not imply that I was doing her some kind of favor. This? This right here is why I don't talk to people.

Because of course she has friends. She's kind and funny and generous. Who wouldn't want to be friends with her? The question is, who *would* want to be friends with *me*?

"I'm sorry, I just—"

"It's fine, Dan. *I'm* sorry. I word-vomited all over you when I was drunk. I made everything weird when you just need a place to crash. And yeah, I'm a little bit adrift at the moment and it's making me a little bit crazy, but I'm trying to channel that energy into something good." She kicks the duffel on the floor. "So you don't have to worry. You can hide from whatever the fuck it is you're hiding from without any interference from me. We're just roommates. Ships passing in the night. And speaking of night, I need to go to sleep, because it's very much past my bedtime."

And then she stomps past me, the sweet smell of her shampoo and something earthy like incense wafting over me as she disappears down the hall, slamming her door behind her.

And I'm left standing in the middle of the living room, wondering how the fuck I screwed that up so royally.

CHAPTER 12
CARSON

"Am I dead? Am I a ghost? Is my sweaty corpse out there on the track?"

A tall, skinny, pale girl named Madelyn, who looks like she's spent most of her life in an art studio, is beside me. She's got her hands on her knees as she pants.

I can't manage to suck in enough breath to answer her.

Because roller derby? Yeah, turns out it's *hard*. Good hard. Powerful hard. I-want-to-kick-someone's-butt hard.

But it's *hard*.

A whistle slices through the thick air of the old community center where the Bloomington Brawlers practice on a slick, shiny basketball court. Violet is standing in the center of the track in full gear while the rest of us, half collapsed on the floor, the rest doubled over and panting, are waiting on the jammer line. We are almost at the end of our very first fresh meat practice, and we've just finished our first attempt at one of the minimum skills required to play the sport: twenty-seven laps in under five minutes.

Only two girls accomplished it the first time, and one of them is a transfer from another league in Michigan—she's been playing for two years already. The other twelve of us in the fresh meat group fell short.

I got twenty-two.

Turns out watching some game tape and having all the right gear doesn't make you an athlete. For the last three hours, we've done skating drills, worked on posture and stride, practiced crossovers and weaving through cones. We started learning stops, which for most of us meant either a slow coast to a wobbly halt or a quick splat on the floor. We balanced on one foot and made some attempts at turns. I was okay at most of it but by no means good. And there were a few times when a voice I recognized came creeping into my brain. It sounded an awful lot like my middle school gym teacher, telling me to *stop draggin' ass, Webber.* Back then, I fully believed that moving my body was awful, that I wasn't good at it, that I shouldn't even try.

But for the last three hours, no one has said anything to me other than *good job* or *great start* or *I can't wait to see that ass in the back of the pack.*

So even though I might be a ghost and my corpse might be in a heap somewhere on the track, I'm still smiling.

A little.

I think I might love this?

"Okay, folks, we've got one final task for you," Violet calls, her voice bouncing around the gym. "It's the last minimum skill you'll be working toward over the course of fresh meat training. Each of you will begin at the jammer line and take off for one lap from a dead start. You need to complete that lap in under thirteen seconds in order to be game-eligible. Remember, this is just a first attempt. Some of you are still new on skates. That's okay! That's what freshie training is for. If you stick with it, you'll get there. This is just to establish your baseline."

I glance around to see if anyone else thinks that thirteen seconds seems like an impossibly short amount of time. A couple of people look confident (namely the transfer, a skater named Maude Forbid who I'm pretty sure managed damn near thirty laps in five minutes), but most everyone is staring at Violet with eyes the size of dinner plates. One girl looks a little bit green.

"Let's go, skaters! Last hurdle—you can do it." Violet claps her hands, her wrist guards making a little clacking sound. Beside her, KO holds a clipboard and looks bored. "Line up!"

Slowly, we all make our way to the line on wobbly legs. I can tell everyone is trying hard to be very cool and also not be first. We sort of bully Maude Forbid to the front, and when Violet blows the whistle, she takes off with three quick steps on her toe stops before digging her wheels into the floor. She hits the turn with her left hand tucked behind her back, leaning deep into her crossovers like an Olympic speed skater.

It looks incredible.

Suddenly I'm not struggling to breathe. Suddenly I'm not breathing at all as I watch her whiz around the track, crossing the jammer line again in a blur. And even though my legs are jelly and my entire body is soaked in sweat, even though I know my face is red as a tomato and there's no way in a frozen hell that I'm going to make this lap in under thirteen seconds on my first attempt, I can't fucking *wait* to try it.

And try it again.

And again.

And again and again and again until I can take those turns with as much speed and grace as Maude.

When it's my turn on the line, Violet gives me a quick wink before blowing the whistle. I try to do that little run on my toe stops that Maude did, but the movement is new to me, and I pitch forward, stumbling a few steps. But I manage to get my wheels under me and push hard into the floor, finding a grip on the short straightaway. When I hit the turn, I lean and cross my right skate over my left, my arms swinging like they can propel me faster. I don't even try to tuck my arm behind me like Maude did, because I know I need both of these babies for balance.

I feel my left foot start to slip as I come out of the turn, but I hang on, my heart in my throat. The straightaway looks endless, and I sprint with everything I have, hitting turn three at a speed I didn't think was possible. As a result, I take the turn a little too wide, but I bend my knees like Violet taught us and push through to turn four.

I cross the jammer line more than a little out of control and have to drop to my knees, sliding like a rock star across the floor in order to stop.

"Twelve point nine seconds!" Violet yells, following it up with a whoop.

Behind me, my fellow freshies erupt into cheers.

Holy shit. *I did it.*

And on my first attempt. Wobbly and awkward and ending in a heap on the floor, but I did it.

Violet skates over and grins down at me, her purple hair spilling out from beneath her black helmet.

"Well done, bitch!" she says, offering me a hand. "Now get your ass off the track before you become roadkill."

———

"I think my blisters have blisters," says Jax, a willowy skater with they/them pronouns on their name tag. They yank off a skate and peer at the hole in the big toe of their sock.

"Epsom salts, everyone," Violet says, weaving through us as we peel off our gear on the floor. "If you have a bathtub, pour a cup into hot water and soak. If you don't have a bathtub, make friends with someone who does."

"Tempted to book a room at the Holiday Inn just to use the hot tub," Emme, another freshie, groans.

"I'll go in on that with you," Georgia says.

There are fourteen of us in this fresh meat class. At the beginning of practice, Violet explained that we'll have six weeks of fresh meat training, during which we'll learn skating skills and game play. At the end, we'll take a skating skills test and a rules test, and if we pass both, we'll be drafted onto one of the league's three teams and be eligible to play in the first game of the season at the end of July.

My fellow freshies, as Violet called us, are a diverse bunch, ranging from eighteen-year-old college freshman Madelyn to Tilly, who looks to be in her forties and has a teenage daughter. About half of the prospective skaters are IU students—mostly under-grads, but Mercedes is working on a PhD in biochemistry.

"Anybody want to go for a drink?" Jax asks.

"I'm not twenty-one yet," Madelyn sighs.

"We can totally go somewhere with NA options," Jax replies, and Madelyn smiles gratefully. "Who's in?"

There's a chorus of yeses as everyone starts shoving gear into bags and climbing off the floor. Tilly bows out so she can pick up her daughter from soccer practice, and Georgia has go home to shower before meeting her girlfriend's parents for dinner.

"What about you, Carson?" Jax asks.

"Oh, I'm actually meeting up with some friends back in Cardinal Springs," I tell them, thinking about the text I sent to Grace and Wyatt before practice began. I dig through my bag for my phone.

"You're seriously going to drive forty-five minutes each way twice a week for practice?" Mercedes asks.

"It's not so bad," I tell them, finding my phone. "I'm an audio-book girlie, so the time is well spent."

"Well, if you ever don't want to make the drive and need a place to crash, Casey and I have a really great couch," Jax says, nodding at their partner, another freshie.

"I'll let you know, thanks!" I say, waving as they file out of the gym.

I shove my skates into my duffel and then reach for my phone, which displays a few missed text messages. My group chat with Wyatt and Grace has a notification, which I figure is about plans for tonight, so instead I open the one from Violet.

Hey bitch! Good work today. Mayhem snapped this pic while you were doing your sprint. Can't wait to see you on the track this fall!

The photo is of me on the last turn of my triumphant sprint lap, approaching the jammer line. I'm crouched low, my blond ponytail flying behind me. One arm is forward, the other back as I sprint. But it's the look on my face that catches my eye. It's one I've never seen before. My brows are knitted, my jaw sharp, my mouth set in a firm line. I look determined.

The feeling of crossing that finish line and hearing my time comes roaring back. Yeah, I have a lot to learn in the next eight weeks, but I'm going to be riding this high all the way through training.

With that fizzy feeling in my body, I click over to my group text with Wyatt and Grace. Before practice, I texted them to see about having a girls' night. It's been a while since we've all gotten together. Grace has been busy with her bookstore and the house her boyfriend is building for the two of them. And Wyatt, on top of falling madly in love with Grace's older brother Owen, has been deep in auntie life. Her sister had a baby last year, and the three of them are living together, along with Wyatt's mother, who recently returned from prison. It's a whole thing.

But it's Saturday, and I want to get together with my girls. I want to tell them all about roller derby and my sprint and how I haven't hit anybody yet, but I want to.

GRACE

I want to hear all about roller derby! But Dad
called a family dinner tonight, so I'll be there.
Maybe next weekend? I have an event at the
store, but we could do a late-night thing after
closing?

WYATT

I'll also be at family dinner tonight with Owen,
but I could maybe do next weekend? I might be
watching Eden so Hazel can go to a movie, but
I'll double-check. What about tomorrow? Sunday
brunch?

GRACE

Decker and I are going up to Indianapolis to look
at tile for the bathrooms. I could be back for
dinner though!

WYATT

I've got plans with Owen tomorrow night. But
we'll figure out a time.

WYATT

Kick ass out there, Carson! I can't wait to hear all
about it!

By the time I've read through all the texts, the fizzy feeling inside
me has gone flat. My best friends are going to be with their best
guys, both at the same family dinner.

Without me.

Because now they're practically sisters.

Maybe Dan wasn't totally off base when he said I needed a
friend.

Trying to fit a girls' night in between all their hot dates is
sounding impossible.

Just when I'm about to sink into the most rockin' of personal
pity parties, the door to the gym flies open with a loud creak. Jax

comes rushing across the floor, their sneakers squeaking on the polished wood.

"Forgot my water bottle," they say, picking up a dented Hydro Flask covered in faded stickers from the bleachers. "You sure you don't want to join us? We're going to Upland."

I glance down at my phone and the encouraging-yet-disappointing text thread, then back up at Jax, my new teammate.

"Actually, yeah," I say, hoisting my gear bag over my shoulder. "My plans fell through, so I'll meet you there."

CHAPTER 13
DAN

wasn't late. I pulled up to my dad's house right on time.

And then I drove right past it.

I've circled the block twice, trying to steel myself to park and go inside for family dinner.

And anyway, it's only five past six. Dad's text calling Archer, Felix, Owen, Grace, and me to dinner at his house told us to show up "around" six.

Not that Archer will accept that answer.

With a sigh, I pull the BMW to a stop behind the trio of pickup trucks belonging to my brothers and Decker's vintage Bronco. The house I grew up in is small and tidy thanks to my Dad, who owns a hardware store and has never once let anything stay broken or unkempt for more than five minutes. He instilled that work ethic in all of us, even if we each went in a different direction with it. I know my dad has always shaken his head at my work in finance, but he's the reason I was able to do it in the first place. Those late nights studying? All those extra hours in the office? That was because of his example.

I love my father.

And I still don't want to go to this dinner.

As soon as I open the front door, I hear the familiar sounds of my boisterous family. They were the soundtrack of my life for the first eighteen years. They were the reason I bought my first pair of noise-cancelling headphones when I was thirteen. When I moved away, I missed them, but I relished having peace and quiet for the first time in my life.

"Do *not* put that hot casserole dish on the table without a trivet!" Grace shrieks from the kitchen.

"What the fuck is a trivet?" Felix calls back, but he's grinning at his twin brother Owen, because he absolutely knows what a trivet is. Teasing is Felix's love language, and annoying Grace is the cherry on top.

"You two are useless," Grace gripes, stomping out of the kitchen with a dish towel thrown over her shoulder, only to watch as Felix places whatever gooey, cheesy monstrosity she's cooked onto a felt hot pad on our old dining room table. There's a card table set up at the end, and I'm barely done counting chairs before the rest of my family descends.

"You're late," Archer says with a brotherly glare. He drops his enormous athletic frame into a chair beside my dad's spot at the head of the table. Archer spent his entire life playing hockey, first at University of Michigan and then in the NHL, until a knee injury ended his career.

He's also a bit of a bossy bitch. Classic oldest brother shit.

"He's fine, Arch," Dad says, patting my brother on the shoulder.

"Good to see you, Dan," says Corianne, my dad's yoga teacher turned girlfriend, from beside him. We all love her, and she's so good for Dad, but I'd be lying if I said it wasn't strange to see a woman sitting at our table beside him. But our mother died when we were so young, and he's been alone for so long, so we've all worked hard to move past whatever hang-ups we might have about their relationship. Of course Archer took the longest to come around, because he's a meddler, but he's on board now.

I give Corianne a nod and a smile and take a seat at the far end of the table, wedged in the corner by the sliding glass door that leads out onto the old deck. Owen sits beside me, his girlfriend, Wyatt, beside him. Grace and her boyfriend, retired Stanley Cup champion Decker Brooks, sit next to her. Felix, blessedly single (and vowing to stay that way), takes the seat across from me.

Everyone begins talking at once.

There are lots of requests to pass things and questions about the food, offers to grab drinks and extra napkins and salt. I scoop a polite amount of casserole onto my plate and fill the rest with salad that apparently—per the shouting across the table—came from Corianne's garden. The noise feels like a physical thing, pressing in on me from all sides. I find myself ducking my head, eyes on my plate, trying to keep it from crushing me, just like when I was a teenager.

I fork a bite of salad into my mouth and realize that one of the very few things I actually missed about Indiana was homegrown tomatoes. I can practically taste that Midwestern sun still warm on the ruby-red skin.

"Grace, this is really great," Wyatt says around a mouthful of casserole. "Is this turkey?"

"Yeah! It's an enchilada casserole with ground turkey and zucchini. I got the recipe from this cookbook a publisher sent me. The author is from Wisconsin, and I think we might do an event with her at the store," she says.

"It's fantastic, babe." Decker leans over and plants a kiss on Grace's jaw that has me staring down at my plate.

"Oh, I made an extra for you to take over to Madeline and Betsy," Grace says to Archer. "I heard they were sick."

"Yeah, they've both got COVID. I think Betsy picked it up on the plane coming back from visiting her dad in Atlanta," Archer says, and a shadow crosses his face as he mentions the trip. Madeline is Archer's next-door neighbor, the single mom of thirteen-year-old Betsy, and every time Archer talks about them, his eyes go all gooey. But if you ask him about it, he immediately starts gaslighting everyone in a five-mile radius.

"Let me know if they need a house call. I'd rather mask up and check on them than bring Betsy into the practice and risk her exposing people," Owen says, ever the town golden boy.

All around me, my family chatters about work and their lives, and I sit in the corner, silently forking food into my mouth. It's been more than fifteen years since I lived at home, and it doesn't escape my notice that the family dynamics haven't changed. Archer is still bossing everyone around, Felix is still fucking around, Owen is trying to take care of everyone, and Grace is still the baby.

And I'm still trying to disappear.

"Okay, I called this family dinner, so eyes on me," Dad says, clapping his hands until everyone falls silent and turns their attention to the head of the table. "I want to share some news with you all." He reaches over and takes Corianne's hand in his. "Corianne and I have decided to move in together, and we've decided that the best plan is for me to move into her place."

Grace gasps. Felix drops his fork.

"Are you serious?" Archer asks.

"I know it comes as a shock, but Corianne's house has a better layout. It's closer to the hardware store. She's been cultivating her garden for decades, and she's got that old garage that I can turn into a workshop."

"But...this is our house," Grace whispers. Decker threads his fingers through hers and gives her hand a squeeze.

"Yes, but you kids are all starting your own lives. You've got places of your own. Grace, you and Decker are moving out to the lake. Felix and Owen have their house. Archer, you've got yours. And Dan..." Dad trails off, because of course I don't have my own place anymore. I have Carson's mom's old sewing room and a mountain of uncertainty.

I look up from my plate and catch Dad's eye, trying to let him know with a look that everything's fine. We don't need to acknowledge any of that out loud. Thankfully, he takes the hint and moves on. And because his news is so shocking, my siblings don't take the opportunity to pepper me with questions like they normally would.

"We're going to put the house on the market in a few weeks, so you'll all have plenty of time to take whatever you want. I imagine it'll take a while to sell in this market, so nothing is going to happen overnight," Dad says. "I know this is hard news. For some of you, it may feel like you're losing part of your mother all over again. But I need you all to know that I will always love her and that none of the love our family shared with her lives in the walls of this house. It lives in all of us, and we'll take it with us wherever we go."

For the first time I can remember, everyone at the table is silent, save for a couple of sniffles from Grace.

"Shit, Dad, did you finally get a therapist?" Felix cracks.

"In fact I did," he says, his voice a low grumble.

"Well, congratulations," Owen says, smiling in a way that looks only slightly forced. I can tell he's doing his best to get on board, to support Dad, and to drag all our siblings along with him, fulfilling his role as the peacekeeper. Owen raises his glass and casts a look around the table until everyone else does too. But I notice that beneath the table, he reaches for Wyatt's hand and gives it a hard squeeze.

Archer's brow is still furrowed, but he seems to be biting his tongue. He raises his glass. Grace raises hers even as she tips her head onto Decker's shoulder. Felix is the only one who looks mostly unbothered by the news. After the toast, he immediately offers to help Dad with whatever fixes the house needs to get it ready to go on the market. That gets Archer's attention, and before long, the three of them are adding to a list on Felix's phone.

Before long, the trademark McBride family din returns. Everyone is leaning in to someone else, chattering, commiserating, planning. And I'm at the end of the table, wondering where I fit in. When I was halfway across the country, I could tell myself that was why I felt so separate from everyone. But now that I'm here, I'm realizing that the physical distance wasn't the problem. I love my family, but they fit me like a wool sweater that has shrunk in the wash. Or maybe *I'm* the one who fits *them* badly.

I wish I felt as comfortable with them as they feel with each other. I wish I could be as unbothered as Felix. I wish I had Archer's instinct to look out for everyone, even if it is stifling. I wish I had the comfort that Owen has with Wyatt and Grace has with Decker. I wish I understood why I can't seem to connect with anyone the way they all connect with each other.

And then my mind goes to Carson, my stubbornly hopeful, defiantly happy, delightfully feisty roommate.

And I wish she were here. Then I don't think I'd feel like I had to stare at my plate. I don't think I'd have to tune out the noise of the room so forcefully.

I know I fucked everything up with her the other night in ways I'm not even sure I understand. And also before that, when I nearly made a pass at her in her kitchen. That's the moment everything went wrong, and I want to fix it. I don't want to avoid Carson. I don't want her to avoid me.

Because the truth is, despite my best attempts to ignore it, when Archer told me I needed a friend, Carson was the only person I thought of.

———

My sister is out on the deck sniffling into Decker's shoulder while Owen and Wyatt start the dishes in the kitchen. Archer and Felix have graduated to walking around the house photographing things they need to fix, like the dent in the wall outside the room that used to be mine and Archer's from when Felix kicked it after we wouldn't let him play Xbox with us in middle school.

While everyone is occupied, I take the opportunity to slip through the living room to the front door. My only thought is getting back to the house so I can talk to Carson. I have no idea what I'm going to say, but I figure I have the drive across town to sort it out.

"Sneaking out?"

My hand is on the doorknob when I hear my dad's voice behind me, and suddenly I'm seventeen again, sneaking out of family dinner to walk around the neighborhood with my headphones on.

I turn and face Dad, trying not to duck my head like I used to. I'm thirty-one years old, after all. I can look my father in the eye.

"If that's okay," I say.

"Of course. I appreciate you coming," Dad says. "I'm always happy to see you. I know you're not in town for the best reasons, but I'd be lying if I said it wasn't nice to get to see you."

"Yeah…" I say, wishing that for once in my life I could find the right words to tell my dad what's going on in my head. "Congrats, by the way. I like Corianne. You guys seem really happy."

"Thanks, son. I'm grateful to have found another person who puts up with my nonsense."

I nod. "You're a lucky man."

"Don't I know it." Dad pulls me in for a hug and sighs into my shoulder. "I love you, Dan. No matter what. You never have to worry about being or doing or saying the right thing on my account. I love you just as you are, you hear me?"

My throat gets tight as I squeeze my dad's shoulders, still broad and strong but a little more stooped than I remember. And for the first time since I walked in the door, I exhale, deep and long. Because in between all the memories from my childhood of escaping or hiding, there are these memories too. Of my father letting me just be, of him reminding me that he'll always be there for me, that he loves me no matter what.

It's a reminder that even when things are hard, I'm still a lucky motherfucker.

"Thanks, Dad."

I pull back but don't immediately reach for the door.

"It's okay, you can go. It seems like you have someplace to be?" Dad says.

"Just a personal thing," I say.

"I hope you've got somebody you can talk to. I get why it's hard to talk to me, or even your siblings. But having Corianne by my side these last two years has shown me how much I needed someone I could talk to. And the craziest part is that I had no idea how badly I needed it until I had it."

I don't know if Dad realizes how far he's drilled down into me. It's like he sees right through me.

For the first time in a long time, it's comforting to be seen.

"Yeah," I say, the word clawing its way up my throat. But I'm trying.

Dad nods, a smile playing at the corner of his lips. "Go on, then. I'll see you later."

CHAPTER 14
CARSON

Three hours of derby practice is followed by two hours of laughing with the freshies and stuffing my face with nachos and beer, then a forty-five minute drive home. By the time I walk in the door, the day has caught up with me.

I'm tired. I'm sweaty. I need something to eat that isn't deep-fried.

I drop my skate bag inside the door and drag my aching body toward the kitchen, praying the fruit salad in the fridge hasn't grown fuzzy.

It's not until I'm in the quiet stillness of my house that I realize I smell. Bad. Like sweat and rubber and—I sniff my arms where my pads were—a moldy old couch. I grimace, already thinking about the bag of lavender Epsom salts underneath my sink and how good it'll feel to slip into a bath hot enough to cook a shrimp.

But when I shuffle into the kitchen, my quads screaming, I remember that I have a roommate.

A very tall, very broody roommate.

And he's sitting at my kitchen table, a notebook in front of him and a pencil in his hand.

Is he...is he *drawing*?

I freeze, because he hasn't heard me, thanks to the headphones he's wearing. He's bent over the notebook, his left arm braced against the table. He's concentrating, but he looks relaxed. His shoulder muscles flex and twitch as the pencil moves across the paper, the only sound in the kitchen the soft *skritch skritch skritch* as the lead scrapes the paper. I can see only a corner of the paper, but I make out a riot of flowers with thick outlines, bursting and blooming and overlapping such that they look alive.

And then all of a sudden, his pencil freezes, his muscles going taut, his shoulders creeping up to his ears. He senses me here. He turns slowly, and when he sees me standing in the kitchen, he quickly flips the notebook over.

Which is when I remember my last words to him the other day. I made a promise to stay out of his way. Out of his business.

So instead of asking any of the fifteen to twenty questions on the tip of my tongue—*You draw? What are you drawing? Can I see? Do you have more?*—I march past him, limping only slightly as my muscles scream at me. I throw open the fridge door and pull out the fruit salad, attacking it with a fork I snag from the drawer.

I'm toying with the idea of taking this bowl of fruit salad into the bath with me when I hear the rustle of paper. I cut my eyes back to the table and see that Dan has flipped his notebook back over. I can see the full illustration now. It's an upside-down horseshoe with intricate shading that makes it look like worn vintage iron. An explosion of peonies and daisies tumbles from the bottom right side of the horseshoe. There are curling leafy vines around the whole piece and what looks like a long string of pearls draped around the picture, dripping off the edges.

"You hang the horseshoe upside down so the luck doesn't fall out," he says, tapping the illustration with the eraser of his pencil.

I don't know what surprises me more: that he drew this, or that he explained it.

"It's beautiful," I say.

"Thanks." He drops his pencil, leaning on his elbow to run his thick hand over his buzzed head. "I like to doodle."

"That looks like a little more than a doodle," I say.

His jaw clenches, like he's literally chewing over his thoughts, before he speaks. "It's, uh, actually a tattoo?"

My eyebrows shoot up. "You draw tattoos?"

He nods, shifting in his chair. "I tattoo," he says. "On people."

There is a very real moment when I wonder if the word *tattoo* means something different in finance, because the notion that Dan McBride is a secret tattoo artist seems as likely as him being a superhero. "Are you serious? You give people tattoos? Like, real tattoos?"

He nods.

"How? I mean, when? I thought…finance?" Oh god, I sound like I'm having a stroke. But also I kind of feel like I'm having a stroke. Dan McBride is seriously an undercover *tattoo artist*?

Dan shrugs, and at first I think it's a signal to walk away, that he doesn't want to talk to me. But he doesn't turn, doesn't look away. He keeps those stormy blue eyes right on me.

So I try again. I lean back against the counter, stab a piece of pineapple, and ask him the first question that comes to mind.

"How does one become a tattoo artist? Like, who signs up to be someone's very first subject?"

He visibly relaxes at the question, his shoulders dropping, his fingers unclenching from around the pencil.

"I tattooed on myself to start."

"You can do that?"

He lifts the hem of his shorts to reveal a pale slice of skin on his upper thigh. It's decorated with a cluster of small tattoos. It kind of looks like what happens when my kindergarteners get hold of a sticker sheet.

"Which was the first?" I ask.

He taps a little lightning bolt. "This one."

His answers are short, but he doesn't seem uncomfortable. After he answers each question, he brings his eyes back to mine as if to invite the next. For the first time since he moved into my house more than a week ago, the man seems like he might actually want to talk to me.

So I keep going.

"How many do you have?" I ask.

"A lot," he replies.

"Where?"

He pauses, cocking his head. "Not in places you can see."

The implications of that particular statement announce themselves low in my belly, curling and warm. And as I'm contemplating what exactly I'm feeling, he doubles down by reaching for his sleeve and rolling it up.

The first thing I see is a rose. Then a small snake. Small black line drawings wind up his arm. There are probably a dozen of them, each one distinct, yet placed such that they make up a full piece.

It's at that moment that I realize he's always wearing long sleeves. I've never seen any of these because he never shows them.

"I'm sorry, is that...is that a hot dog?" I ask, catching the bottom of a design that peeks out from his sleeve.

He grins. "Yeah. I always get one when I go see the Mets play."

His sleeve stops mid-biceps, but it's clear that's not where the designs end.

"Are there more?" I ask.

He nods.

The way he looks at me turns my insides molten. Suddenly all those carved muscles I've envisioned beneath his perfectly tailored clothes are covered in ink. I didn't think I had a thing for guys with tattoos, but I know now that I was very wrong.

Or maybe I just have a thing for broody, quiet, buttoned-up Dan McBride covered in secret tattoos.

"Why do you always keep them covered up?" I ask. His jaw clenches. "Sorry if this feels like an inquisition. I can stop."

"I don't mind," he says, the words coming out quickly.

"You sure?"

"Yeah," he says, and this time there's the barest hint of a smile on his lips. "When I started getting tattooed in college, I stuck to places I could hide easily for internships and work. I wanted to make sure I still read as clean-cut in interviews and networking situations. People tend not to want to entrust huge chunks of their wealth to someone with knuckle tats."

I nod. "And now?" I realize too late that we've tiptoed back to the question of his troubles, and I prepare for deflection. I even consider taking it back. Anything to keep him from shutting down again.

Instead he gazes back at the intricate design in his notebook, cocking his head as his eyes trace the lines. "I don't know. I guess I'm waiting to see if I need to be respectable anymore," he says, then blows out a breath like it's the first time he's actually said that out loud. And maybe it is. I still have no idea what's going on with him, but this is the closest he's ever come to telling me. "Listen, I wanted to apologize for the other day. I totally messed that up. I'm not really very good at talking, in case you hadn't noticed."

I nod, because I absolutely have noticed. "It seems like you're doing just fine now," I say.

"We'll see how long I can keep this up," he says with a rueful laugh. Then he takes a deep breath and blows it out. "What I meant to say that night was that *I* could use a friend. I'm pretty short on them these days."

My heart aches at the sight of this man sitting in my kitchen, asking me to be his friend.

"I'd love to be your friend, Dan," I tell him gently. "And I should probably apologize too. I was kind of high on this new roller derby thing that night. I was a little feistier than usual."

He lets out a quiet laugh. "How's that going?"

Even though I feel nervous and fizzy, I can't help the smile that spreads across my face. Because just the thought of derby and what I accomplished today—hell, the fact that I showed up at all is a wild accomplishment—is like an ember glowing inside of me, threatening to burst into flame.

"It's awesome," I say, dropping into the chair across from him. I pause and glance at him to see if I should keep going. I don't want to overwhelm Dan with my enthusiasm. I'm a yapper, and he's decidedly not, but when he leans back in his chair, his arm slung over the empty chair beside him, the corner of his lips almost twitching into a grin, I decide to talk.

"There were fourteen of us today, and we could not have been a more motley crew. Some of us had more skating skills than others, but none of us had ever played before except for this one girl named Maude Forbid who transferred from somewhere in Michigan, I think?"

"Maude Forbid?"

"Yeah. We get to pick derby names, if we want. Violet is called Violet Rage, and KO is Knockout. I actually don't even know her real name. It's kind of awesome. I've never had a nickname before. I've always just been Carson. I mean, the only real way to shorten it is to call me Cars, and that's sort of…I don't know, it lacks something. So I need to do some thinking. If you have any ideas, definitely let me know."

He nods, his full attention still on me. So I go on.

"We practiced a bunch of skating skills and finished with a speed test and an endurance test. For endurance, we had to do twenty-seven laps in under five minutes, which I definitely did not do. But then we did a sprint, which was supposed to be a single lap in under thirteen seconds, and I did it. I freaking *did it*. On my first try! And when I crossed the finish line, everyone was cheering, and I don't know, it was just cool to be in this room full of badass women cheering each other on. I just…I just loved it."

He smiles, and it's a real one—I can tell because there's a dimple in his left cheek that I've never seen before. "That's amazing, Carson."

The sound of my name coming out of his mouth nearly sucks the air from my lungs. Thank god I'm already sitting or my knees might have given out.

"It really was," I say. I clear my throat and continue. "I mean, it was really hard. My body is definitely not used to doing this stuff, and I haven't even gotten hit yet. I have a feeling my muscles aren't going to know the difference tomorrow, though. I'm going to be *sore*."

He nods. "Taking up something new is always an adjustment. My arm was exhausted after the first couple of weeks of tattooing. Holding the gun steady, the physical concentration. I had to ice my shoulder every night."

I eye his arms, his sleeves still rolled midway up his forearms. He's obviously jacked, his arms carved and veined. Woe betide the pickle jar that tries to best him.

"I can help you out," Dan says, and my eyes suddenly jerk away from the wonder that is his arms.

"With what?" I stutter.

"I can take you to the gym. Teach you how to lift."

I grimace like he just suggested I eat my neighbor's cat. "Ugh, I fucking hate the gym."

He laughs. "That's the first time I've heard you swear."

"Hazard of teaching five-year-olds. Your vocabulary becomes decidedly PG."

"Funny that the gym is what brought it out of you."

I sigh. "It makes me think of my mother saying, 'A moment on the lips, a lifetime on the hips.' As if my weight were something I could control and not, you know, part of my genetics."

Dan's jaw clenches, and he's silent for a long moment. Too long. Long enough that I start shifting in my chair under the force of his glare. When he finally speaks, it's only after a long, slow inhale and a harsh exhale. He leans across the table, and the heat of his gaze is enough to make me sit back in my chair, like his attention could actually burn me.

"Carson, I don't want to take you to the gym to make you smaller. I want to take you to the gym to make you bigger," he says, like he can't believe anyone would ever suggest anything else. And then his full lips curve into the most devilish grin. "We put a little more muscle on that ass, you're going to knock girls into the stands. And that's something I want to see."

I blink, swallowing hard to keep from choking on the chunk of pineapple lodged in my throat.

"I, uh—" I sputter. "Okay."

"Yeah?"

I nod.

"Monday?"

Oh crap, I thought I'd have more time to try to get out of this.

"Sure," I concede, even though I'm far from it.

"Seven a.m. okay?"

I grimace. "Do we have to?"

He grins. "Best way to start your day."

"Fine." I might regret talking to him after all.

He rises from his chair and opens the fridge to pull out the orange juice, and the motion of the door produces just enough wind to send my taped-up sample of lemon-printed wallpaper fluttering to the floor. He bends and scoops it up, studying it like he's committing to memory every sunny yellow curve, every green leaf.

"What's this?" he finally asks.

"Just a wallpaper sample. It's been hanging there for months. I'm surprised the Scotch tape held on so long," I say.

He glances up. "You still considering it?"

"No...yes? I mean, I love that wallpaper. It's so bright and happy. I can imagine it perking me up on even the darkest day of a Midwestern winter. I definitely want that wallpaper."

"I could help you put it up. Since you're letting me stay."

I shake my head. "Oh god, no. You don't need to earn your keep. And anyway, you've already done more than enough by picking my drunk ass up in Spencer. I just...I don't know, I haven't really been able to commit to anything in here yet." I stand and walk past him to deposit the now-empty fruit salad Tupperware in the sink. On my way, I pluck the wallpaper from his hand.

"It would look good," he says. "It's a good choice."

"Thanks," I say, sticking the sample back on the wall with a mental note to find another piece of tape. I love this wallpaper. I loved it from the first moment I saw it. I *want* this wallpaper. I just...I don't know if I want it *here*. Which makes no sense, because this is my house. My kitchen. I have no idea where else I'd put it. I just need to suck it up and order the rolls, break the seal and put it up. Grace is right—I need to start focusing on myself and my future. And I should start with this wallpaper.

I turn away from the sink and see Dan studying me in very much the same way he focused on his drawing. It makes my skin prickle. His lips part like he wants to ask me more about the wallpaper, but I say, "I'm going to shower. Seven a.m.?"

He nods. "Seven a.m."

CHAPTER 15
DAN

I t's a hazy Monday a week later when I pull into the parking lot of Gene's Gym, the sky turning purple as the sun rises.

But Carson isn't looking at the horizon. She's peering through the windshield at the double doors of Gene's like there's a combination root canal/colonoscopy waiting for her inside.

"Are you okay?" I ask, shutting off the engine.

She nods very hard for way too long. "Yeah, totally! Totally, totally fine," she chirps. When I raise an eyebrow, she sighs. "It's just that at this moment, my nervous system seems to think I've traveled back in time to middle school gym class."

I laugh, but she doesn't. "There won't even be that many people in there this early. Gene's isn't that popular. There's nothing to be scared of. "

I can practically hear her eye roll. "Uh, says *you*. You look like you were designed in a lab to be in there. I look like I star in some jerk's TikTok about what a disaster I am in there."

I clench my jaw, the thought of some asshole tormenting her making me want to tear the doors off this car. "This gym has a no filming policy, and even if they didn't, if I saw anyone filming you in there, I'd remove their teeth from their head."

Her cheeks turn pink, but she still looks skeptical, and I have to remind myself what it was like to be new at the gym. I was in college when I first started going. Jameson dragged me there after much protestation. Growing up, my brothers were always in the weight room at school, Archer and Felix for hockey and Owen during baseball and track season. But I never took to sports growing up. I figured one of us had be unathletic, and that was me. I was the quiet one, the serious one, the one who would rather stay home and play video games than get up early for practice. I was the kid in gym class who was happy to be hit early in a dodgeball game so I could sit in the bleachers and flip through the paperback I'd smuggled in. My only goal in high school was to get the hell out of Cardinal Springs, and sports were not part of that plan.

When I got to Princeton, I assumed my real life would begin. I was in a new place where nobody knew me. Everything had to get better. But that first semester, my classes kicked my ass, and the social thing didn't go much better. I couldn't figure out why it was so easy for everyone else to make friends and find their place. I'd see groups in the dining hall laughing and talking, people spread out on blankets in the quad, and gaggles trudging from house party to house party together. Where had they all met? Had I missed some kind of make-a-friend event where they'd all exchanged numbers? The only person I managed to talk to in the first month of freshman year was Jameson, and that was only because he was my roommate.

But after six weeks, Jameson finally had enough of me rotting in my extra-long twin bed between classes, my laptop cooking me as I watched Netflix and perused message boards. He dragged me to the gym, walked me through the space, showed me how to use every machine and dumbbell, and make me lift.

But I don't know how to tell Carson about my pathetic social trauma, or maybe I don't want her to know just how awkward I can be, so instead I say, "I wasn't always built like this. I worked up to it by going there." I point at the double glass doors, and she sighs again.

"Fine." She climbs out of the car, plants her feet on the cracked asphalt of the parking lot, and squares her shoulders, her brows knitting together in determination. Her lips move as she gives herself a silent pep talk, and then she gives the slightest nod. "Let's do this."

I take her to the front desk, where a barely awake teenager stands behind a desktop computer that probably predates him. I flash my laminated membership card.

"And I've got a guest," I say, nodding to Carson.

The sleepy teen says nothing but pulls a sheet of paper out from beneath the desk, nodding at a chipped mug full of mismatched pens, most of them missing their caps.

"This place is delightfully low-tech," Carson says while she fills out the bare-bones release form. "No app? No key tag to scan? No influencers in candy-colored spandex?"

"Gene's does not do frills. I don't think the membership cards have changed since the eighties, when Gene got a laminator," I say. "That's what I like about it."

"Well, it's certainly not the smell."

I lift an eyebrow. "You don't love eau de gym socks and rubber?"

"I usually lean more toward citrus and bleach, but this will do," she says with a grin, and I think she might be working through her anxiety. But as soon as we start to walk toward the machines, she tenses.

I reach for her arm to stop her. "Hey, look at me," I say, and when she turns tilt her chin up with my finger. I wait until she meets my gaze, and then I have to take a beat, because looking straight into her big eyes the color of a summer sky damn near knocks me out. "I'm going to be by your side the entire time. I won't let you get hurt, I won't let you embarrass yourself, and I won't let anyone give you any shit. But if at any moment you need to tap out, you can do that. Okay?"

There's a long pause, and for a minute I think she's going to march past me and straight out the door. Instead, her lips quirk as she says, "Can we have a password?"

"A password?" I ask. "You mean like a safe word?"

She blushes, and I have to beat back all the thoughts that come along with that particular fantasy. I told her I needed a friend, after all. Anything else would be ungentlemanly.

"Yes," she says.

I nod. "Name it."

She thinks about it. "Lemon."

My mind immediately goes to the wallpaper sample in her kitchen and the look on her face when she told me about it. She loves it, clearly, but something is holding her back. She isn't ready to explain what, and I'm certainly not going to push her to talk. But I like that she's bringing it up with me now. It's like she sees me as safe.

I like it a lot.

"Okay," I say. "You want to leave, you just say 'lemon' and we'll get out of here."

She nods. "Yeah. Okay. Let's do it."

"Attagirl," I say, and give myself three seconds to enjoy the rush of pink that floods her cheeks. Then I shake it off. She's nervous. I told her I would help her. And that doesn't include objectifying her, no matter how good she looks in her black leggings and pink tank top, the crisscross straps of a green sports bra sticking out tantalizingly underneath. "Okay, let's do legs today. Quads will help you skate, and glutes will help you hit."

She nods, her brow set like I'm her drill sergeant.

"We'll start with some mobility to get warmed up."

I take her over to an open space in front of a bank of mirrors and grab two mats, then lead her through some basic stretches and gentle joint movements. She watches me closely, sometimes pulling her pillowy bottom lip between her teeth, sometimes letting out these breathy little sounds as she sinks into a stretch.

I thought the gym would be a safe space. I've never once walked into this place, which smells like sweat and old sneakers and has a soundtrack of eighties hair metal and the occasional male grunt, and thought of sex.

But that was before Carson was standing next to me in front of a full-length mirror, her ass encased in black spandex, her strawberry-blond hair pulled back in a bouncy ponytail that begs for me to wrap it around my hand and yank.

But, you know, in a fun way.

It takes every ounce of my concentration not to let my body react to her. But I manage to lock it down, because I don't want to be a fucking creep. And also my gym shorts don't leave much room for error.

And then a welcome distraction appears in the mirror behind us.

"Always with the stretching," Norm grunts, because he's forever teasing me about how mobility is new age woo shit and not the number-one way to make sure I'll be able to get out of bed without wincing when I'm eighty.

Then his eyes land on Carson.

"And who's this?" he asks.

For the first time in the year that I've been working out beside him, Norm isn't glowering. No, suddenly there's an actual gleam in his eye.

"This is my, uh, friend," I say, glancing at her as I try the word on for size. Friends—that's what we are. Roommates too, I guess, but I hope that even after I move back into Decker's apartment, if the plumbing ever gets fixed, Carson and I can stay friends. I don't make many of them, so I'd like to keep her, if I can. And from the smile she gives me, I think she might agree. "This is Carson Webber."

She smiles and holds out a hand, which Norm seems to find charming as all get-out. When he takes her hand, he pulls her in a little, dropping his voice as he says, "He's not giving you any trouble, is he?"

And then the smooth motherfucker winks.

Suddenly, grumpy, sullen Norm is goddamn charmer. Mr. Shut

Up and Lift looks like he's ready to sit down for brunch with Carson and yap about whatever the Real Housewives are up to.

"He's been really helpful," she says, glancing at me with a smile. "I'm a little bit nervous, to be honest."

Norm chuckles. "Oh, it's not so hard. Just pick up heavy things and put them down again. That's all there is to it."

Carson giggles, and I'd glare at Norm for hitting on my girl, but she's not my girl. And his words also seem to have calmed whatever nerves she was still holding on to, so I guess I should be grateful to the motherfucker.

"You know what the hardest part is?" he says.

"What?" she asks.

He points toward the front. "Walking in that door," he says. "Congratulations. Now get to work."

CHAPTER 16
CARSON

Dan leads me to the back of the gym, where a row of contraptions that look like playground equipment lines the rear wall. Giant weights hang on racks like enormous wheels of cheese, and damn, I wish I were at home eating cheese right now instead of standing here in spandex, wishing I had a moment to pick my thong out of my butt. Dan made me eat scrambled eggs before we came, and they're sitting in my stomach like sour lead.

Dan drops his gym bag beside the rack in the far corner. He's wearing a pair of gym shorts and a black hoodie. I don't know how's he's not burning up. I haven't even done anything, and I'm already sweating in here. The air conditioning in this place seems like a mere suggestion, the thick air circulating mostly thanks to a couple of those big orange fans you see on industrial construction sites. They sound like jet engines and do nothing to change the temperature.

"Okay, we'll start with some Romanian dead lifts. They're good for hamstrings and glutes, both of which you'll want to be good and strong for skating." He grabs one of the thick, shiny barbells and steps back. "You want your feet about shoulder width apart, and you're going to push your butt back like you're using it to close a door, lowering the barbell down your legs like you're shaving your shins with it."

I stifle a laugh. "Wow, that's very…descriptive."

"Just trying to be as clear as possible," he says as he prepares to demonstrates the movement. "Watch."

And oh, I watch. I could watch him all day. Because this man's ass, which is pushed back and flexing, is a work of art. He's caked up like it's my birthday. You could haul mountains with that dump truck. You could bounce an entire roll of quarters off those cheeks. When he stands up, his hips move forward in a way that makes a lot of very explicit images flit through my mind.

Good lord, ten minutes in a gym and I've become a Neanderthal. At least I was already pink-cheeked from the heat, so he can't tell that I'm blushing while imagining him doing something very different with his hips.

He does a few reps while I try not to blush so hard my cheeks sizzle, then places the bar back on the rack.

"Okay, you try," he says, his voice both gentle and authoritative.

"Are you going to put any weight on it?" I ask.

"The bar weighs forty-five pounds, and right now we're just learning form. So no."

My nose scrunches up as I step toward the bar. "Isn't that embarrassing? To use just the bar?"

I can tell Dan's working to hold back a smile. Damn, I love infuriating him. He's usually so stoic. It makes me want to see what happens when he really lets loose. "I only used the bar just now. Carson, nobody here is judging you. Most people are so busy staring at themselves in the mirror that they'll never even notice you at all."

"Not even a little bit?" I ask with a wink as I reach down to grip the bar.

"Cute," he says with an eye roll and a little smirk. "Now, show me what you got."

Hot damn, I did not know the gym was quite so flirty.

The bar is rough beneath my palms. I adjust my feet, then adjust them again, then adjust them a third time. I look forward into the mirror and see my red cheeks and wide eyes. I look like I've been tasked with lifting weights while riding a roller coaster. It's really super cute. I'm remembering why I never come to places like this.

"Stop judging yourself and just go," Dan chides. "Were you this freaked out at your first roller derby practice?"

I wasn't. Which in hindsight is pretty insane. But I loved it from the very first moment I put skates on—the movement, the way my heart pounded, how my breath came in gasps. I'd never felt so inside my body before, never been so aware of every muscle and joint. So in control of a body that, for my whole life, has felt very out of my control. My mother spent every day telling me what foods were good and what foods were bad and in what quantities, and still I woke up each morning in a body that was fiercely determined to be what it was. My body's will has always been stronger than whatever fad diet my mother put us on. But on skates, for the first time in my life, I felt like I was using my body in a way it was made to be used. For the first time, I didn't feel like it needed to be any different.

The difference, of course, was that I had a whole crowd of newbies to look stupid with me.

But I didn't look stupid. Or if I did, I didn't care.

I liked not caring.

I *loved* not caring.

So I give it a go now.

I set my jaw, stare into the mirror, and bend.

And I wobble.

I have no idea what this is supposed to feel like, but it doesn't feel right. I simultaneously feel like I'm going to tip forward and rock backward. I jerk up, the bar going cattywampus in my grip.

"Okay, we need to adjust your form a little—you're using your back too much," Dan says. I appreciate that he's pretending I got the movement even close to correct or have any idea to fix what I did. He steps behind me. "Is it okay to touch you?"

I nearly drop the bar on my feet.

"Uh, yup," is what I mange to reply. "Sure, definitely. That's fine. Touch away."

Very cool, Carson.

His hands are warm when they land softly on my hips, heat licking at my skin. His fingers press into my hip bones, pulling back slightly. My body bows, my hips hinging as I let his firm grip lead me.

"You're going to bend here, pushing your hips back. Go," he says gently, and I do, trying so hard not to think about the fact that I'm pressing my hips directly back into his lap that it's actually *all* I can think about. As I bend, one of his hands coasts up the column of my spine, leaving a trail of fire across my skin. "You want to keep your back neutral. Don't round your shoulders or arch your back here."

One of his palms stops at the small of my back, right at the waistband of my leggings. I freeze, every muscle flexing, and lean into his hand. I blow out a breath that I hope sounds like exertion and not pure lust.

Do not sexually harass your roommate. Do not assign sexual intent to his coaching. This man is helping you out of the kindness of his heart. He's let you into his sacred gym space. He's talking, which is a thing he never does. Respect that, and respect him, and get your freaking mind out of the gutter.

Maybe it's his touch or the distraction provided by my hormones, but I suddenly stop panicking about being at the gym and doing things wrong and getting made fun of. I'm simultaneously focusing on my body and not focusing at all, my mind drifting into a meditative state where all I feel are my muscles stretching and flexing, the weight of the bar in my hands, and the pounding of my heart as I lower and rise.

"Good, that's it," Dan says. "That's perfect."

My heart stutters. This is all too much—the weight in my palms and the sound of his voice and the feel of his hands on my body. I need to calm the fuck down.

But then I glance up into the mirror.

I find his eyes, which are trained on my body. As if he can feel my gaze, his eyes come up to meet mine in the mirror. The sound of Def Leppard on the crackly sound system fades away. The air in the gym seems to still.

And for a moment, Dan McBride looks at me with fire in his eyes.

"You guys at the beginning of your workout or the end?"

The tether between our gazes snaps as Archer bounds up behind us like a human Saint Bernard. I think I might hear Dan let out a small groan, but I'm probably imagining that. Wishful thinking.

"We're just starting," Dan says after dragging his eyes away from mine. "It's Carson's first time."

Archer's grin widens. "That's awesome! Is Dan going easy on you?"

No, I'm more turned on than I've ever been.

"Yup. Definitely. He's great," I say, plastering what I hope isn't a manic grin on my face. I want to rerack the empty bar, but I worry I won't know what to do with my hands without it, so I just stand there holding it like an idiot.

"You guys doing just legs today or you hitting a full body?" Archer steps up to the rack beside us and starts doing a few squats and lunges. He's approaching his mid-thirties, still lean and muscular, evidence of his former life as a professional athlete. There's a long scar on his knee from the injury that ended his career.

"Legs," Dan grunts.

"Cool, same. Mind if I join you guys?"

Dan's jaw flexes, but I just smile wider. Archer's good looking, but his oppressive big brother energy is the cold shower I need right now.

"Yeah, absolutely. The more the merrier," I say with a wild grin.

Dan's face shutters.

The rest of the workout is filled with Archer's loud, happy chatter, which I work to keep up with as Dan quietly explains and demonstrates different movements and machines.

He doesn't touch me again.

For the next forty-five minutes, we visit different stations around the gym. I learn about leg extensions and calf raises and glute bridges, Dan and Archer and I taking turns on each machine just like I teach my kindergarteners to do on the playground. We end up in an area filled with rows padded benches and several racks of dumbbells lining the wall in front of a bank of mirrors.

"Let's finish with a single leg movement," Dan says. "Curtsy lunges."

"Do Bulgarians," Archer says with a devious grin.

"Curtsy lunges, because I'm not trying to kill her on her first day," Dan replies with just a hint of venom.

And as he's done at every other station, Dan calmly and quietly explains both the movement and the mechanics. He demonstrates, and just like at every other station, I try to watch him without ogling him. Because as I've learned today, nearly every movement a person makes in the gym is damn near pornographic.

I'm going to need a cold shower when I get home.

Dan has me try the lunges without weight, and when I earn his delicious approval—the smallest nod of his head, which hits me like the sexiest praise I've ever received—he brings me a set of ten-pound dumbbells and sets them on the floor in front of me. I reach for them, but Dan shakes his head.

"Rest," he says.

"But I didn't do anything," I say. "That was just practice."

"Listen to the boy," Norm says, ambling over to an empty bench beside us. He drops his little shaker cup that all the men in this gym seem to carry around, then pulls a pair of fifty-pound dumbbells from the rack. My back hurts just from watching him pick them up, but Norm, despite his advanced age, seems to find their weight a mere annoyance. "Rest is just as important as the work. Rushing through is how you get injured."

Dan gives me a look that says, *See?* I roll my eyes in response and sit down on my bench just as my phone emits the weird little ding that indicates I have a new match on Hinge.

"What the hell was that?" Norm grunts, the dumbbells over his head.

"Sounds like I might have a date." I unlock my phone and swipe to the app. I avoided it for a couple of days post-Gabe, but then my lust for Dan coupled with our agreement to be friends drove me back into the arms of digital dating. For the last day or so I've been chatting with an MBA student at IU who doesn't seem like he'll murder and/or abandon me.

"You're on the apps?" Archer asks. He drops his weights with a thud so loud that I jump.

"Dude, it's more impressive if you control them all the way to the floor," Dan grumbles, but Archer isn't listening. He's too busy trying to peer over my shoulder at my phone screen.

I shrug. "To quote our savior Sabrina Carpenter, 'since the Lord forgot my gay awakening,' I'm not going to meet anyone playing roller derby. So it looks like it's the apps for me."

"In my day, we just met women in the wild and asked them out on dates," Norm says. He cuts a look at Dan, who drops his eyes to the floor.

"Surely there's got to be a better way," Archer says.

"When you find it, let me know. In the meantime, I'm going to meet, uh"—I squint down at the screen, reading the name of my newest love connection—"*Jack* tomorrow night at Hoosier Brews in Bloomington."

"Please tell me you're driving yourself this time," Dan says.

I give him a saucy smile. "Yes, I am. I learned my lesson."

"Good girl," Dan says. His voice is low, and I don't think

Norm and Archer hear him, since they're both mid-lift. But I do, and the blood in my veins goes molten. Our eyes meet in the mirror, that spark from earlier returning.

But then Archer's weights hit the floor again, and my stomach leaps into my throat, my eyes tearing away from Dan's gaze.

"What do you know about this guy?" Archer asks, because apparently he's *everyone's* big brother.

I roll my eyes but scroll through the profile anyway. "According to his profile, he's six feet tall—"

Archer scoffs. "He's five-ten. *Maybe*," he says.

"I'll be sure to bring my tape measure," I say with another eye roll, then peer back down at my phone. "He's getting his MBA at IU, and he likes road biking, bar trivia, and spy movies."

"Let me see his picture," Archer says.

He takes my phone and begins swiping. Norm uses his rest period to peer over Archer's shoulder. From what I can tell, Jack is your standard-issue college town white boy. He's got an orthodontist smile and wears a lot of khaki. His sunglasses are on a leash in every photo. He looks like a basic bitch, and honestly, at this point I'll take it. If the man is polite to servers and doesn't comment on my weight or my diet, I will happily crawl into bed with him. If this gym outing is any indication, I need to get laid *yesterday*.

Archer shakes his head when he reaches the end of Jack's photos. "This guy is giving big steak-well-done vibes," he says.

"That boy looks like a hangnail would take him out," Norm grunts.

I snatch my phone back. "You guys are more judgmental than Grace and Wyatt."

"Maybe you should listen to your friends," Dan says.

I glare at him. "My friends are busy. And anyway, it's one date in broad daylight in a public place. How bad can it possibly be?"

"That's what people say right before they end up on Dateline," Archer says.

I glare at the lot of them. "Yuk it up, but both of you are single, and I haven't seen either of you go on a date in two years, so maybe shut your smug, stupid faces!"

"My face isn't stupid!" Archer cries, then looks at Dan for backup.

Dan, as usual, says nothing.

CHAPTER 17

DAN

arcel's text came through an hour ago, and I walked straight out of the house and got into my car, leaving behind the stack of documents I was trying to commit to memory. I was supposed to fly to New York next week to give testimony in the SEC investigation regarding the missing money from Holt Capital. I've been subpoenaed. But that meeting is now on hold.

Again.

Marcel hopes it means that I'm not on the verge of getting indicted, that the investigators believe my side of the story and plan to turn their focus to Anders Holt.

It's a nice thought, but the problem is that Anders Holt has hundreds of millions of dollars and a suite of lawyers, each of whom makes more money in an hour than Marcel makes in a month. Even with the truth on my side, I'm expecting this to drag on forever.

Which means I'll stay adrift for a good long while.

But the only thing I can think about?

Carson. My roommate. My *friend*.

So I drove.

I should not be here.

It is categorically insane that I'm here at a crowded college brewery on a Friday night.

And not just because there are fourteen televisions over the bar, each playing a different sporting event, and one television the size of a Winnebago on the wall to my left that's showing a football game that looks like it happened in 1974. The sound is blessedly muted, but the flashing colors and silent screaming fans are still a nightmare of overstimulation.

No, there's no reason I should be sitting in a sports bar in Bloomington, trying to hide from my roommate/friend/object of my unfortunate affection while she has a fucking internet date. Not a good reason, anyway. Not one I want to examine very closely.

I sigh. This whole place reeks of Axe body spray and mediocre conversation.

I should not be here.

But Carson is sitting near the largest television, her back to me, as a guy with an uppercase body and a lowercase head talks at her. Not *to* her, because for most of the time I've been here, his mouth has not stopped moving. He's definitely talking *at* her.

Carson and I have been to gym twice more since our initial lesson. She's getting stronger and more confident. She no longer looks like she's second-guessing her every move.

And watching her use her body, even under fluorescent lighting in a smelly public gym, hasn't gotten any easier for me.

Which is why I'm in this fucking bar on a Friday night.

"Cucumber melon IPA?" The bartender slides a coaster in front of me.

I grimace. "That can't be real."

"It is, and it's awful. Hence why it's two dollars a pint today," the bartender says.

I glance at the taps and pick the one that looks least like it'll taste like something someone threw up at a tailgate. "B-Town IPA," I say.

"Good choice," he replies. "Anyone joining you?"

I glance back over my shoulder. Carson has slumped lower in her seat, but her date doesn't seem to have noticed. He's still yapping and gesticulating like he's giving a private TED Talk.

"Just me," I say, turning back around.

The bartender slides my pint across the bar to me, then leaves me to my own insanity. I glance back over my shoulder for the ten thousandth time, then pivot back on my stool so fast I nearly tweak my neck. In an effort to calm my nervous energy, I reach for a napkin and the bartender's pen and start doodling—swirls and flowers and a couple of lemon slices—imagining each ink stroke on skin.

On *her* skin.

She'd look gorgeous with a cluster of strawberries on her arm or a wisteria vine climbing over her shoulder. My fingers twitch as I think about the needle traveling across her skin, marking her forever.

I shouldn't be here.

But when she said her date was in the MBA program, all I could imagine was every douchebag I went to grad school with. The guys with their two-hundred-dollar haircuts and their boat shoes. The guys who used to talk unabashedly about the women they wanted to make their wives and the women they wanted to make their mistresses. The guys who had favorite strip clubs, the guys who talked about women like they were commodities to be traded. I imagined Carson ending up in the bed of a guy like that and suddenly wanted to throw the biggest dumbbell in the gym directly at the mirror.

At least that's what I told myself.

But the truth I pushed down—the truth I hid away, the truth I barely want to admit to myself—is that imagining Carson in *anyone's* bed makes me want to break things.

And that's fucked up.

Because she's not mine. She didn't ask for my protection. She full-on *told* me she just wants to be fucked, and I have absolutely no right to get in the way of that. Maybe she shouldn't be with this guy, but I don't think she should be sitting across from me, either.

It's getting harder and harder to remind myself of that.

I groan, wadding up the napkin in my fist. I've got to get out of here. If she sees me, I'll have no explanation. Not one that makes sense, anyway.

But then my phone lights up with a text, and the name on the screen makes a smile spread across my face.

CARSON

I see you over there at the bar, you creeper. And thank god, because this guy is a grade A douche canoe. Please come save me so I don't have to fake pass out and go to the ER just to get out of this date. That would be very expensive.

CHAPTER 18
CARSON

This man is polite and kind and clean, and he smells like fresh laundry, and he is *boring*.

"And then I clicked the wrong Zoom link, so I'm sitting in a meeting trying to talk about crypto markets when these guys are only interested in bonds. *Bonds!*"

Oh my god, he is *so boring*.

For about five minutes, I thought this date was going to be good. Jack pulled out my chair, then asked what I wanted to drink and ordered it for me. He told me that my dress, a fluttery little white number with a pattern of blue hydrangeas, brought out my eyes. I was already starting to plan how I could get back to his place. I was starting to imagine him without clothes, imagine his hands on me.

And then I asked him about his grad program.

I haven't spoken since.

The beer on the table in front of me is half gone, completely flat, and warm. My stomach is growling. And all hopes of getting laid are drifting away like my attention as this man continues to talk.

Men sleep with women they don't care about and aren't particularly attracted to all the time, so for the past few minutes,

I've been giving it the good old college try. What looks like studious attention to his jabbering is actually me focusing really hard, trying to imagine what it would be like to sleep with him. Could I get it up for this man?

Unfortunately, every time I try to imagine him hovering over me, all I can picture is his sunglasses—which are on a red neoprene leash around his neck—slapping me in the face. Even in my smuttiest fantasies, he remains the kind of guy who wouldn't take his sunglasses off to have sex. I bet his dirty talk is about pivot tables. I bet he comes to the sound of the New York Stock Exchange opening bell. I bet his kink is a good midyear review with HR.

Kill me.

I hope I remembered to charge my vibrator.

"And so the earnings report said the DOW was in spaghetti and sneezing the treasury yield dropped the price of ham."

Okay, that's not what he just said, but the actual words make about as much sense to me as those. Would he like it if I held him hostage at this table and talked to him about IEPs and curriculum benchmarks for an hour? I doubt it! But that's not stopping him from yammering on about the DOW and blue chips and an "epic run" on precious metals.

Oh my *god*, this man is boring.

There is no way I can sleep with him.

I can't even pretend to pay attention to him anymore.

I give up on pretending to listen and let my gaze drift. Which is when I spot him. Shoulders hunched, jaw ticking, he's bent over the bar, a pen in his hand.

Jack is still talking, something about derivatives and absolute returns, and I don't even bother to hide it as I pull out my phone and tap out a text. Luckily, Jack is so far up his own ass, he doesn't seem to notice.

I watch Dan receive the text. Watch the way his body uncoils. Watch his smile unfurl, the dimple in his left cheek deepening.

I sit back in my seat, take a swig of my warm beer, smile at Jack, and wait.

It doesn't take long.

"Carson?"

Dan is standing over our table, his broad shoulders blocking the light from the window, casting a shadow over the us.

All at once I have absolutely no trouble imagining what it would be like to have sex with *this* man. In fact, a series of images flashes through my mind like I'm looking through one of those old-fashioned viewfinder toys. His hands, his lips, his muscular ass. Oh god, asking him to save me might have been a mistake.

"Yeah?" I say, the word scraping up my throat, coming out breathy and filled with all the need in my body.

"I thought that was you," Dan says. He bites his lip, dropping his eyes to the floor. His thick dark lashes brush his cheeks. When he slowly drags his attention back up to my face, there's a light in his eyes. A playfulness I've never seen before. "I've missed you."

What?

"Oh," I breathe, feeling heat climb up my chest. I was prepared for him to claim a family emergency or just wordlessly drag me out of here. But a fake dating ruse?

I'm in.

"Yeah. I never should have let you go," he says.

I nearly leap out of my chair, throwing myself at him and locking my legs around his waist. I don't know exactly what he has planned, but I'm ready to commit to this bit. I'm in it to the bitter end, baby. *Yes, and.*

"I'm sorry, who is this?" Jack asks, his eyes moving between Dan and me.

"I'm the sorry-ass idiot who let her get away," Dan says, never taking his eyes off me. His voice sounds like a roll of thunder before a summer storm. I feel it deep in my belly. "Tell me it's not too late, Carson. Please."

"Carson? What's going on?" Jack asks, but it sounds more like a whine than a question. Which means I have absolutely no problem letting a smile spread across my face.

"I could never say no to you, Dan," I say. I rise from my chair, then look down at Jack, who looks like the stock market just tanked. "I'm so sorry, Jack, but this is the love of my life."

His mouth drops open. "Are you serious?"

Dan slips his hand into mine, his long, strong fingers giving me a squeeze.

"Sorry to do this to you, man," he says. "But you spent some time with her. You know she's special. I just couldn't go another minute without hearing the sound of her voice."

I nearly bark out a laugh. I'm not sure Jack could pick my voice out of a lineup. I'm surprised it didn't come out as a croak when I finally got to use it upon Dan's arrival. I'm surprised Jack isn't hoarse from all the talking *he's* done. But I bite down on my lip and gaze up at Dan, trying to mask my laughter with a lustful look.

Which, let's be real, isn't too damn hard.

I'm afraid if I open my mouth, I'll laugh, so it's good that Dan gives Jack a shrug and then turns, still holding my hand, and tugs me through the brewery. By the time we get out on the sidewalk, I can't contain myself anymore. I break into a fit of giggles as the hot, muggy June air envelops me. It's a welcome reprieve from the overly air conditioned brewery. It's also blissfully quiet.

Summer in Bloomington has always been my favorite, which made it extra sad that I always had to move home during it, since I lived in a dorm and then a sorority house. I'd work at the church nursery, help with Vacation Bible School, and babysit, but Cardinal Springs was still deadly boring. Grace was there, of course, and it was great to be reunited with her. But every chance I got, I'd drive the forty-five minutes back to Bloomington, enjoy the quiet, sleepy college town, empty of students, and wish I had an apartment or a room in one of the old craftsman bungalows in Vinegar Hill. The summer before my senior year, I planned to sublet an apartment and get a job working with the orientation office at the university, but then my mom broke her ankle right before the end of the semester, so I ended up moving home to help her.

"I hope that was okay," Dan says, his bravado from inside the brewery melting into nervous energy.

"It was great!" I assure him. "You have no idea how much I appreciate you right now."

"From your text, I wasn't sure if I should come over swinging or not."

"Oh god, no. He was fine, just really boring. Like, *so* boring. And into crypto, which he kept talking about like I had any clue what he meant."

"Crypto is just multilevel marketing for white dudes without personalities," Dan says. "It's the Amway of international banking."

"How do I keep matching with these losers?" I groan, then raise my fist at the sinking sun. "Which god have I angered? Did I kick puppies in a past life? Burn down an orphanage? At this point, I don't even know what a good date is supposed to be like anymore!" I look around for something to kick, but all I find is an empty Dasani bottle discarded on the curb. I pick it up and toss it into the trash can, but hard. You know, to make a point. "Ugh, I wore good underwear to this. What a waste!"

"It doesn't have to be."

I spin on my heel so fast my dress flutters. Is he still doing a bit? Is this more of the *You're the love of my life, Carson* thing he was doing inside? Because I would be happy to riff on that idea all night.

"What do you mean?" I ask, because I want this to be clear. I don't want to embarrass myself by assuming. I want him, but only if he wants me.

Dan shrugs, looking casually past me, his Adam's apple bobbing as he swallows. He seems to weigh something in his mind, engage in a little mental tennis match, before taking a deep breath.

"You want a good date? You can have a good date."

"With you?"

"Yeah. So you can see what a good date is supposed to be like. I'd hate for you to get duped again." He swallows, then shrugs. "If you want."

I want. I am *made* of want. Want is coursing through my veins in such a high concentration that I may simply combust right here on this sidewalk, leaving behind a charred black circle on the pavement and the lingering scent of desire.

Luckily that doesn't happen, because as Dan just pointed out, this isn't a real proposition. It's basically research. Desire is not a factor.

I mean, it shouldn't be. It very much is for me, but I'll shove that down like all the other feelings we Midwesterners are so good at ignoring.

Though when I open my mouth and something that sounds like "Ummughhhh*yes*" comes out, its doesn't feel significantly less embarrassing than the combustion thing.

"Good. Meet me back at the house," he says. He pulls his keys out of his pocket and spins them on his finger, then gives me a lazy grin that's hot as fuck. "I'll take it from there."

———

Because I learned my lesson from my date with Goober Gabe and drove myself to meet Jack, I have a forty-five minute drive back to Cardinal Springs to think about what the hell is going on.

The drive is torturous.

If this proposition had come from anyone else, I'd call Grace and ask her for a pep talk. But I'm not entirely sure she wouldn't try to talk me out of whatever is about to happen with Dan—*a good hang? A real date? Something more?*—and I don't want that. I know all the reasons why crossing the line with Dan could be a bad idea. He's my best friend's older brother; he's my temporary roommate; he's going through some heavy shit that I still don't understand.

But what about all the reasons it could be a great idea? He's my best friend's older brother, which means I know him. I know he's not going to yammer on about bond markets or intermittent fasting or some questionable ideas about vaccinations. I know he's not looking for anything serious, and I know that his time here has an expiration date.

I *know* him.

And I trust him.

And I want to see where that little spark in his ice-blue eyes might take us.

I beat Dan home, thanks to my nervous lead foot, so I dart into the house and double-check that I didn't spill anything down the front of my dress or sprout a new zit I need to cover up. I figure he'll come in when he gets here, so the knock at my front door comes as a surprise.

"What are you doing?" I ask when I find him standing on the stoop.

"Showing you what a good date is like," he says. "It doesn't start with a man sitting in his car and honking his fucking horn."

The way he glowers as he refers to Gabe makes my heart skip several beats. So many I damn near pass out on the stoop.

And then there's the fact that he said this was a date. Not a real one, obviously. But still…a date.

"Such a gentleman," I say. It's very hard to keep the excited trill out of my voice.

It's harder still when he doubles down, reaching for my hand and leading me down the front steps. He closes the door behind me and locks it. Then he trots past me so he can open the passenger door of his BMW. The buttery leather seats are as comfortable as I remember. The last time I was sitting here, I was too drunk to appreciate how fancy the car is, but now, as the engine purrs and we glide away from the curb, I can see that it's a really fine piece of machinery.

And I'm deeply grateful that he doesn't seem to want to tell me anything about it.

"If this were an actual date, I'd take you to a good restaurant, but you've already eaten, so instead we'll just do dessert," he says. "Sound good?"

My brain snags on the words *actual date*, a reminder that this is all just pretend. I seem to keep forgetting.

"Sounds great," I say, hoping that my body will get the message that this is just a dry run—emphasis on *dry*.

CHAPTER 19
DAN

have no idea what I'm doing. All I know is that when I took Carson's hand to lead her away from that business school bro, I didn't want to let go. I didn't want her to walk away from me. I didn't want to go back to the house and keep pretending to be just her roommate or just her friend.

Running that bit with her felt too good. If I'm going to pretend with her, I want it to be a different kind of pretending.

At the bare minimum, I want to show her what she deserves.

CHAPTER 20
CARSON

Dan settles into the driver's seat, the engine purring as we pull away from the curb. He's wearing aviator sunglasses, his wrist draped casually over the top of the steering wheel. If this were a real date, the sight of him would have me climbing over the center console to straddle him right now. He looks like how I used to fantasize my Ken dolls would look in the driver's seat of my Barbie convertible if they were human. It's too much, and I squeeze my thighs together to alleviate the ache between them.

It only takes about five minutes to get to the Dairy Barn, a walk-up ice cream stand on the outskirts of town that's open in the summer. It's an old wooden structure that's been here for decades, built to look like a barn, but each wall is painted a different pastel color. There's a copse of trees on one side and a cornfield on the other. It's Friday night, so there's a decent line of families and teenagers on dates. At the counter, haggard-looking teens scoop ice cream. I remember longing to be one of them in middle school, fantasizing about meeting the love of my life while scooping mint chocolate chip in the heat, but my mother always made me help out at the church during the summers.

I throw the passenger door open, but I've barely started to

climb out before Dan appears, towering over me, a hand out. My thumb brushes over the back of his warm, strong hand as I take it.

Fake date. Fake date. Not real. For research purposes.

"We used to come here every Sunday after church when I was kid," I say, because Dan is doing his silent thing again, so of course I've come down with a major case the nervous chatters. "It was the only time my parents would let me have dessert. They were sort of granola heads, though my mom cared less about health and more about toxic diet culture. Classic almond mom shit. I always wanted to order the biggest, chocolatiest thing on the menu, but she would tell me that was too much sugar. A plain vanilla cone was it for me. When Grace and I started coming here by ourselves in high school, I embarked on a mission to try everything on the menu. Spoiler alert: my favorite thing wasn't a plain vanilla cone."

I finally pause my monologue of embarrassing childhood memories, taking a breath before I also tell him about the time I wet my pants riding the Scrambler at the county fair when I was in fifth grade.

Dan and I join the line behind a family of five, three wild little kids running in circles around their haggard parents. They're loud, and Dan has to step out of the way before the littlest one crashes into his knees.

"So sorry," the mom says with a wry grin. She grabs her son by back of his collar. "We should definitely be putting more sugar in him, huh? That'll make things much better."

Dan gives her a tight-lipped smile and a nod, but he doesn't say anything. He stuffs his hands in his pockets, his shoulders bunched. The obvious explanation is that the kid annoyed him, but as I watch him, I realize that's not it at all. It was the mom, the interaction with a stranger. The line of people in this small town, all gossiping and looking at each other.

I take a step forward, angling my body so I cocoon him in a little circle that's just us.

"Did you come here a lot as a kid?" I ask, then immediately

second-guess myself. "Sorry, you don't have to tell me. I mean, we can just be quiet."

Dan's eyes flick up, and I see him realize that despite my small stature, I'm blocking him from the rest of the line. I watch his shoulders relax as he breathes out; in this moment, despite the crowd, it's just him and me.

And then he speaks.

"My brothers and I used to ride our bikes out here every Friday night when we were kids."

I remember that, of course. I loved escaping my quiet, watchful home to spend time at the fun and chaotic McBride house. Grace's brothers were always loud, always banging around. Sometimes I'd convince my mom to let me spend the night there, and Grace and I would watch the four McBride boys ride off into the night, leaving us behind with Mr. McBride, who usually fell asleep on the couch watching baseball. Mrs. McBride died when Grace was born and Dan was just eight years old. The McBride boys had to grow up quickly, and Mr. McBride was left to care for an infant and four rowdy boys on all his own. They definitely got to do things my watchful, worried parents never would have allowed.

To say nothing of the superior snacks full of artificial colors and flavors that lived in their pantry. Were it not for the McBrides, I'd never have been introduced to the wonders of Pop-Tarts and Fruit Roll-Ups and Cookie Crisp.

"I remember watching you guys ride off with flashlights in your back pockets, hoping that cars would see you," I say.

"Probably not the safest," he admits. "I can't believe we never got in an accident."

"I bet Felix was a mess out there," I say.

"His head was always on a swivel, distracted by every little thing."

"He's still like that," I add.

"If we hadn't been there to keep an eye on him, he probably would've followed a butterfly and wound up in Illinois."

"What did you used to get here?" I ask.

He thinks for a moment, like he can't remember. "Root beer float," he finally says.

"Seriously? Were you born sixty-five years old?"

He makes a mock-wounded face. "Hey, don't yuck my yum."

"I'm just saying, you had the entire Dairy Barn menu at your disposal and no parental supervision, and you ordered root beer floats?"

Dan shrugs. "I like what I like," he says, and then I swear his eyes sweep the length of my body in such a way that I feel his gaze in my bone marrow. Goose bumps spring up all over my skin, and I have to swallow *hard* to keep my cool.

"Grace and I were always so jealous that you guys got to run off," I say, thankful that I manage to get the sentence out despite the pounding of my heart. "We tried to follow you around like little ducklings."

"Yeah, we were assholes for ditching her all the time. We just always thought of her as so fragile, and none of us wanted to be responsible for her."

The McBride family is a huge part of my childhood memories, but hearing Dan talk about the past feels precious. Like holding a firefly in your cupped hands, waiting for it to illuminate again. I want to hear more. I want to see all those memories through his eyes.

"Luckily she had you," he says.

"You remember me from back then?" I ask, because it's the first time he's ever referred to the fact that he's known me since I was a kid. That I was there too, not as loud as Grace about wanting to be included but yearning for it nonetheless. I figured he'd barely noticed me, and in his defense, it wasn't like I had my eye on him back then, either. Or I did, but I had my eye on…well, *everyone.* I was a stereotypically boy-crazy little girl who looked at each of the McBride brothers and imagined what it would be like to be on his arm. Together, they were just this nebulous blob of hot guy that was always around but never available to me.

Dan laughs. "I remember you. Always there to back up Grace when she wanted to play video games with us, even though I'm pretty sure you had no interest in *Assassin's Creed*."

I roll my eyes. "Less than no interest. Frankly, those graphics make me motion sick. But I've always been a loudmouth where my best friends are concerned. And I am definitely still salty that you never took us with you on your bike excursions."

He shrugs. "They weren't very exciting."

"Excuse me, you just told me you got to eat ice cream without parental supervision *every Friday*. Sounds pretty good to me."

"I'm sorry your mom made you feel like you shouldn't eat dessert," he says.

I suck in a breath. I wasn't prepared for that.

"She was just looking out for me," I tell him. I didn't mean to barf out all that minor childhood trauma. I certainly don't want the pity. Not from him.

But Dan's face isn't filled with pity. It's serious—more serious than I've ever seen it, which is really saying something.

"Anyone who ever made you feel like you were less than perfect was seriously misguided," he says, his voice a rumble that I feel under my skin. "I know you've had a bunch of shitty dates lately, so maybe you haven't heard it in a while. But please hear me now when I say that you're gorgeous, Carson. An absolute knockout."

Dan looks at me with an intensity that makes all the sights and sounds around me fade away. Suddenly it's just him and me and this one hot look. I stand so still I can feel my blood rushing through my veins. Everything in my body is telling me to reach up and feel his five o'clock shadow against my palm, to stroke a thumb over his mouth, to rise up high on my tiptoes and press my lips to his.

I swallow hard, that little voice inside my head reminding me that this isn't real. It's just a fantasy that a man would take me out, buy me ice cream, and tell me I'm beautiful without showing me pictures of fish he's hooked or telling me about treasury bonds.

My breath feels ragged, and I squeeze my fists at my side. My nails bite into my palms, the pain a reminder not to get carried away.

I finally manage to summon a smile. "You're putting on a hell of a master class in how to be a good date," I say, forcing out a little laugh, like I'm in on the bit.

Dan blinks, the fire in his eyes flickering. "Hey, that isn't—"

"Hey, you guys!"

I don't get to find out what it is or isn't, because Owen and Wyatt are here.

Dan's younger brother has all the trademarks of a McBride, from the height and the ice-blue eyes to that thick, dark hair. But while Dan is quiet and wears his height like an uncomfortable sweater, Owen is a walking, talking ray of sunshine, a golden retriever in human form. He's got his arm around the waist of Wyatt, Grace's and my other best friend. She's grinning, her purple-tipped curls held back by a pair of hot-pink cat-eye sunglasses, her swirling tattoos peeking out from under a vintage band T-shirt she's hacked up and sewn back together to fit her body like a glove.

The two of them could not look more mismatched or more in love.

"Hey, girlie-pop, what are you up to?" Wyatt asks, cutting her eyes over to Dan. I don't know how long ago they spotted us, but if it was any amount of time at all, then Wyatt definitely saw the way Dan was just towering over me, the intensity of our gazes in that moment. Nothing gets by her.

But intense Dan is gone. So is the Dan who leaned casually against a brick wall and talked about his childhood. Now Dan is standing up straight, his shoulders tight, his hands pressed deep into his pockets. He looks like the human embodiment of a door that's just been slammed.

"Just getting some ice cream," I say, trying to catch Wyatt's eyes, but they're too busy roving over us. She studies the two of us like we're a murder board, taking in Dan's posture, my flirty dress, the way I suddenly can't figure out what to do with my hands. If I don't deflect—and fast—Wyatt and her powers of perception are going to read me for filth. "What about you guys?"

Whatever they've been up to must've been pretty good, because Wyatt immediately breaks into a wide grin, her suspicions suspended.

"Well, we've got some big news," she says.

I drop my gaze to Wyatt's left hand, because she and Owen, who danced around each other for months last year, have been attached at the hip ever since they finally admitted their sizable feelings to each other. They didn't even have to tell the rest of us, because they'd been walking around with big cartoon heart eyes and everyone else could see it. I guess some people have to spend a little time being idiots before they can become lovers.

But Wyatt's left hand is bare.

"Not yet, Grandma!" Wyatt cries, swatting at my arm.

"Ouch!" I cry, rubbing at the spot where her hand landed. Next to me, Dan lets out a low sound that damn near sounds like a growl.

"Someday," Owen says, giving Wyatt a hot look that has her absolutely melting, but then he turns to us with a wide grin. "But first, we're moving in together. We bought a house."

Wyatt gives him a pointed look. "*He* bought a house, and I'll be living there with him."

"I bought a house for *us*, and I'm putting your name on the title, same as mine. It just passed inspection, and we're closing in two weeks."

I squeal, bouncing in my wedge sandals, then drag Wyatt in for a hug. "That's great, you guys! I'm so happy for you!"

"Thanks, friend," Wyatt says, but as she leans in close, burying her face in my hair, she whispers, "What the fuck is up with you and Lurch?"

When she pulls back, I give her a stern look that I hope says *Cut it out, you meddler*, but she just volleys one back that I'm pretty sure says *I'm going to blow up your phone later, you absolute minx.*

"Congrats," Dan says. He nods in what I think is an attempt at brotherly love.

"Where is it?" I ask.

"It's actually only a block from Archer," Owen says. "It's an old craftsman that needs some updating. The kitchen and bathrooms were last renovated in the seventies, so it has the finest avocado-and-burnt-orange color palate. The linoleum is old enough to collect social security."

"And I do not care, so long as it means we won't be woken up by a toddler screaming at five a.m. or your brother starting a new home renovation project at midnight," Wyatt says. Owen currently lives with his twin, Felix, a contractor with a penchant for hyperfixating on projects just long enough to get them started. And things aren't better at Wyatt's house, which she shares with her younger sister, her baby niece, and her formerly estranged mother, recently released from prison. The four of them have done some serious healing while crammed into the tiny house, but I can see why Wyatt is ready to get the hell out.

"McBride!" a teenager calls from the pickup window, and two heads whip around. Owen jogs toward the window and grabs two big cups, whipped cream and maraschino cherries spilling over the top.

"Wait, how did you get that so fast? You just got here!" I ask Wyatt.

"Brynne's one of his patients." She nods at the blond girl working the window. "Whenever Owen shows up, she knows to make an extra-thick chocolate shake, and when I'm with him, she makes two. My sweet man is an excellent tipper."

Owen's the beloved town pediatrician, so I'm not surprised that ice cream appears as if by magic when he arrives.

"We're heading back home to celebrate," Owen says with a grin.

"He means sex, and a lot of it." Wyatt winks, and Owen blushes adorably. If I didn't love them so much, I'd find this exchange absolutely disgusting. But I'm happy for them, truly. And not jealous. At all. Not a bit.

I glance up at Dan, whose face is still a closed book.

"See you later." I wave and give Wyatt a stern look when she mouths *We'll talk* with a pointed look at Dan.

It's another ten minutes before we make it to the front of the line, and Dan maintains his frosty demeanor for every last one of them. His discomfort is practically a living thing, its breath blowing my hair back. I want to lead him back to the moment before his brother arrived, when he was just…talking. When he didn't look like he was measuring every word, carefully uttering as few as possible. I ache to hear his voice again, to feel him open up like a safe, letting me see what treasures he's got hidden inside.

"What can I get you, Miss Webber?" Brynne asks. I was her little sister's kindergarten teacher last year, so now I'll be Miss Webber to her until the day I die.

"I'll have a strawberry shortcake cone," I say, then turn to Dan, who shakes his head. "What?"

"Nothing for me," he says to Brynne with a tight smile. Even when he's reticent, he's still always polite.

But I don't want *nothing* for him, or from him. I want more.

"You can't get nothing," I say.

"I don't really do sweets."

Okay, a full sentence. A terrible full sentence, but a full sentence nonetheless.

"That's…no. That's unacceptable," I say.

He shrugs. "I'm more of a savory guy."

I roll my eyes. "That's bullshit," I say without thinking. Brynne gasps behind the counter, and Dan's eyes go wide. Oh, so I guess I've hit the moment in the summer when my cursing ban fully falters. But I can't even be bothered to care, because suddenly I know exactly how I'm going to draw him back out. "You know what's not a good date? Making me eat ice cream by myself. You picked this place, Dan. You're getting ice cream."

Dan's eyes narrow, suspicious, and I can tell he's on the edge of shutting down. But then he says, "Okay, then pick something for me."

I give him a long look, a smile unfurling across my face. Then I turn to Brynne and order a triple brownie delight.

"What the hell is that?" he asks as we walk away from the window and around the side of the candy-colored building to wait for my name to be called.

"You'll see."

It doesn't take long for the sullen teenager at the window to holler my name. He hands me my cone—strawberry soft serve dipped in pink and white cake pieces with a white chocolate drizzle—then slides a bowl the size of a baseball cap across the counter.

"That's yours," I say to Dan, nodding at the mountain of ice cream topped with Oreos, brownies, hot fudge, whipped cream, and sprinkles. Three maraschino cherries perch perilously on top, glistening red in the sinking sun.

Dan stares at it for a long moment like it's a bomb that requires defusing. Then he glances back at me over his shoulder, but I just give him a saucy little smile.

"Scared?" I ask, cocking a hip.

I half expect him to walk away, maybe even exit the parking lot, stomping silently down the road until he gets all the way back to his house. But then his lips twitch, and I don't know if it's a trick of the light or if he's getting feisty, but I swear I see a sparkle in his eye. He reaches for the bowl, his biceps flexing as he lifts it, then turns and follows me to an open picnic table behind the Dairy Barn. I settle in across from him and take a long, lascivious lick of my rapidly melting ice cream.

But Dan just stares at his bowl. "What the hell did you order for me?"

"Triple brownie delight," I say around a mouthful of ice cream. Because this isn't a real date, so who cares if I talk with my mouth full?

"What's the delight? A sugar coma?"

"If you finish the whole thing, you get a free T-shirt," I say. I nod at the back window of the Dairy Barn, which sports an array of faded, dusty T-shirts in the colors of the building.

"Lucky me," Dan says.

"I would like to see you in the pink one," I say.

Dan plucks a cherry off the top of his sundae and places it between his teeth. He snags my gaze with his, his lips quirking into a smile before he gives the stem a tug. "If you want to see me in the T-shirt, I'll just buy the T-shirt," he says.

My entire body goes molten, and I'm surprised my ice cream doesn't melt into rivulets dripping down my wrist.

"Now, this is a good date," I say, watching him scoop a heap of ice cream and baked goods onto his spoon.

"That's what I like to hear."

CHAPTER 21
DAN

've spent many hours of my life sitting on these picnic tables behind the Dairy Barn, usually some combination of hot, sweaty, mosquito-bitten, and sticky. I wasn't kidding when I said I'm not much of a sweets guy. I never have been. I came to the Dairy Barn to make sure my brothers stayed out of trouble, but I wouldn't say I formed precious memories here.

Sitting across from Carson is different.

That's in spite of the metric ton of ice cream she has sentenced me to. Despite all my grousing, I manage to get through about half, and I only feel a little bit like I might die.

"That was good, but the serving size was diabolical," I say as I toss the reminder into the trash.

"Grace and I tried to take one down as a team in sixth grade, but we barely got farther than you did."

"What were you going to do with one T-shirt?"

"Joint custody, duh," she says. She turns to head for the car, but I make my way back toward the line. "Where are you going?"

"I told you I'd buy the T-shirt."

"Come on, I was just kidding," she says.

I lift an eyebrow. "I wasn't."

Thankfully, there's a temporary lull, and I'm able to get the pink Dairy Barn T-shirt without too much of a wait. I throw it over my shoulder like a bar towel, then pull out my keys. "Okay, next stop," I say.

"You mean the triple brownie delight didn't end your night?" she asks.

"I mean, I think I'll probably sugar crash like a toddler at a birthday party in, like, forty-five minutes, but I can power through," I tell her, leaving out the part about how the triple brownie delight was actually really delicious and I enjoyed every bite. Especially the ones she took off the spoon I offered her. I focused entirely too much on her tongue, wishing I could taste her, covered in vanilla and chocolate. It's that thought that inspired the idea for our next destination. "The night is young. The sun hasn't even set yet."

"Okay, then. Where to?"

"It's a surprise."

———

I almost never talk about my childhood. People I met in college heard I was from a tiny town in the middle of Indiana and immediately tuned out. Not that I minded. My years in Cardinal Springs were defined mostly by my desire to escape it. My earliest memories are of the aching emptiness and confusion when my baby sister came home from the hospital but my mom didn't. After that, I remember trying not to disappear in a house full of chaos and grief until I got old enough to realize that disappearing was actually exactly what I wanted to do. As part of a big family who experienced a big tragedy in a tiny town, I always felt like I was being watched, studied, picked apart. My teen years were an exercise in finding places where nobody noticed me. Where nobody *saw* me.

And to my utter surprise, I find myself telling Carson all of this as we head down the rural highway leading out of town. Whenever I pause, she gently asks another question, and suddenly I'm talking again. I keep my eyes on the road and the passing cornfields, but I can practically hear her listening beside me. And it feels good, revealing parts of myself to her. The more I talk, the more I want her to see me. I want to let her into every part of myself. It's the same feeling I get when I see something I want to sketch, my fingers itching for a pencil so I can explore it on paper. I hear a question in that gentle-yet-confident voice of hers, and I *want* to talk.

"So, how did you find this place?" Carson asks as I flick my turn signal and ease off the highway and onto a dirt road that disappears into a thick patch of trees.

"I used to ride my bike out here just for the quiet and the exercise. I wasn't as into sports as my brothers, but I definitely always felt better when I exhausted myself. It made that itch I always had under my skin calm down. I did a lot of exploring, and that's how I found this."

We bounce down the dirt road until it ends, my headlights hitting a thick row of trees. Carson bounds out of the car, thrilled by the adventure. I like that she trusts me. Leading a woman out into the woods is pretty sketchy. I certainly hope she wouldn't do this with the chucklefucks she's been going on dates with, but I'm happy she'll do it with me. I told her this is just a pretend date, and maybe for her it is, but the way I want to be out here with her isn't theoretical. Being with Carson, just existing in her presence, beside her, talking to her...I don't know how to describe it. It's a level of comfort I've never felt with anyone before.

And it's with that thought in mind that I reach back to take her hand, leading her down the little dirt path between the trees. When her hand slips into mine, I hear the smallest gasp, but I don't look back.

I'm afraid that if I look back, I'll lose my nerve.

I'm afraid that if I look back, I'll let go.

CHAPTER 22
CARSON

don't know which shocks me more: the wide-open expanse of the limestone quarry, or the fact that Dan is still holding my hand.

Emerging from the trees, we stop to take in the moonlight shining down on the water that fills the quarry, sending glittering ripples across the surface. The quarry is massive, probably the size of a couple of football fields, with high limestone walls surrounding three sides. I've heard about quarries like this all over central Indiana, but I've never seen one myself. Decades ago, the whole place was mined for stone that would become sculptures, monuments, and buildings at the university or in downtown Indianapolis. But now all that's left are the even cuts in the walls and a placid swimming hole. It's wild that it's just here, peaceful and quiet, among the trees and cornfields.

"How have I never heard about this place?" I ask, keeping my voice low like I used to in church when I was a kid.

"The guy who owns the property is pretty private," Dan says. His grip tightens on my hand, sending a zing of electricity up my arm. "And squirrelly about trespassers."

"Are we going to get in trouble?"

"Nah. I met him my junior year. He told me if he ever caught me drinking or doing drugs out here, he'd turn me in to the cops. But once he realized it was always just me and a book, he let me be."

"Can you swim here?" I ask, then wince. I worry that he's going to tire of my questions, but I can't help asking them. I love pulling little bits of information out of him, mining him for gold. Every new piece of Dan lore he shares with me is precious.

"Yeah. There's a dock over there that you can jump off. The water's really deep, but it's clean," he says. "It's not safe to swim here alone, though, so I haven't done it very much."

Standing here beside him, I feel like I've stepped outside of my life. Summer always feels a little bit like that for me, when I'm free of the structure of the school day and the pressures that come with being responsible for a roomful of five- and six-year-olds. But this dark, silent, beautiful place makes me feel like I've stepped through a portal with Dan by my side.

Already this summer has been so different from any other. I'm living on my own for the first time in my life. I joined a roller derby team. I've been lifting weights. I made friends with Dan McBride.

As the sounds of the water and the breeze echo off the stone walls, filling my ears with gentle white noise, I start to wonder what else I could do. How else I could step outside of who I've always been, past the boundaries that were set up for me—that I maybe even set up for myself.

"I want to swim," I say, my eyes on the water.

"We can come back tomorrow," Dan says.

"No," I tell him. I squeeze his hand, then let go. "Now."

"But—"

I take a few steps away and then whip around, taking a deep breath as I look directly into his eyes. "I want to do things. New things. Take risks. I've spent my whole life with a list of things I couldn't do or shouldn't do. But I'm learning that the can'ts and shouldn'ts are where the fun lies. I want to *do* things, Dan."

And then, before any of those pesky little voices in my brain can pipe up and tell me to stop, I reach back and tug on the zipper of my dress.

Dan sucks in a breath, his lips parting as the fluttery fabric floats down my thighs, pooling in the dirt at my feet. His eyes rake over the white lace bra and matching panties I'm wearing, and I revel in it. I want him to look. I want him to see me.

When I reach back for the clasp on my bra, his eyes shoot skyward.

"What are you doing?" he asks, like he's new to this planet and has never seen a woman get naked before.

"I'm going skinny dipping," I tell him, the plan forming as the words come out of my mouth.

My bra hits the ground.

I hook my thumbs into the waistband of my panties, and Dan plants his heel in the dirt and spins.

"What are *you* doing?" I ask, laughing.

Dan clears his throat, and I watch the way his shoulders tense with probably a little too much pleasure. "I think the point of skinny dipping is the thrill that you *might* be seen. But the goal is *not* to be seen."

I'm standing here, naked in the dirt beneath a nearly full moon, and this man is staring at the trees? Absolutely not. I've stripped down to nothing in the woods, and I want to be looked at, dammit.

"Then what's the point of doing it with someone else?" I ask.

Dan clears his throat again, then blows out a long breath. "Well, uh, there are circumstances...I mean, there are scenarios where...if you and I...I mean, we said this wasn't a real date, but —so, uh, I mean...we probably should have had a conversation before the clothes started coming off, don't you—"

Is he...oh my god, is he *babbling*? Steely, controlled, one-word-and-a-grunt Dan McBride is *babbling*. It's almost too much. I squeeze my thighs together, desperate want for him coursing through my body. I'm desperate for him to *look*.

"Turn around," I say, interrupting his stream of half-formed thoughts.

His steady stream of interrupted sentences screeches to a halt.

"What?" he asks, his voice raking over the word like tires over gravel.

My heart feels like it might pound out of my chest, but not because I'm nervous. No, it's because my need for him feels like sitting at the top of a roller coaster, waiting to tip over onto that first drop. I desperately want to go on this wild ride with him.

"Turn. Around," I tell him, my voice husky with desire.

He pulls in a breath and holds it for a beat.

And then he turns.

He meets my eyes first, his jaw set, his brow furrowed, like I'm an exam he's studying for. Then his blue eyes, glowing in the moonlight, begin their descent. They trace down my neck and along my collarbone, caressing my bare shoulder before sweeping across my breasts. I breathe in, lifting them toward him. His tongue sweeps across his full lower lip, and a small sound very close to a moan escapes my throat. His gaze continues to rove over my body, heat licking at every inch of my bare skin that he studies. He's probably five feet from me, too far away for me to reach out and touch him, but I feel every movement of his eyes. It's like he's tasting me from afar, and from the way his teeth sink into his lip, I think he likes my flavor very much.

Being looked at by Dan McBride feels better than any sex I've ever had.

When his eyes retrace their journey up my body, finally meeting mine again, I nearly step back from the force of his attention. It's almost too much.

And without a second though, I spin on my heel, sprinting for the dock. When my toes reach the end, I leap, my hair flying out behind me as I squeal into the night sky, then hit the water with an impressive splash.

When I surface, I brush the water from my lashes and look up to see that Dan has followed me down to the dock—and at quite a clip, if the way he's breathing is any indication.

"You coming in?" I call from the inky blackness of the water.

For a moment I think he won't. For a moment I think he won't even say anything. For a moment I worry I've gone too far, that he might leave.

But then he grins and reaches for the buttons on his shirt, his strong fingers making quick work of them. He shrugs the shirt off onto the dock, and for the first time, I can see all his tattoos. Every last one.

Glowing in the moonlight, the ink Dan hides beneath his shirt swirls and cuts across his skin. There's a cardinal and a sunset and an abacus. There's a rose with thorns and a hammer and nails and a tiny string of numbers just over his heart. There are designs that wrap around his ribs that I can't quite make out, and there are leaves and vines and flowers winding between them all. His chest, his shoulders, his arms, all marked.

He waits for me to finish perusing his art, but when my eyes drift down to the waistband of his shorts, a fleur-de-lis curving over the waistband, he reaches for the button. He flicks it with his fingers, working the zipper down until the slutty little shorts drop to the dock, leaving him standing there in a pair of black boxer briefs.

I swallow.

He hooks his thumb into the waistband.

I suck in a breath, can practically feel my pupils dilate.

He tugs them to his hip bones.

And I disappear beneath the water.

CHAPTER 23
CARSON

Dan hits the water with a splash, and my heart jolts. When I surface, he's bobbing nearby.

"Talk a big game, dontcha?" Dan grins.

My eyes dart to the dock, where his boxer briefs lie in a little pile beside his shorts. My mind is still on the image of him peeling his boxers down his thighs. In the moment before I submerged, I thought I saw something glinting in the moonlight. It looked like—

No. It couldn't—

"Do you have piercings on your dick?" The question explodes out of me, and I immediately want to sink back under the water, never to emerge.

A devilish little smirk appears on his face. "I do."

"You have tattoos *and* piercings."

"Yup."

My mind is whirring, the image of the metal bright in half my brain while the other half spins out, wondering what one is even supposed to do with this information. While not a beginner, I am definitely firmly in the intermediate category when it comes to sex. But dick piercings? That's advanced shit.

"Do you want to ask me any question?" Dan asks from a few feet away, where he's treading water.

I swallow hard. "I—uh, did it hurt?"

"Like a motherfucker," he says, which makes me laugh. I mean, obviously it hurt, but I kind of expected him to be all stoic about it. "There were supposed to be more, but I couldn't get past three."

"And what's…well, what's it do? I mean, what's the…point?"

"It provides enhanced sensation, both for me and for my partner," he says, then laughs quietly. "Plus it looks cool."

I laugh, but I'm stuck on the enhanced sensation, which I sort of feel like I'm experiencing right now, just imagining it.

"I'm sorry, we don't need to be talking all about your—" I gesture in a way that I hope conveys what I mean.

Dan swims toward me, stopping just out of reach. Which is especially mean since my fingers are twitching, wondering what it would feel like to have him in my hand. What those metal bars would feel like against my skin. I know he's trying to keep a respectable distance, but I don't have any interest in being respectable right now.

"So, how's it feel? Skinny dipping?" he asks.

"It feels…" I pause, letting myself really experience the cool water pressing against every inch of my body. "I like it."

We swim in silent, lazy circles for a while, my nervousness unspooling as we listen to the crickets and the rustle of the leaves. I get brave and turn over on my back, staring up at the stars as I float, aware that my tits are pointing skyward. Aware of Dan's eyes on me.

I take a deep breath and revel in his attention.

I can't believe I'm floating naked in a quarry with Dan McBride.

I can't believe I'm floating naked in a quarry with Dan McBride and it's the most peaceful I've ever felt.

Until a distant car horn sends my heart into my throat. Even though it sounds miles away, I still gasp, ducking under the water like I used to duck under my covers to avoid monsters as a kid. I hold my breath until I feel like my lungs might explode, my mind conjuring images of Sheriff Woods with his flashlight, ordering us out of the water. Would we get arrested? Would I have to spend the night in the Cardinal Springs jail? Would he let us get dressed first?

When I emerge, Dan splashes me gently.

"I thought the thrill of skinny-dipping is that you might be seen?" he asks with a smirk.

I glance around, but there's no flashlight, no headlights. There's no sound of tires crunching over the path, no slamming of car doors. We really are alone out here.

"The threat of being seen is one thing, but *actually* getting spotted is another thing entirely," I say, trying to slow my pounding heart. "Oh my god, if someone sees me naked out here, I will never live it down. It will definitely get back to my mother."

"Doesn't your mother live in Florida?"

"You think the Cardinal Springs phone tree doesn't make long-distance calls?"

"I think you should worry less about what your mother will think and more about what *you* think."

"*I* think that I don't want the entire town talking about me baring my ass in a quarry."

Dan nods. "Well, that I can understand."

"Right? And if they're talking about me baring my ass in a quarry, they'll probably also be talking about *you* baring *your* ass in a quarry. And I'm pretty sure I can guess how you feel about that."

He visibly shudders.

I splash him. "You don't even live here! You get to leave! What do you care, really? I, on the other hand, have to stay and run into them in the grocery store and sit in the next booth at Pete's and teach their children how to count to ten."

Dan looks confused. "You don't have to stay here."

Now it's my turn to be confused. "What do you mean?"

"I mean, you can teach kindergarten anywhere, I would think."

"Right, but…I have the house."

He shrugs. "It's in your name. That makes it an asset. You can sell it and take the money wherever you want to go."

The sound of him talking finance bro to me turns me on, but I'm also stuck on the idea that I could leave. It's never occurred to me that I could sell the house. My parents gave me that house. I grew up in that house. It's full of memories, and selling it just seems…I don't know, like bad manners? It would be like returning a Christmas gift for cash. I have always worn the scratchy sweater, used the perfume that gave me a headache, lied about how excited I was to read the book I already owned rather than be rude to the people who gave those things to me.

But it's not my dream house. It's just the house that was given to me. Believe me, I know how unbelievably lucky I am to have it. But it's a house, not an obligation. Not a museum.

"I could sell the house," I say, trying it out. I say it again, louder this time, so it echoes around the quarry. "I could sell the house!"

Dan grins. "Where would you go? If you could go anywhere?"

I pause. "I don't know," I confess. I've never been very far from home. My four years at college forty-five minutes away are as far as this little bird has ever flown from the nest.

"Well…what's someplace that makes you happy? The mountains? The beach? A big city?"

I think for a moment, then a moment longer, because my initial answer feels too boring. Too safe. And I'm trying not to be either of those things anymore. That's why I'm naked in a quarry in the middle of the night. But nothing else comes, and I don't want Dan to stop talking, so I confess.

"Bloomington," I say.

"Bloomington?" he asks.

I nod. "Yeah. I mean, I know it's only forty-five minutes from Cardinal Springs, but it feels like another planet. And I actually like a smaller town, the slower pace of life. I'd just like to live in one where everyone hasn't known me since the day I was born. One where people don't know all the embarrassing stories from middle school that I was supposed to be able to grow up and escape. And I love Bloomington. It's really artsy, and it's got good restaurants. I like being close to the university. The energy is really good, and there are always things going on—concerts, speakers, festivals. And I like the idea that I could take a class if I wanted. Like, if I wanted to pick up some Italian or learn art history or take jiujitsu. Plus the houses are gorgeous, especially downtown, not that I could afford one even if I sold my house. There's this one neighborhood that has all these gorgeous Craftsmans. It's walking distance from a huge park and a community pool, and when I think of my dream life, it's having a kid someday and being able to walk them to the library or the playground or ride bikes around the park, all steps from my big old house with a wide front porch and a fenced-in backyard for cookouts or reading in a hammock. I want gleaming old wood, polished mahogany, not some all-white millennial nightmare. I want a banister and built-in cabinets and a window seat. And I want that lemon wallpaper in my kitchen so I can look at it while I bake or cook dinner while drinking a glass of wine. I want my kitchen to be sunny even on the coldest, snowiest, grayest days of January."

I don't know if I'm nervous-babbling or confessing.

But Dan still seems to be listening.

I've been staring at the sky, taking in the dark expanse of night and the twinkling stars, but when I glance over at Dan, he's looking right at me. He's treading water, the inky darkness rippling out around him with his sure, steady movements. And his focus is entirely on me. I can practically see him listening.

My cheeks burn at his attention. I immediately try to play back everything I've just said, scanning the tape for errors or missteps, cataloguing potential embarrassments. I try to imagine what it was like for him to hear me say those things, what he thinks, if I've come across how I imagined I would.

And as if he can hear the steady thrum of my intrusive thoughts, his brow furrows.

"That sounds perfect, Carson. I want that for you. The house, the park, the jiujitsu classes," he says, then swallows. "The kid."

Something in my brain sizzles, like on those medical shows where they futz around in someone's brain with probes while they're awake and suddenly the patient starts speaking gibberish.

Unfortunately, the weird thing I say in this moment, naked in a quarry with Dan McBride, is, "Do you want kids?"

If I could close my eyes and magic myself straight to hell right now, I would.

But of course I can't, because I'm already there. This—being naked in a quarry with my best friend's notoriously private, broody, mysterious older brother, asking him if he wants *kids*—is for sure one of the circles of hell.

"You don't have to answer that. Oh my god, I'm so sorry. What a weird thing to say. And rude too. I know better than to just ask someone if they want kids. It's so personal and not at all my business, and I'm—"

"I do."

I suck in a breath so fast I nearly choke on quarry water.

"You do?"

"Yeah," he says. "I mean, it's hard to imagine right now, what with, you know, all the legal shit. So a lot of other things would have to fall into place first—and I'm not counting on it, to be honest—but I think I could be a good dad. I'd like to try."

"I think you'd be a *great* dad," I answer, a thing I can say to him while we're in this liminal space, alone in a quarry on a fake date. If all of this is just pretend, that means none of it counts. None of it's real. I can say anything out here, floating beneath the moonlight.

The quarry is like Vegas. What I say out here stays out here.

That's how this works, right?

I'm spiraling again, ready to barf out another embarrassing

word salad, when I feel something cold and slimy slip against my foot. My mind immediately says *snake*.

And I scream. So loud it echoes off the water and bounces around the limestone walls of the quarry like surround sound. So loud that whoever honked a mile away probably just heard me.

If there weren't cops coming before, they might be coming now.

Dan immediately cuts through the water until he's right in front of me. He reaches for my shoulders.

"What happened? Are you okay?"

I'm panting, trying to decide if it was a figment of my imagination, or maybe just a fish. It could have been a fish, right? Are there fish in quarries? Because I know there can be snakes. Big, scary, fat snakes that slither out of the woods and disappear beneath the water, only to rise up from the bottom and sink their fangs into your flesh and *oh my god I need to get out of here*.

"I-I felt s-something against m-m-my foot," I manage to stutter, but Dan is already pulling me toward the dock. He's got an arm hooked around me like a lifeguard, his muscles flexing as he pulls us through the water. I could probably swim myself, but that would mean not being pressed against Dan's warm body, and suddenly that is taking up far more of my mental real estate than the possibility of a snake.

When we get to the dock, he places my hands on the spongy wooden ladder, making sure I'm holding on. Then he reaches down into the water, his hand ghosting down my calf until he reaches my ankle. He circles it with his large hand, gently tugging up until I let him pull my foot above the water line.

"Did something bite you?" he asks as he studies it, his fingers coasting over my skin, looking for a wound.

"No, I just touched something slimy," I say, shivering. I still can't catch my breath, but it's not because I'm worried about snakes anymore. Now it's because Dan is holding my ankle in his hand.

Dan is touching me, and I'm naked. And he's naked. We're

both still hidden by the water, but there's no longer any distance between us.

"Don't scare me like that," he says, looking up to meet my eyes. He reaches out and brushes a wet curl away from my cheek, his thumb tracing a path down my jaw. I lean into his touch, my eyes fluttering shut. He grips the ladder just behind my head. His breath, shuddering but steady, is warm on my cheek.

"I want to kiss you," he says.

This is not real.

I so want this to be real.

For a moment I can't say anything, lost in the fear that maybe I'm dreaming. Or hallucinating. That beyond this being a fake date, I've gone and made up this whole moment. It's all too perfect. There's no way this could actually be happening to me.

"But this is just pretend," I whisper, and I'm not entirely sure if I'm asking him for confirmation or trying to convince myself.

Dan gives the slightest shake of his head. My heart skitters in my chest.

"Carson, the only pretending I'm doing is pretending I don't want you."

"Since when?"

"For so long I've forgotten there was a time when I didn't. I know I said this was for research purposes or whatever bullshit I said, but I lied. This is real to me."

"Then kiss me," I say, and brace for everything to change.

CHAPTER 24
DAN

Kissing her feels like I've been writing with my left hand my whole life only to discover that I'm actually right-handed.

Kissing her feels like I didn't actually know what kissing was until tonight. Whatever I was doing before was just a poor imitation.

I could stay in this water and kiss her all night.

I could stay in this water and kiss her forever.

When she pulls back, there's an instant feeling of madness that this might be over. But thankfully she's grinning and flushed, the picture of pure delight.

"Can we get out of the water?" She nods to the wet wooden ladder she's still using to support herself. "I'd really like to use both hands right now."

I match her grin. "Absolutely."

I watch her climb the ladder, the water sluicing over the curves of her hips and ass as she emerges. I follow her closely. I've spent so long keeping a respectable distance from her, trying always to walk that line, shoving down my desire for her. But now that I've tasted her lips, I want to be as close to her as I can. As soon as my bare feet hit the dock, I reach for her wrist and tug her back into me, taking her mouth. She tastes like sweet strawberry ice cream and every dirty thought I've ever had, and I know immediately that I'll never get enough of her.

And there's no way she doesn't know much I'm enjoying this, because she's naked and against me. The evidence of my desire for her is hard and pressing into her soft belly, the three metal bars in my dick against my stomach.

"Can I?" she asks, her cheeks red, her lashes brushing her cheeks as she casts her gaze downward at my cock.

Oh right, *this* is why I got those piercings. This exact moment, when a beautiful woman, bold despite her shyness, asks if she can touch them. I'd endure an infinite number of needles just to have this experience with Carson.

"Yeah," I try to say, but my voice gets trapped in my throat.

Her hand drifts down my chest, her fingers dancing across my tattoos like a game of connect-the-dots as they move toward my length. Just before she reaches the head, she pauses, and I damn near cry out from how badly I want her to touch me.

"Will I hurt you?" she asks. "If I pull too hard?"

So much blood rushes south at that question that I start to feel lightheaded.

"You won't hurt me," I tell her, then take her hand and guide it down. She wraps it around my shaft gently, gasping as her fingers meet the metal. She gives me a few tentative strokes that feel so good it sets my teeth on edge. If I'm not careful, these curious, gentle strokes are going to make me come all over her.

We probably shouldn't be standing here, naked and bathed in bright moonlight. Because if the soft little moans that escape her lips as she strokes me are any indication, this is going to end with me inside her. In all my times coming out here, I've never encountered another person, but still I'm not willing to take the risk now. Not with her. I know what it would mean for her to be found like this.

It takes every ounce of my willpower to step back from her grip, but I do it. I reach for my clothes, then take her hand in mine. As I march down the dock, I bend down to scoop up the clothes she left behind like a dirty Hansel and Gretel. When I reach the car, I throw open the back door, shoving the clothes over the front seat. Then I step aside and gesture toward the back seat.

She looks at me skeptically. "But I'm covered in lake water," she says.

"And?"

She huffs out a little laugh. "Your really nice, really fancy, totally spotless car—I'll get it all wet."

"Yeah, I'm counting on it," I say, a smile on my face. "Now get in the fucking car, Carson."

I wonder for a moment if the order was a little too harsh. I've known Carson for so long, but I've only really *known* her for a few weeks. And I've never known her in a sexual context. I don't know how much sex she's had or how comfortable she is. I don't know if I should be going slow, easing her into this. I don't know if we're even going to have sex tonight. But the memory of her voice pleading *I just wanna get fucked* has been the soundtrack of every minute of our time together, and I to know if she meant it. I won't push her. Not far, anyway. Just enough to see if she likes it.

But I have to know.

And then all my hesitations and second guesses are obliterated by the wicked grin that unfurls across her pretty pink lips.

"Oh, you want me to crawl into the back seat of your car, Daniel? I can do that." She turns, bends over, and literally crawls in, her knees sinking into the soft leather upholstery, her gorgeous ass wiggling seductively. She peeks over her shoulder, her wet curls falling across her face, and purrs, "Did I do it right?"

Oh, game *on*.

"You did great, baby," I tell her, then reach into the car and grasp her hips, flipping her over onto her back. In an instant, I'm in the car, hovering over her. I brace one hand on the window and slip the other beneath the nape of her neck, my fingers threading into her wet hair. My cock rests, hard and heavy, at the juncture of her thighs. It would be so easy to slide inside her. Easier still when she parts her legs, wrapping the left one around my waist. Her heel digs into my ass, pulling me closer.

It would be so easy to be inside her right now.

But I want this to last.

I also want this to last longer than tonight, but I quickly shove that thought away. It brings with it way too many questions, too many caveats, too many doors that I fear are closed and locked. If tonight is all I have, then I'm going to make tonight last until the sun comes up. I'm going to take as much of her as she'll give me.

I'm so fucking greedy for her.

I drag my fingers out of her curls and coast them down her body, pausing to pluck at her pert pink nipple. As my hand continues its journey south, I replace my fingers with my tongue, pulling her nipple into my mouth, toying with it between my teeth, urged on by the gasps and pleas that spill from her lips. Her skin is warm, but she shivers beneath my touch.

And when my fingers reach her sex, when they part her folds to discover how slick she is, her entire body jerks beneath me.

I groan, bringing my lips back up to hers so she can taste the rumble.

"Please," she begs into my mouth as my fingers ghost over her clit, exploring the soft, wet skin. Her eyes are closed, her head tipped back. I press kisses into the column of her neck as she writhes beneath me. She's trying so hard to get the pressure of my fingers right where she wants it, but she's not in charge right now.

I am.

"Please what, Carson?" I murmur, enjoying teasing her far too much. "Please make you come?"

"Oh my god," is her answer, but that's not good enough. I stop moving my fingers.

"Use your words, sweet girl," I urge her. "I know you know how."

She tilts her chin down, her lashes brushing her cheeks as she blinks at me with hooded, wanton eyes.

"Make me come, Dan," she says. Her lips are a deep red, flushed with need. I want to bite them. "Please. Don't make me beg."

Oh, I want to. I want nothing more than to hear her beg me to please her, to hear my name trip off her lips as she writhes beneath me.

But I want to see her fall apart even more.

I let the pads of my fingers slip across her swollen clit, playing in her slick heat. Her back arches off the seat, her breasts rising toward my lips. I'm all too happy to accept her offering.

"Oh my god, it's too much," she moans, but my sweet girl has no idea how much she can take.

Thank god I'm here to teach her.

I let my fingers explore lower, slipping one inside her as I use my thumb to circle her clit. She lets out a moan that trips into a whine as she grinds against on my hand.

"You want more?" I ask, and she nods. "Words, Carson."

"More," she cries, her fingers pressing into my back, her nails biting into my skin.

I slip a second finger inside her, beckoning her closer with a curve of my fingers, and press into a spot inside her that makes her cry out. My thumb keeps up a steady rhythm against her clit as she rides my hand. My cock is weeping with need, but my focus is on coaxing her orgasm out of her.

Although the word *coax* indicates a gentle effort.

It's obvious that my sweet girl doesn't like gentle.

She bucks against my hand, chasing her pleasure, and I'm all too happy to give it to her. Her orgasm feels so close, but then she abruptly sits up, hooks her hands underneath my arms, and yanks.

"What is it?" I ask, even though I know full well what she wants. But once again, I want to hear her say it. I like when she asserts herself. It's my favorite version of Carson. "What do you want, sweet girl?"

"Get up here and get inside me," she demands, and I swear if we were standing, she'd stomp her foot in the dirt. "I want to feel you. I want to know what that metal can do."

"Yes, ma'am," I reply. I press my lips to hers, and her tongue swipes into my mouth. The head of my cock slips across her center, warm and pulsing and ready to welcome me, but I pull back.

"What?" she asks, her eyes wide, and I know the feeling I see in them. I feel it too. It's fear that this is over.

"I don't have a condom," I tell her.

She sits up so fast she nearly smashes her forehead into my chin. I jerk back, my head hitting the roof, and we nearly tumble off the seat into the floorboards, a tangle of arms and legs.

"I think I have one," she says, scrambling over the center console and dragging her purse into the back seat. She starts rifling through it, but it's not bright enough to see into the black hole. With a frustrated growl, she turns it upside down and dumps the contents onto the floor: an assortment of tampons and broken crayons, some dusty mints, and what looks like six months worth of wadded-up receipts.

But no condom.

"Shit. Fuck. Okay," she says, lying back down on the seat and gazing up at me, a look of sheer determination on her face. "It's okay. I'm on birth control. Have been for years. I'm religious about taking it. I have an alarm on my phone so I never forget."

She blinks up at me, hopeful, and god, I wish it was enough.

"I haven't been tested in…" I stop, counting backward to my last physical, because with everything that's been going on and the loss of my health insurance, well… "It's been a long time."

Her mouth drops open in an adorable display of shock. "What?" she cries, like I've just told her that I live a secret hidden life as a puppy-kicker or a person who tells children Santa isn't real just for fun.

"I've been distracted by other things!" I explain.

Carson stares up through the moonroof like she's mad at the sky. "I can't believe this!" she cries.

And as much as I want her right now, want to be so deep inside her I forget what it's like not to be connected to her, I still can't help but laugh at the little temper tantrum she's throwing right now. She's still flushed from the pleasure she experienced beneath my hand, making a mess on my leather seats, on the precipice of an orgasm she begged for, and she's pissed she can't have more.

"You can't believe that I don't have current STI results in my back pocket at all times?" I ask, because if I can't fuck her, then I at least want to laugh with her.

She glares at me. "I can't believe we're naked in the back of your fancy-ass car and we're *not* going to have sex."

A grin spreads across my face. "I guess that depends on your definition of sex."

With the car door still open, I slide down her body, my lips and tongue and teeth exploring her soft, pale skin, until my knees are in the dirt. Then I grab her ankles and yank her across the seat until her legs are over my shoulders, her pussy wet and open and begging to be devoured. And when I drag my tongue up the length of her, she lets out a scream that makes me smile into her wet heat.

Then I close my lips around her clit.

Her body shudders, her thighs pressing into me as I lave her heat with the flat of my tongue and suck her clit like a starving man. Her back arches, her hands pressing into the door behind her head, her heels digging into the leather as she presses her pussy into my tongue.

"Good fucking girl," I mutter, my lips fluttering over her, the vibration of my voice going straight to her core.

Her orgasm rips through her body like a freight train, her ankles pressing into my back, her hands reaching down to dig her fingernails into my shorn scalp.

"Fuck fuck *fuck*, Dan!" she screams, the words catching in her throat between gasps.

I suck her through it until her thighs are quivering and she starts to scramble away from me, overstimulated. I give her clit one last flick with my tongue, then plant soft kisses along her inner thigh and over the crease of her hip.

Her chest is heaving, her eyes wide as she stares out the moonroof, the light catching her blue eyes. When she looks down at me, still kneeling in the dirt before her, she smiles.

"That was fucking incredible," she says, panting. There's a red flush on her chest, her cheeks are pink, her lips are crimson, and she's smiling. She's lit up like she just won the lottery, like she just found out that world peace is within her reach. It suddenly strikes me that I would do anything for this girl.

My sweet girl.

My needy, demanding, dirty, tough-as-nails sweet girl.

As I gaze down at her, all I can think is that I can't believe she keeps going out with the poorest excuses for men on the planet. And I can't believe those poor excuses for men don't realize how Powerball lottery–level lucky they are to be in her presence.

Because I sure as shit know how lucky I am even just to have gotten to look at her tonight. The fact that I got to taste her? I've never been good enough in my life to deserve that. And as much as my cock is aching to be inside her, even if I never get there— even if this is all we ever get, even if when the sun rises tomorrow, she decides that this was enough, I'll somehow both mourn the fact that it's over and thank my lucky stars that I ever got this far.

If I thought for one second that I was good enough for her, I'd sweep her off her feet and promise her that beautiful house with the hammock and the lemon wallpaper. I'd move mountains to give her anything and everything she wants and pray every single day that that list continues to include me. I can't believe that all the ways I've fucked up my life both brought me to her and keeps me from giving her everything she deserves.

But I can't think about that right now.

Right now, all I can do is gather her into my arms, press my lips to her neck, and kiss the spot just below her ear that makes her huff out a low moan. If this is all I can give her, I'll give it to her for as long as she'll let me.

"This is stupid," she says, shattering the silence in the car, and I still. And then I practically hear her grin. "We have an empty house, and there's a CVS between here and there."

CHAPTER 25
DAN

My shirt is buttoned wrong, and Carson's hair is sticking to her face in frizzy, half-dry clumps, but we don't care, because the CVS by the highway is open twenty-four hours.

Though truth be told, I'd drive to Indianapolis if I had to, as long as I got to end the night inside Carson Webber.

Thank god there were no cops on the way here, because I tested the limits of my BMW's suspension as I plowed down the dirt road, skidding back onto the highway like we were in *The Fast and the Furious: 2 Horny 2 Stop*. I pointed the car toward town and stomped on the gas pedal.

The CVS doors whoosh open, and I take Carson's hand, a thing I wasn't able to do just a few hours ago. But now it feels as natural as speaking her name. And the way she threads her fingers through mine, squeezing like she wants to make sure I don't let go? It's as good as kissing her.

To say nothing of the white lace panties that are currently in my pocket. We played a brief game of keep-away back at the quarry before she shot me a saucy little grin and told me to hang on to them. The thought of her bare ass beneath that little dress makes me walk faster.

As we enter the too-bright store, I notice her craning her neck toward the registers.

"You okay?" I ask.

"Yeah, I just want to make sure I don't know anyone working tonight," she says. "The one time I bought condoms in Cardinal Springs, when I thought I was going to get lucky with this guy I went on two dates with—he turned out to be in a vegan cult, I think? Anyway, that's not important. The point is, I drove out to the gas station on the county line so no one would report back to my mother."

I laugh. I love her nervous babbling and how she lets slip little bits of accidental Carson lore every time she talks. I suspect she thinks I'm not listening, or that I don't like it, but the truth is that I collect those little bits of treasure that make up *her*.

"You remember that your mother doesn't live here anymore, right?" I remind her. It's funny how easy it's become to talk to her. I suddenly get the connection Owen seems to have with Wyatt, that relaxed, lived-in ability to just...talk. In all my relationships, fleeting as they've been, I've never been able to relax into conversation with anyone the way I can with Carson.

"You remember the Cardinal Springs phone tree?" she shoots back.

"Right," I say, dragging her toward the family planning aisle. I'm all too familiar with the way gossip spreads in Cardinal Springs. I know I've been the chief topic of conversation for quite some time, ever since the Securities and Exchange Commission officers showed up at Wyatt's niece's birthday party looking for me.

But I'm not thinking about that right now. I can't, not if I want to do all the things I want to do to Carson.

We stop in front of the shelves full of condoms. "Preferences?" I ask.

"Isn't that a you question?" she replies.

"I think in an ideal situation, this would be a cooperative decision," I tell her.

She glances at the shelves, her nose wrinkling. "Nothing neon or fruit-flavored."

"Noted. Latex allergy?"

"Nope."

I stop, turning to tip her chin up toward me, locking in on her wide blue eyes. Fuck, she's gorgeous. And I'm not going to fuck her over.

"And you're sure?" I ask. "This isn't a heat-of-the-moment thing? We don't have to do this. Not tonight. Not ever."

Her pretty pink lips quirk up into a grin. "Dan, we're standing under the harsh fluorescent lights of a CVS. There's no heat in this moment."

I cock an eyebrow at her. "Speak for yourself," I say, then reach for a blue box of standard-issue Trojans. But before I can grab them, Carson gasps, then ducks.

"What?" I ask, my body springing to attention, ready to protect her from a drug store attacker or a bear.

"It's Mrs. Eberle!" she whispers, pointing over at the next the aisle.

I don't even bother to look, just drop down into a crouch beside her.

"I knew we should have gone to that sketchy Exxon," she mutters.

"I'm sorry," I say. "Do you want to try to escape to the car? I can buy the condoms."

"If she sees you, she's going to have questions."

"I don't have to talk to her."

"She'll still have things to say!"

"I'm willing to fall on that grenade for you, Carson," I say, and I mean it. As much as I hate the way this town gossips and hate being the subject of that gossip even more, I'll let them all talk if it means I get to end this night in bed with her.

Carson looks like she's considering it, but then her brow furrows, and she huffs out a sigh. "No. This is stupid. I'm in a

CVS, hiding from my high school English teacher. I'm twenty-five years old! I can buy condoms!"

She stands, squares her shoulders, and reaches for the Trojans I was going for. "These?" she asks, her voice quivering only a tiny bit. When I nod, she grabs them, turns, and starts walking to the register.

I keep my eye on Mrs. Eberle, who hasn't noticed us. She's in first aid, contemplating the virtues of various Band-Aids. Carson leads me straight to the self checkout, which I think is a good move until the damn machine starts talking.

At maximum volume.

"Please scan your Extra Care Card," it screams, shattering the silence of the too-bright drug store, and like a dog hearing a potato chip bag opening from three rooms away, Mrs. Eberle's head pivots straight toward us. I feel like I'm in a horror movie trying to escape a killer, and from the pricks of sweat at my temples, my body thinks so too.

It seems to takes Mrs. Eberle a minute to place us, but as soon as she does, she plucks a box of Band-Aids from the shelf and makes her way directly toward us.

Carson frantically smashes buttons on the screen, desperately trying to make the automated system work faster, but it just keeps yelling at her about her fucking Extra Care Card.

"Forget it, we're caught," I mutter, seconds before my least favorite high school teacher stops right in front of us, a smile on her face but questions in her eyes.

"Well, hello, you two," she says, her eyes dropping down to the blue box in Carson's hand. Carson's eyes follow Mrs. Eberle's gaze to the condoms, then dart toward the door, and for a wild a moment, she looks like she might simply throw the box and run.

I ready myself to bolt with her like a thief in the night. I'll willingly participate in whatever crime she wants to commit.

Instead, Carson plasters on her fakest smile. "Hi, Mrs. Eberle."

"What are you two doing out so late?" she asks with a pointed look at the condom box.

I'm seconds away from telling the old bat to mind her own business when Carson shrugs. "Wyatt called for a refill. She and Owen cannot keep their hands off each other. We're on our way over there for movie night, but I highly doubt the two of them will make it through *Space Jam* without sneaking off. You know how in love they are!"

The computer beeps and spits out a receipt, which Carson rips from the printer before pivoting on her heel and marching out. She's clutching the box of condoms so tightly in her fist that the cardboard crunches.

"*Space Jam?*" I ask as we tumble back into the car. She's already giggling hysterically.

"It's the first movie that came to mind!" she says, hiccupping with laughter.

"I hate to tell you this, but I don't think she bought it," I say, gesturing to my mis-buttoned shirt and her wet, wild hair. I laugh. "Mrs. Eberle's going to have quite the story to tell."

"Owen's going to kill me," she says, gasping.

"Owen and Wyatt would absolutely fuck while watching *Space Jam*, and you know it," I say. I fire up the car and stomp on the gas pedal. That whole scene was hilarious, but now the reality is setting in that there's a box of condoms in Carson's lap and an empty house waiting for us no more than a five-minute drive from here. "If you need me to put on *Space Jam* when we get home to put you in the mood, just let me know."

"I don't think I'll have any trouble getting in the mood with you, Dan McBride," Carson purrs, sending all the blood in my body straight to my cock.

I barely register the drive home. By the time we screech to a halt outside the little house, I'm practically ravenous for her. I throw the door open and race around the car, taking her hand and dragging her out, then plant a kiss on her lips and slip my hand up her dress before I tug her up the path to the door.

"Down, boy," she giggles, trotting after my long strides.

"It's your fault for being so goddamn fuckable," I grumble.

While she fumbles with her keys, I press against her from behind, dragging my lips and tongue along the shell of her ear. I coast my hands up her thighs, grasping her hips and pulling her ass back into my lap.

"Do I need to wait until we're in your bedroom, or can I strip this dress off of you and fuck you against the inside of this door?" I growl.

"Why not both?" she murmurs.

A groan rumbles out of me as the door clicks open. With my hands firmly on her soft hips, I shove her inside, the two of us tripping over each other. I'm reaching for the zipper on her dress when Carson goes rigid.

And that's when I notice we're not alone.

There's a woman sitting on the couch, her gray hair in a curly bob, a T-shirt reading TRUST IN THE LORD ALWAYS stretched across her ample bosom. She's been flipping through a magazine, but now she's looking at us with a wide—if suspicious—smile.

"Surprise!" she says.

I can't see Carson's face since I'm standing behind her, but I can picture her wide eyes, her lips parted in silent shock.

"Mom?"

CHAPTER 26
CARSON

My mother is in my living room.

My mother is in my living room, I'm holding a CVS bag full of condoms, and my panties are in Dan McBride's pocket.

Oh. My. God.

"Mom, what are you doing here?" I ask, feeling red splotches creeping up my chest and into my cheeks. I try to ease the condom bag behind my back.

"Your aunt Gladdie scored front-row seats to see the Mormon Tabernacle Choir at IU, so I flew up on a whim! Isn't that wild? I booked my flight this morning! I figured I'd surprise you." Mom is grinning, but her eyes are sweeping over my wet hair and the mascara that's probably pooling beneath my eyes.

"I'm definitely surprised!" I reply, taking one giant step into the living room and away from Dan.

"Daniel, it's nice to see you again," she says. Her eyes go straight to the hem of his shirt, hanging unevenly since he missed a button after our skinny dipping session. Then she looks back at me. She doesn't say anything out loud, but the question is all over her face: *What is going on, Carson Jane?*

God, did she hear the filthy things he said to me out on the porch?

"I offered Dan the guest room after a pipe burst in his apartment," I say.

Her brow furrows. "Is that why you're wet?"

"I, uh—" Why is the only thing going through my head right now *that's what she said*?

"I was showing Carson a place I used to swim out on Highway 9," Dan says.

I suck in a breath, bracing for more questions.

"Swimming at night? Goodness, that can be dangerous. I hope you were safe," Mom tuts.

"Absolutely," I sputter, squeezing the condom bag in my fist.

"Good. I was wondering why you were out so late. I got in two hours ago and have just been sitting here waiting. I finished the book I got at the airport and was dang near finished with this issue of *People*. I was really starting to get worried," she says, then yawns. She closes the magazine in her lap and stands up. "I'm pooped from the trip. I went ahead and put my things in my room."

"You're staying here," I say—not a question, just an attempt to process this insane reality in which my mother, who never goes to the grocery store without a strategic plan and four different lists, hopped on a plane this morning.

And is in my living room.

Where I was hoping to have hot, filthy, depraved sex with the man who lives here with me.

Oh fuck.

"Hey, Mom, I'm just going to put this stuff away," I say, shaking the bag, throwing up a prayer to Jesus—if He still listens to me—that my mother can't see that there are extra-large Trojans inside.

Mom waves me off in her *I don't want to be any trouble* Midwestern way, even though she is being, at the moment, a metric fuck-ton of trouble. "Oh, I'm just planning to head to bed. And you should too. It's really quite late, Carson."

"Absolutely," I tell her, even though it's barely ten, then glance over my shoulder at Dan, silently ordering him to follow me.

As soon as we get to the kitchen, I open the pantry and hide the bag of condoms on the top shelf behind the ancient salad spinner we never use. Then I whirl around to face Dan.

"So I guess this will have to wait," he says, giving me a look so hot it nearly melts the rest of my clothes right off.

"This isn't funny!" I hiss. I give my hands a shake, like that'll help me release some of the stress that's currently approaching a boil inside my body. But no. No matter how hard I shake, my chest still feels tight. Suddenly I'm sixteen again, worried my mother is going to find the romance novels I hid in the back of my closet, the sex scenes dog-eared and underlined.

Dan seems to catch on to the fact that this is not a joke, because he steps forward, his voice dropping low in a way that is entirely too sexy for my state of mind right now.

"I didn't want my parents to know I have a boy living here!" I whisper-shout.

"A boy?" His eyebrow quirks, and I can tell he still doesn't quite grasp the seriousness of this situation. And why would he? Dan grew up practically feral, one of many wild kids barely supervised by an overburdened father. Mr. McBride is incredible, but it's not a stretch to say that as teens, the McBride boys practically raised themselves. Dan has no idea what it's like to be *raised*. To be watched, worried over, monitored like you have your own personal NSA agents living in the next room. I had to achieve international life of crime levels of slick to get away with *anything* in my house, and if I stacked up all my sins, they'd still look pretty tame. Mostly I just had that closet full of bodice rippers procured from library sales and candy hidden all over my bedroom like a Gen Z Claudia Kishi.

"What, you think 'I have a man living here' would go over better?" I ask, backing into the counter, because I need the support right now. The whiplash of this night—going from panty-melting orgasm to greeting my *mother* in my living room—is making me lightheaded.

"She doesn't have to know we're sleeping together."

"She absolutely *cannot* know that," I say, horrified.

Dan looks confused. "Carson, you're twenty-five years old."

"And my parents still think I'm thirteen. To say nothing of the fact that my mother is the church lady to end all church ladies. If she found out you and I were planning on fucking tonight, I wouldn't put it past her to call Pastor Steve over here tomorrow. And by the way, that would be the very first time she's ever acknowledged the existence of sex to me."

This does not seem to compute with Dan. "You never got a talk?"

"I got whatever my public school saw fit to offer, plus a 'check yourself before you wreck yourself' lesson in Sunday school. Frankly, I was floored my mother signed the sex ed permission slip. I'm guessing she didn't realize what it was, because if she had, my butt would have been in the library during 'Family Life Class.'" I make sarcastic finger quotes so aggressively I fear I've given myself carpal tunnel. "We are an abstinence-only household, Dan."

Dan bites his lip to suppress a grin. "Not from where I'm sitting."

"This isn't funny!"

He shrugs, and it's infuriatingly adorable "Come on. It's a little funny."

"Just...you have to sleep in your room. I'll sleep in mine. My mom will sleep in hers, and for the duration of her stay, we will pretend you haven't seen me naked."

Despite his teasing, Dan doesn't argue. He nods, accepting my terms, because apparently, despite my advanced age, to be involved with me is to participate in parental subterfuge.

"Okay," he says, his voice even. He leans back against the counter opposite me, his hands in his pocket, and nods. Then he gazes at me from beneath hooded eyes. "But just know that every time I look at you for the rest of the weekend, I'm thinking about this." He reaches into his pocket and pulls out my panties, letting the white lace hang off one of the long, strong fingers that brought me so much pleasure earlier this evening. Then he holds them up to his nose and inhales.

My head fills with static, and I nearly throw myself at him, mother in the other room be damned. I want him so badly, my desire is practically a living thing. I don't know how I'm going to fall asleep tonight when I'm so wracked with need, my mind filled with all the filthy things I'm eventually going to get to do with Dan.

"Honey, where are the towels?" My mom's voice dissolves the thick cloud of desire that surrounds me like French perfume. "I checked the linen closet, but I didn't see them."

"I moved them to the laundry room," I shout back.

"Why would you do that?"

I sigh. "Because I'm turning the linen closet into a coat closet."

Mom shuffles into the kitchen just as Dan shoves my panties back into his pocket.

"Well, that's silly—that's what the coatrack's for."

I close my eyes and take a deep breath. I can't tell her that the coatrack is currently in a regional sorting facility for the Goodwill of Central and Southern Indiana, because she will thoroughly lose her shit. My parents never got rid of anything when I was a kid, and they didn't start with their big lottery win. Instead, they left almost everything in the house when they absconded to Florida, choosing to outfit their new condo with the finest *Golden Girls*–style décor—lots of pastels, seashells, and wicker. I'm pretty sure my mother bought out the word art section of the Boca Raton HomeGoods. No ocean pun goes un-punned in the Webber retirement condo.

To hear that I offloaded her coatrack (to say nothing of the coffee table, end tables, and a whole collection of vintage-style lamps that looked like they were acquired in a particularly vintage win on *The Price is Right*) might kill her.

But I don't know what else to tell her, because I'm horny as fuck and my brain is scrambled eggs. For the first time in my life, I don't know if I can come up with an appropriate lie to tell my mother.

And then Dan saves me.

"Mrs. Webber, can I make you a cup of tea?"

"Oh, that would be lovely, Daniel," she says with a warm smile, "but I'm completely exhausted. I think I'll just head to my room."

Daniel? I mouth at him when she turns to take a mug out of the cupboard.

He shrugs and winks, and I mouth *thank you* in return.

I try not to bristle at her calling it *her* room. I mean, yeah, it's the bedroom my mom and dad slept in for the entirety of my life until last fall. It still has hunter-green walls with an ivy wallpaper border and contains the dark wood bedroom set they bought as an anniversary present to each other in the early nineties, before I was born. It's practically a time capsule, a museum = of my over-protected childhood.

But it's not *theirs*. This house is mine. And just because I haven't changed it yet doesn't mean I won't. In fact, I should probably plan to move into that room. It's the primary bedroom, the one with the en suite. It's ridiculous that I'm still sleeping in my childhood bedroom, my childhood *bed*.

But then I realize that this is the very reason why I haven't taken over the primary bedroom. Because even though this house is mine, even though I've made a few efforts at making it feel like mine, somehow it will always be theirs.

You could sell the house.

The thought simultaneously excites me and makes me exhausted.

"You know what, I think I'll crash too," I say, giving my mother a tight smile.

She pads across the kitchen and wraps me in a hug, her signature apple-spice smell enveloping me. I breathe in and let myself feel the comfort of being really, truly loved. I don't take it for granted. Grace grew up without her mother, and I know that even in her worst moments, I'd still rather have Mom here than not.

I do wish she wasn't *here* here, though. Not at this very moment.

"Good night," I say into her hair.

"Good night, butterbean," she says. "I love you."

"I love you too, Mom."

Over her shoulder, I see Dan drop his eyes to the linoleum, before gazing up from beneath his thick lashes. *Good night*, he mouths.

Soon, I reply.

———

I wake with a deep inhale just at the moment that dream Dan is about to slide inside me. Even my subconscious is cockblocking me. I sigh and turn over, but it quickly becomes apparent that I'm not going to fall back asleep easily.

I crawl out of bed and drag myself to the bathroom, hoping the bottle of melatonin I'm picturing in there isn't also a figment of my imagination.

I trudge down the carpeted hallway, half thinking about someday putting in wood floors and half thinking about finding a whole new house that already has wood floors, so I don't immediately notice the strip of light coming from beneath the bathroom door. Not until I'm directly in front of it. Not until the door flies open and Dan steps out.

I gasp. He's wearing a pair of gray sweatpants and no shirt, so his carved chest and the ink decorating it are on full display. Without thinking, maybe because I actually am still half asleep, I reach out and trace a flower—a dogwood, I think. He stands still, his eyes following the path of my finger along his smooth skin.

When I reach the stem of the flower, I let my finger wander down the valley between his pecs, over the ridges of his abs, to the waistband of his sweatpants. I can see the outline of his cock, thick and heavy. I felt it pressing into my belly on the dock and so tantalizingly close in the car. I want to spend time with it, lavish it with attention until he's as undone as I was earlier tonight.

The idea of taking apart broody, controlled Dan McBride is the sexiest fantasy my mind has ever created.

I start to crook my finger into the waistband, but I only get the very tip inside when he reaches down and circles my wrist with his big, strong hand.

For a split second I worry that while I've spent my time alone in my bed conjuring dirty dreams, he's spent the time alone in his bed deciding that sleeping with me would be a terrible mistake. Maybe he's decided he doesn't want me.

But that terrible thought lasts only as long as a breath, because Dan takes a step backward into the bathroom, pulling me in after him. He pushes the door shut with his foot and then presses me up against it, his lips covering mine.

He presses his body into me, cradling my jaw as he kisses me. When one hand coasts down my body to my ass, I raise my left leg, hooking my thigh over his hip. Open to him, I grind against his thick length, the pressure of him on my clit delicious. Again, he's so close. *We're* so close. I want him to yank my panties to the side and slip inside me. I want him so badly.

Dan pulls back. "Not tonight," he whispers against my lips, and I let out a little whimper that would embarrass me if I weren't so turned on right now.

His lips drift along my jawline until they brush the shell of my ear. "Let me be clear," he rumbles in a low voice that brings me to the edge of madness. "Carson, I want you so badly that I can't see straight. I've been lying in that bed, staring at the ceiling fan and thinking about all the things I'm going to do to you when I get the chance. But not tonight."

"Please?" I beg. "I can sneak into the kitchen and get the condoms."

"No," he says, his voice low and firm, and when I let out another small whine, he takes my chin in his hand and tilts it up until I'm looking directly into his eyes. The hot look on his face makes my knees go weak. "Carson, when I fuck you, I want to hear you scream."

CHAPTER 27
CARSON

don't know how I manage to fall asleep. The adrenaline from our middle-of-the-night kiss has me wired. But thank god I do, because every time I close my eyes, my mind serves up a carousel of images from the back seat of Dan's car. I revisit the best orgasm of my life at least three times.

It isn't enough.

Unfortunately, I can't stay in bed with my imagination (and my vibrator), because I wake to my phone vibrating itself off the edge of my bedside table.

God, with everything that's happened after, I almost forgot that we ran into Wyatt and Owen last night. Of course Wyatt has questions.

WYATT

So you're sleeping with him, right?

Because SOMETHING was going on between you two last night

There were vibes

I MUST KNOW!

> I'll be at the bar all day, we have deliveries in the morning and then trivia tonight GET YOUR ASS OVER HERE AND SPILL

And one text from Dan:

DAN

> I'm at the tattoo shop getting in some apprentice hours. Figured I'd make myself scarce with your mom around. But if you need a wingman, call me

It's funny—just a day ago, a text from Dan with this many words would have been a sure sign that he'd been kidnapped. Or that his phone had been stolen by particularly thoughtful thieves.

I read his text three times, kicking my feet beneath my covers and letting out a silent squeal. This is *real*. It really happened.

And we're not done.

I just need my mother to get the hell out of my house.

"*My* house." I whisper it out loud to myself. I'm certainly going to need the reminder when I leave this bedroom and have to face her again.

I text Dan first.

CARSON

> I'll be fine. I have derby practice at noon, and she's leaving for the concert while I'm gone. Just have to get through the morning

DAN

> Don't let her push you around. And don't forget how fucking incredible you are.

This time the squeal I let out isn't so silent.

"You okay, hon?" my mom calls through my closed door.

"Fine! Just getting up," I call back, then sigh. I stare at the ceiling and take a few deep, cleansing breaths. I love my mother. Really, I do. And I know she loves me. She means well.

She just doesn't often come off that way.

And I've never had the kind of strength required to tell her that.

I dress quickly, pulling on a pair of cutoff shorts and a T-shirt, then trudge into the kitchen.

"Look at you, sleepyhead!" my mom says from her perch at the kitchen table, a half-drunk mug of coffee on the table in front of her. "I've been waiting for you to wake up. Let's go to breakfast. Then I want to swing by the fabric store—I miss Libby's. All we have down in Boca is a Hobby Lobby, and their customer service is just not up to par. And then we should hit the grocery because honey, there are no vegetables in your kitchen. Do you need some financial help? Because you know Dad and I would be happy to send you money."

I suppress a sigh. It's not even eight on a Saturday morning and I'm standing in my kitchen fully dressed, but sure, I'm a sleepyhead. And of course she doesn't ask whether I have any plans, just assumes I'll tag along on her errands.

"Breakfast sounds good," I say, plastering on a smile. "And I was already planning a grocery trip today, before you surprised me with a visit. If I'd known you were coming, I'd have stocked the fridge. I just need to be somewhere at noon."

I brace for her to ask me where I need to be, at which point I'll need to tell her about roller derby, which I'm dreading. But instead she just smiles.

"Let's go to Pete's," Mom says, reaching for her purse, the same brown leather Coach bag Dad got her for Christmas when I was in middle school. The lottery win may have changed their retirement plans, but it hasn't changed much else. "I miss their pancakes. I shouldn't, though. So many calories for breakfast. But I'm on vacation, so maybe I can be bad."

I bite back the desire to tell her that eating a pancake doesn't make her bad, that the food we eat has no moral value. I want to tell her that food is simply fuel, and since I have roller derby practice later, I'll need plenty of that.

Instead I smile a tight-lipped smile and take my purse from the counter.

"Pete's sounds great, Mom."

———

The Half Pint is dark and quiet at nine thirty in the morning on a Saturday. The chairs are upside down on the tables, and the speakers are blasting Taylor Swift. Wyatt is behind the bar, inventorying the bottles on the wall behind her.

"I have to make this quick," I tell her, slinging my purse onto the bar and sliding onto a stool. "My mom stopped into the fabric store, so I should have about twenty minutes before she texts."

Wyatt looks confused. "Your mom is here?"

"Surprise!" I say, pulling a face. "Yeah, she showed up last night."

She grimaces. "Wow. And here I thought you were getting lucky with Dan."

"Yeah, me too," I grumble.

The bottle of tequila Wyatt is unboxing lands on the bar with a thud. "Wait, seriously? I was teasing," she says.

"Why does me hooking up with Dan seem so crazy?" I say.

"It's not crazy, just surprising," she says, raising her hands in surrender. "I'm surprised. He's not the easiest person to get to know."

"Well, it doesn't feel surprising to me. Frankly, the only feeling I have about it is *good*." And then I feel myself flush from head to toe.

Wyatt's eyebrows shoot up. "Okay, get it, girl," she says. "Where are we at with this thing?"

"Well, last night after we saw you, he took me to this old quarry, and, uh, we went swimming..."

"I'm guessing you did not pack swimsuits?" Wyatt waggles her eyebrows.

"We did not," I say with a grin. "But the evening got interrupted when we rolled into the house to find my mother sitting on the couch."

"Yikes," she says. "What a cockblock."

"No kidding," I say.

"Just be careful," Wyatt warns.

My mother has only been back in town for twelve hours, and already I'm exhausted from hearing all the ways I need to slow down, be safe, make good decisions. She still talks to me like I'm fifteen, so hearing Wyatt join in gets my hackles up.

"You know, I'm twenty-five years old. It's perfectly normal for me to sleep with people," I snap. "I don't need to be babied about my sex life."

Wyatt reaches across the bar and rests her hand gently on my arm. "Hey, I'm not trying to baby you. I'm only saying…Dan isn't just anyone. It would be easy to get wrapped up in the moment and forget that there are all kinds of very real obstacles in your way. Like your lifelong best friend."

"Yeah, Grace already made it clear that she's not happy about the idea, but she'd come around," I say.

"She would. But that's not what I mean," Wyatt says.

"Okay, well, don't leave me in suspense. Please do tell me all the reasons why sleeping with Dan is a mistake."

"Girl, sleeping with him is fine. Encouraged, even! By me, at least. I just don't want you to get caught up and find your heart in a position it shouldn't be. I mean, it's not like he's staying in Cardinal Springs."

"How do you know that?"

Wyatt looks at me like I've asked her to explain the end of *Old Yeller*. "Carson. Come on. It's obvious he hates it here. As soon as whatever legal situation he's dealing with is resolved, I imagine he's going to go back to New York. Get back to his real life."

The words hit me like a slap. Because yeah, I know he doesn't love Cardinal Springs. But he hasn't really expressed any love for New York either. He hasn't talked about going back. He certainly hasn't waxed poetic about his old job. I still don't know exactly what his situation is, but I haven't spent a lot of time thinking about him going back to New York.

"Okay. Well, I don't know if that's true," I tell her, and hate that I sort of sound like a pouty teen. "But also, who cares? What if we just have a fling?"

"You want to have a *fling* with your best friend's older brother?" Wyatt asks gently.

"You did it," I retort.

"Okay, well, way to throw that in my face." She laughs, tossing a bar towel over her shoulder. "All I'm saying is, be careful. When I was messing around with Owen, I knew what a dangerous game I was playing. I love Grace, I love her family, and I love this town. If anything goes wrong between the two of us, I know I'll wind up on the wrong side of that equation. And that's with Grace's encouragement! I somehow suspect you won't get the same reception from her."

I sigh. "I don't see why not."

"Carson, I say this with all the love in my heart. You are the sunshiniest of days, and that man is a walking black cloud. It doesn't exactly seem like a match made in heaven," she says.

"Maybe not everybody is looking for the love of their life. Maybe I'm just looking for a good time."

Wyatt looks at me like she can see right through me. "Carson, that's not you."

"Wyatt, has it occurred to you that maybe nobody really knows who I am, least of all me?" I reply.

There's a long pause during which Wyatt studies me. She blows out a breath. "That's kind of a big thing to say."

I sigh. "I know, but I'm realizing that this is the first time in my life that I'm actually running the show. I may be late to this blooming thing, but I'm here now. And I don't know what things are going to look like when I'm done."

Wyatt nods. "Okay, well, I'm certainly not the one to lecture you on being careful. So I guess all I can say is, go get 'em, tiger."

My phone vibrates on the bar with a text from my mother. She's waiting outside, because for her, walking into a bar is like walking through the gates of hell.

"If you'll excuse me, I need to go grocery shopping with my mother now," I groan.

"May I be so bold as to offer some advice?" Wyatt asks.

"Isn't that what you've been doing this whole time?"

She laughs. "Fair. I just want to say that if you're doing some blooming, you might try to grow a couple of thorns where your mother is concerned. Take it from someone with a truckload of mommy issues. I know she means well, but put her in her place, okay?"

———

The grocery store trip is fine, though Mom definitely gives me a look when I put a new box of Lucky Charms in the cart. She also sighs awfully loudly at the pint of Jeni's ice cream and the plastic clamshell of M&M cookies. But because I'm trying this whole growing-up thing, I do not point out that my cart is also full of the protein I need now that I'm lifting. That I have plenty of fruits and vegetables, to say nothing of the multivitamins I'm buying. Instead I bite back the lecture and refuse to take the bait.

"Are you sure you don't want to go to the concert with us? I could probably find another ticket for you," Mom says as I load the groceries into the trunk of my Prius.

"I actually have another commitment." One that can't come soon enough. We're going to practice hitting today for the first time, and I could use the physical outlet, seeing as I'm filled with equal parts irritation and abject lust.

"What is it?" she asks as we settle into the car.

Well, I guess now is as good a time as any to get this out in the open. I imagine a few carefully placed new thorns as I tell her, "I joined a roller derby team."

She looks at me like I've said I joined the circus. "A what?"

I throw the car into reverse and back out of the parking spot, thankful I have something else to focus on while we have what I'm sure is going to be a deeply irritating conversation.

"Roller derby," I say. "It's a women's sport."

"Isn't that like wrestling? Where the girls hit each other?"

"It's not like wrestling, it's more like…rugby on skates. It's full contact, but it's a real sport with rules." I can't keep the smile out of my voice. I cannot wait to throw my body around today.

Mom, as expected, tuts. "Hitting people on skates? Oh, Carson, that seems dangerous," she says. "I thought you joined the Women's Auxiliary at the church."

Oh, I joined the Women's Auxiliary. I went to exactly one meeting. Their next service project was ministering outside the Planned Parenthood. I stood up and walked out.

"It wasn't for me, Mom," I say. "And I really like this. It's great exercise."

"You'd really rather risk your body hitting other women when you could just do Zumba?"

"Yes, Mom. I'd really rather do this than Zumba," I tell her through gritted teeth.

We pull into the driveway, and not a second too soon. If I have to keep having conversations with my mother about the way I should be living my life, I might just snap and shout, *Dan brought me to a screaming orgasm using only his tongue last night, so maybe it's time to treat me like an adult!*

I unload the groceries from the trunk and follow my mother into the house, falling into the familiar rhythms I remember from when I was a kid. We move around the kitchen like a ballet, unpacking groceries and putting them in their places. My mother acts baffled about where to put the Lucky Charms, but I simply pluck them from her hand and place them on top of the fridge. When the unloading is done, I put the reusable bags in the cabinet by the back door and wad up the receipt to throw away. But when I open the lid of the trash can, I spot a flash of yellow.

My wallpaper sample.

It's in the trash.

I pull it out, brushing toast crumbs off of it and smoothing out a bent edge. I clutch the paper as my heart ping-pongs from my gut to my throat. There's a noxious combination of sadness and rage simmering inside me.

"Mom? Did you throw this away?"

My mother looks up from her place at the kitchen table, where she's already paging through a new copy of *People* magazine.

"It was on the floor. I just assumed it was trash," she says.

"It's not trash. I was—*am*—thinking about putting up this pattern in here."

"Oh, honey, that yellow is much too bright," she says, flipping to the crossword in the back of the magazine. She barely gives the wallpaper sample a glance, and somehow that infuriates me even more. "With the sun you get through that window, you'd be blinded every morning! You know what would be nice? A calming blue. You could do a Wedgwood pattern! I saw some on Martha Stewart's Instagram. That would look gorgeous with the cabinets. I'll order a sample for you."

She continues to chatter on about Martha and east-facing windows, but I can't hear her anymore. Or maybe I just refuse to. All I can do is stare down at the yellow lemons in my fist, picturing the sample sitting in the trash can. She's wrong about the sun. This yellow might be a smidge bright on the sunniest of summer days, but during our long, cold, gray winter and the rainy days of spring, it's going to be an absolute balm. I have plans for these lemons to get me through from October to April.

I have plans.

Don't I?

The lemons should already be on my walls. *My* walls. Why haven't I hung the wallpaper yet? What am I waiting for?

"Do you have time for lunch before you go? I could whip up some egg salad," Mom says.

"No," I say, clutching the wallpaper sample to my chest. "I need to get ready and head out."

I rush out of the room before she can say anything else. I throw on my derby clothes: a pair of short spandex shorts, knee socks, and a cropped T-shirt with the Bloomington Brawlers logo on it. I braid my hair into two pigtails so it'll stay out of my face beneath my helmet, then grab my duffel bag from the corner of my room.

As soon as I get back to the living room, I realize the tactical error I've made.

My mother peers up at me over her glasses, a book open in her lap. "Honey, what are you wearing?"

My molars grind, but I try to form something that looks like a smile. "Shorts," I say.

Her eyebrows lift. "Those look like underwear."

"They're not," I grit out. I fear my smile may look more like bared teeth, but it's the best I can do.

"And you really shouldn't be wearing cropped shirts. They make your torso look short, and with the tight waistband on those shorts, well…" She waves her hands in the direction of my body. "The whole outfit isn't doing you any favors."

I take a slow, deep breath. "I don't need my clothes to do me favors, Mom. I need them to cover my body."

She laughs. "Well, they're not doing a very good job of that, either."

"Mom, please," I say, trying to hang on to the last shred of my patience.

"What? I'm just trying to help," she says. She looks genuinely baffled by my irritation.

"I didn't ask for help."

She throws up her hands in surrender. "Okay, fine. I'm sorry I said anything," she says in that way that means she's absolutely not sorry and is in fact waiting for me to apologize for shutting her down.

It's a great personal victory that I don't. As is the fact that I don't tug on the hem of my T-shirt or hunch over to try to make it look a little longer, try to cover myself a little bit more. I don't suck in and roll my shoulders back like she taught me to do because it makes me look "more fit" (translation: thin).

Instead, I stand up straight. I breathe in, filling my rib cage, and breathe out, ignoring the curve of my belly. Baby steps.

"Honey, can I be honest?"

There's no indication that you can be anything else, I think. But I don't say that.

"Sure, Mom," I reply, and brace myself.

"Well, this new attitude of yours is concerning," she says. She pulls off her glasses and studies me. "This just isn't you. It's not you at all, and I worry it's the influence of this new crowd you're running with. I just looked up those roller derby girls on my phone, and I am not impressed. I mean, all those piercings and tattoos! I don't think this is who you should be spending time with," she says, then folds her hands in her lap.

"Right. Okay, well, I'll take that under advisement," I say, and now I'm sure my smile really does look like that of a predator ready to attack. "In the meantime, I have practice. You'll be gone when I get back?"

"What time will that be?" Her tone of voice sounds so much like it did when I was sixteen and going out with Grace. I half expect her to give me a curfew.

"Four," I tell her.

"I won't leave until five, since the concert's not until seven. Maybe we can buzz over to Crimson 'n' Cream. I want to get some muffins to take to Gladdie," Mom says, slipping her glasses back on and returning to her book.

"Can't wait," I sigh, and head out the door.

CHAPTER 28

CARSON

"Remember—no elbows, no arms, no hands. Use the asses your preferred deity gave you," Violet shouts from her coaching command center in the center of the track.

All the freshies are skating in two parallel lines, and for the first time, we're going to hit each other—at speed—on skates. We've practiced in sneakers to get the movement right. We've done some stationary hitting on skates.

But now it's time to go full-out.

I'm paired up with Jax, who is nearly a head taller than me but has half the ass.

"On my whistle!" Violet calls, her voice echoing around the rec center.

In the moments before she blows the whistle, my mind is a cacophony of instructions: lead with your hip; bend your knees and drive up; finish contact with your shoulder; hit *through* your opponent's body, controlling position until they're out of bounds or on the ground.

And then there's also the white noise of my personal frustrations humming beneath it all. *Be careful, Carson. Go easy, Carson. Be safe, Carson. Don't get hurt, Carson.*

And none of those warnings are about this drill.

But as soon as Violet blows the whistle, my mind quiets. There's no hesitation, no second-guessing, no last-minute nerves. I hear that sound, and my body responds on instinct, like I'm some kind of roller derby sleeper cell, the whistle calling me to action. I angle my inside skate toward Jax and lunge, shooting across the track. Just before we collide, I bend my knees and spring upward. I connect with Jax's hip, the upward motion rocking them onto their back wheels. I follow through with my shoulder, shrugging into their chest until their skates go out from under them. Jax lands ass-first on the floor.

"Hell yeah!" they shout from behind me, because my momentum has carried me down the straightaway.

"Nice one, Carson!" Violet calls from the middle of the track.

I skate back and offer Jax a hand, unable to wipe the smile off my face.

Violet skates over. "Jax, don't forget to bend your knees to absorb a hit. You're tall, and the instinct to pop up when someone comes at you is gonna end that way every time. In gameplay, you can use those long legs to make you a more difficult target."

"Will do, Coach." Jax nods, giving Violet a little two-finger salute. Then they turn to me. "Again?"

Hell. Yes.

———

By the end of practice, I've got Velcro burns on my arms from rubbing against everyone's elbow pads, a fresh bruise is blooming on my outer thigh from landing on Mercedes's skate wheel, and my quads are screaming at me from all the skating and hitting.

But I've put every single one of my fellow freshies on the ground.

"Fuck, it feels good to be right," Violet says as we're packing up. I'm physically exhausted, but my mental energy is off the charts. I'm positively glowing from the experience of hitting people and doing it *really well*. "I knew the first time I saw you that you were gonna be a killer blocker."

"Well, I have a good coach," I tell her.

"Do not inflate her ego," KO says as she shoves her skates into an old WFIU tote bag.

"My ego is a self-sustaining organism, thank you very much," Violet says with a grin, then turns back to me. "But seriously, you did great. Next practice we're going to start running gameplay drills. The first freshie scrimmage is going to *rule*."

Our fresh meat training culminates in a full regulation scrimmage at the beginning of July, a little more than three weeks away. The freshies will be divided into two teams that will be rounded out by a few of the vets. We'll play two thirty-minute halves, after which we'll get drafted onto one of the league home teams. After that, we'll get to start practicing with our teams and getting ready for the fall season.

I'm dying to play a real game.

We finish packing up and file out of the rec center. Violet holds the door open for me, and as I walk out past her, she lets out a low wolf whistle. "Truly, your ass is incredible."

I blush. "Dan's actually teaching me to lift weights so I can hit harder," I tell her shyly. I'm not used to such direct compliments about my body.

Violet's eyes go wide. "Please tell me you're doing more than working out with him. Or that you're also doing cardio with him? Sorry, my brain isn't functioning properly. Imagine I said something clever that amounts to, 'Please tell me you're fucking him.'"

I grin, because this is the kind of conversation I want to have about Dan. Not ones full of warnings to be careful and go slow. I want to squeal about the hot man who wants me and can do unspeakable things to my body.

"Not yet," I tell her, my excitement burbling out of me in a frantic string of words. "But we're definitely fooling around. Or we did. Once. Last night. And we would have gone further, but my mother showed up for a surprise visit, so that interrupted us.

But he told me he definitely wants to sleep with me, and long story short, I think I might have some idea what blue balls feels like."

Violet stares at me, mouth agape. "Good lord, woman. No enhanced interrogation tactics are needed on you, huh?"

I blush. "Sorry. It's new, and I'm kind of excited about it."

"Don't be sorry! I love this for you," she says. We stop at her old Toyota, and she pops the trunk and drops her gear in. "Just promise me you'll guard our strategies a little better. I don't want some Cincinnati honeypot pulling a con on you to find out about our jammer strategy."

"Scout's honor," I say, holding up three fingers in a mock salute.

"Good girl." She slams the trunk, then turns. "So what now? Where are you off to?"

I think of my mom on the couch in my—*my*—living room. I can already picture the look she's going to give me when she sees the angry red marks on my arms and the purple skate wheel bruise on my leg. The way she's going to wrinkle her nose at how my sweaty crop top clings to my skin. I look at Violet, with her purple hair and her septum ring and her constellation of tattoos. Violet, who thinks my body is perfect just the way it is. Then I gaze around the parking lot, where the vets are all loading up. At KO, who sometimes requests permission to slap my ass "as a sign of respect." At the rest of the players and their short shorts, their tattoos, their piercings. Even the skaters with no body mods carry themselves like they've got them.

Not my crowd?

I've never felt more like I belong.

And I know that I'm not going home.

Instead, I fire off a text to my mother, telling her practice is going long and to have fun at the concert. Then I get in my car and open my GPS.

CHAPTER 29
DAN

The shop has been dead today. That's partly because it's summer, when business naturally slows without all the students around, but there's also a tattoo convention happening downtown. All the shop's other artists are there. I volunteered to hold down the fort because crowds like that are my own personal hell. But Drake called twenty minutes ago and told Rosie, who's working the front desk, to close up.

While she shuts everything down out front, I stay back in my booth, my iPad in hand. I'm not in a hurry to get back to Carson's, not with her mother around. She seems like a nice enough lady, but I hate the way she talks to Carson, her criticism veiled as support. I can see the way it picks at Carson, slipping under her skin until she folds in on herself. It's not a side of her I'd seen before her mother showed up unexpectedly. It's only because I didn't want to make trouble for her that I managed to keep my mouth shut as Mrs. Webber threw little barbs at her.

That's why I escaped to the shop today and why I plan to stay here sketching even though we're closing up.

That doesn't make it easy to be away from her, though. That moment in the hall last night? It took every bit of control I have not to fuck her against the bathroom door. I want her so badly I can taste it, the phantom flavor of strawberry ice cream on my tongue.

It's hard to focus on sketching, but I try. I gave a guy a thistle tattoo earlier today, and it made me want to expand my portfolio of weeds. But a scuffle outside my booth, the sound of footsteps hurrying down the hall, breaks my concentration.

"We're actually closing," Rosie calls just as Carson turns the corner and appears at the entrance to my booth. She's in a pair of sinfully short black spandex shorts and a cropped T-shirt, her hair in two disheveled braids down her shoulders. She's sweaty and smiling, and she's never looked more beautiful, my gorgeous little bruiser.

"Hey," she breathes, a wide smile on her face.

Rosie looks from me to Carson and back again. "Did you finally make a friend?" she asks.

"No," I say, then cross the floor in two strides, take Carson's round, flushed cheeks in my hands, and kiss her. She sinks into me with a soft moan that I devour with my tongue, the sound going straight to my cock.

"Hey," I whisper against her pretty pink lips, then glance up at Rosie. "It's okay. She can stay."

"Whatever, I'm out," Rosie says, turning to head back to the front. "I'll lock the door. Make good choices!"

Carson laughs.

"What are you doing here?" I ask. I'm still crowding her, unwilling to let even an inch of extra space come between us. I'm dizzyingly aware of how close we came last night and how soon we'll be alone.

"I want a tattoo," she says.

Well, that's a surprise. "I'm sorry?"

She takes out her phone, tapping the screen to pull up an image of her lemon wallpaper.

"This. I want this, right here." She taps her left forearm, the skin soft and smooth and free of any marks. "And I want you to do it."

I glance at the pattern, my brain already formulating an image. "You sure?"

She nods. "I want you to give me my first tattoo."

Oh *fuck*. That is way hotter than it should be.

I kiss her again, tugging on her braids and letting my hands roam down to her hips. Getting to tattoo her, to be the first to mark her skin…the prospect is too good. I want to devour her, swallow her whole.

Instead, I take her by the shoulders and walk her backward toward the large chair in the center of my booth. I press her down into it. "Let me draw for a second," I say.

I drop onto my stool and reach for the iPad. I feel her watching me, and my attention is torn between her and the drawing. The image comes together quickly, because I'm more familiar with those lemons than I'd like to admit. Ever since she showed me that wallpaper, I've been doodling them in every spare moment.

But I haven't put a single one of those sketches on a flash sheet. It's like I was saving them for her.

"This look good?" I flip the iPad around to show her the bisected lemon, a leaf peeking out from behind it. "I can take the leaf off if you want, just do the lemon."

She shakes her head. "No. It's perfect."

"Color or black and white?"

Her nose wrinkles as she debates. "Color? I don't know. What do you think?"

"It's your body, but for what it's worth, you've always been full shining color to me."

She smiles. "Okay. Color it is."

I print the image onto a stencil and set about preparing my station. I could do this setup in my sleep, but I find myself taking extra time now, checking the needle and the ink, laying out all my supplies, wrapping my machine in grip tape. I want her to feel at ease, but I also want to be sure that I take good care of her.

I think too many people have been a little too careless with Carson.

I work methodically through the steps, explaining everything as I go. And before I know it, I'm next to her, tattoo machine in hand, needle hovering over her skin.

"Ready?" I ask.

She bites her lip, the first indication that she's nervous. But before I can try to put her at ease, my sweet girl sucks in a deep breath. She closes her eyes and blows it out slowly. I watch her take control of the moment, of herself. Then she opens her eyes, her pupils wide, and nods.

"Ready," she says, and fuck, if I weren't gloved up and sterile, I'd thread my fingers into the curls at the nape of her neck and pull her in for the kind of kiss that leads to other things.

But she wants a tattoo.

And I'm going to give it to her.

"Let me know if you want to stop. We can take a break at any point. There's no rush, okay? We're literally the only ones here."

"Okay," she says, her eyes on me.

"Okay." I tap my foot on the floor pedal, making the machine buzz to life, and begin the first line.

When the needle bites into her skin, she doesn't jump or hiss. She doesn't even wince. If anything, the pain just makes her more stoic. More determined.

She's more in control than I am, that's for sure. I'm fighting for my life over here, because the feeling of tattooing her—permanently marking her with *my* art—is entirely too erotic. Every stroke of the needle feels like a stroke of my tongue on her skin, a claim. The needle vibrates, and my brain hears *mine mine mine mine mine mine mine mine mine.*

"Talk to me," I say, trying to interrupt my filthy thought spirals. "If you can."

She laughs. "I'm fine. This isn't that bad. Just sort of…uncomfortable? Irritating?"

"That sounds about right," I tell her.

"Who was the first person you ever tattooed?" she asks. "Other than yourself, I mean."

"Eamon, the guy who taught me how to do this. I put a spade on his arm."

"Were you nervous?"

"Not really. Tattooing relaxes me. Same as getting tattooed."

"You find *this* relaxing?" She glances down at the needle marking her skin, then quickly looks away.

"I find the whole thing meditative. The rhythm, the pain, the art of it. It requires you to be incredibly present in your body and the moment. You have to leave all your anxieties at the door and focus on what's happening in front of you. That's relaxing. Certainly more so than my other job."

"Do you even *like* working in finance?"

"I was good at it," I tell her, then notice I've used the past tense.

"You understand that that's not the same thing, right?" she asks, then winces. I pause the machine, thinking she needs a break, but she shakes her head. "Sorry, you don't have to answer—"

I laugh and start the machine up again. Of course she's worried about her questions and not the needle driving into her skin several hundred times a minute.

"It's cute how you always feel like you need conversational consent," I say, glad to be able to pivot away from her questions about my former career and what happened to it.

"I'm sorry! I worry that my questions bother you. You're not a very talkative person."

"I don't really like to talk," I say, my eyes on my work. "But I love hearing your voice."

She sucks in a breath, and for a moment I worry I've hurt her —more than I'm supposed to, anyway. But when I look up, her lips are parted and curved, a smile tugging at the corner of her mouth.

Fuck, I want to kiss her so bad.

"Can I ask *you* a question?" I try, bringing my focus back to the tattoo. I'm so lucky I get to do this. I absolutely cannot fuck it up.

"I mean, you're certainly owed a few," she says.

"What made you come here today?"

She sighs. "I've been on my own for nine months, and I felt like I was just starting my real life. I joined the roller derby team. I skinny-dipped. I told a terrible date to go fuck himself. I was making progress. But then my mom showed up, and suddenly I felt sixteen again. It was like nothing had changed. I just stood by silently while she kindly, sweetly, in that supportive mom way, took me apart piece by piece."

My grip on the tattoo machine tightens, my molars grinding. The rage I feel that anyone has made her feel this way turns me feral.

"But then I went to practice, and Dan? I kicked *ass*. Literally. I laid skaters out using my body. The very one my mom is always telling me I need to change, hide, minimize. Like I should be embarrassed about who I am and what I look like. And I want to commemorate that feeling I had on the track today. I want to remember that I can do this. That I can be tough and strong just as I am."

"I'm honored that you came to me," I tell her, putting the finishing touches on the shading. I set the machine down on the tray, wipe away the excess blood and ink so she can see the final product, and look up at her.

She gazes down at the tattoo, her bottom lip between her teeth as she fights a grin.

"I love it, Dan," she says, and dammit, the sound of the word *love* falling from her lips does dangerous things to me. Then she reaches up and takes a fistful of my shirt, pulling me down to her lips.

CHAPTER 30
CARSON

Adrenaline is coursing through my body. The bite of the needle, Dan being so close, the enormity of this permanent decision…and now Dan's lips are on mine. Kissing him only amplifies the burning tension sizzling through my veins. Our connection is immediate and intense, his tongue tangling with mine. I moan into his mouth, and he devours the sound. The contours of the room melt away until it's just Dan, me, and the need between us that's so intense it feels like a physical presence.

I release the fistful of his shirt so I can wrap my arms around him, pulling him closer, as if I could ever get close enough to him.

And Dan obviously agrees, because in an instant, he springs off his stool and sends it rolling backward across the floor, pressing his knee into the vinyl of the chair just beside my hip. His large, strong body covers mine, one hand holding him up, the other cradling my cheek. I'm so lost in him that I barely notice how narrow the chair is until Dan grasps my hips, flipping us so that I'm sitting astride him. His rakes thrusts upward, his blue eyes burnished with lust.

"So fucking gorgeous," he mutters, and I can't help myself. I giggle. His eyes narrow. "Something funny?"

I glance down at my shirt, sweaty from skating, a black smudge on the shoulder from Jax's eyeliner. I've lost the elastic at the end of one of my braids, and the hair is rapidly trying to stage an escape. I have scrapes and bruises, I probably smell, and there's a fresh tattoo on my arm, already bleeding beneath the protective shield Dan applied.

But Dan, who looks at me like he can hear every one of my intrusive thoughts, digs his fingers into my hips.

"Carson, I'm not fucking around here. You? Like this? Undone from spending your afternoon being a fucking badass? You look happy and strong and like you don't give a fuck, and you've never looked more beautiful."

"I don't," I reply. "Give a fuck, I mean."

The word tumbles out of my mouth, no hesitation at the profanity, no need to hold it back. The realization that I have never felt more myself is too powerful.

"I don't give a fuck how my body looks. I give a fuck what it can *do*. It can skate, and hit, and lift," I say, running my hands up Dan's chest, across his shoulders, and down his firm, rounded biceps. "And I know what else it can do."

I roll my hips, grinding into the stiff length beneath me, straining at the zipper of his jeans. Dan lets out a low, masculine groan, his head tipping back. His jaw flexes as he works to hang on to the fraying ends of his control.

But I don't want him to be in control.

I reach for the hem of my shirt and drag it over my head. It lands in a pile on the linoleum. Then I reach for the thick band of my sports bra.

"Let me," he says, pushing my hands away.

"Dan, this is an industrial-strength sports bra," I tell him, but he scoffs.

"And I'm a big boy, Carson. I've been dreaming of peeling this thing off you since you wore it to the gym last week. So *let me*."

His strong fingers grip the material, his forearms flexing as he pulls. I lean forward to help him with the angle, so when the spandex comes off, I'm left leaning over him. My breasts, heavy and aching, hang just above him. He grins. "See? This worked out perfectly."

He tilts his head up and sucks my nipple between his lips, his free hand kneading my other breast. The sensation is too much, and my back arches to offer him more and less at the same time. Lost in the moment, I tip my head back and let myself feel it, an explosion of pleasure that fills my vision with a glittery brightness.

And then I catch sight of us in the mirror hanging on the back wall of his booth.

I look wild and wanton, my skin flushed as I writhe atop him, his lips on my breasts.

I have a momentary flash of anxiety, just a hint of that old shame that always hides in the back of my mind. But Dan's tongue, lavishing my full breasts with attention, chases it away.

"Like what you see?" he asks, catching my eyes in the mirror, his lips curling up.

I reach down for his shirt. "I'd like it a lot better if you caught up."

"Yes, ma'am," he says, grabbing the back collar of his T-shirt in his fist and tugging it off in one swift, shockingly sexy move.

But it's nothing compared to the sight of a shirtless Dan, all his ink on display beneath me, my hands free to roam.

I trace my nail over a sunrise inked just above the waistband of his jeans and delight in the shudder of his breath. "Someday you'll have to give me a tattoo tour," I say. I roll my hips again, grinding my needy pussy over his desperate cock.

"Any time other than right now," he rasps as he looks up at me from beneath his dark lashes. "I fear I'm about to lose the power of speech."

I arch an eyebrow at him. "If I recall, turned-on Dan is the mouthiest version of Dan."

A slap lands on my ass, the delicious sting of his palm going straight to my clit.

"Aren't you the little sass mouth?" he says with a smirk. "I'll show you mouthy." He snaps the waistband of my shorts. "Take these off."

CHAPTER 31
DAN

For as long as I live, I will remember the sight of Carson standing before me, eyes wide, cheeks flushed as she peels down her shorts.

Especially when I discover that she's not wearing anything beneath them.

She reaches for her braids, her delicate fingers making quick work of them. When she shakes out her curls, they cascade over her shoulders and dance around her breasts.

Then she squares her shoulders, her sparkling eyes tangling with mine like a challenge, and I know I'm done. The confidence she exudes standing naked in my booth, daring me to look as long as I want? I know this woman is it for me. Even if I only get to have a moment with her, I know that no one else will ever live up to this.

"You next," she says, a single eyebrow rising.

I stand up and crowd her, gripping her hips as I walk her backward. I steal another kiss and press her down into the chair. Never taking my eyes off her, I pop the button on my jeans. I revel in the way her blue eyes widen, then go dark as she realizes that I am also not wearing anything beneath them. Her eyes fix on the three barbells that cross the top of my shaft. I like that they seem to excite her. I like that I'm introducing her to something new.

I want to do so many new things with her.

"Laundry day," I say with a smirk, then take my swollen cock in my fist and give it a long, hard stroke.

"Tell me you have a condom," she whispers. Her tongue swipes across her bottom lip, and *fuck* that gives me ideas. But that's for later. Right now, I want to be inside her.

I reach for my messenger bag next to the toolbox full of tattoo supplies and pull out a strip of condoms. "I paid a visit to the cabinet, behind the salad spinner," I say with a grin. "There was no way I was going to be caught unawares again."

"Smart boy," she purrs.

"Lucky boy," I reply as I stalk toward her, dropping to my knees. Thankfully, our discarded clothes provide a decent landing place, because I plan to spend some time down here, getting her ready for me. "Now spread your thighs for me like a good girl."

"*Fuck,*" she groans, her knuckles going white as she grips the chair.

"That's right," I growl, spreading her open and taking in the slick heat of her. "You're going to need that dirty mouth."

And then I feast like a starving man.

Carson lets out a string of moans and expletives and pleas as I lave her clit with the flat of my tongue, sucking and swallowing as I work to make a mess of her cunt. I know how badly she wants me to fuck her—almost as badly as *I* want to fuck her—but I also know that she needs to be ready to take me.

Luckily, this is my favorite part.

Her gorgeous tits heave as she gasps for breath. She squirms, but I press my palm into her belly to hold her still. With my free hand, I curl two fingers inside her, beckoning her orgasm closer.

"Dan, fuck, I'm going to come. Please…" She begs for release, and because I'm in the business of giving her whatever she wants, I add a third finger, thrusting inside her as I suck her clit between my lips.

Her orgasm is glorious, a screaming, shuddering experience, her inner walls pulsing against my fingers, her thighs closing around my neck as I lick and suck her through it and pray my weeping cock doesn't betray me by coming simply at the existence of her incredible orgasm.

When the aftershocks subside and she goes boneless in the chair, I rise and take my cock in my hand, stroking as I watch her. There's a mottled blush climbing up her chest, and her cheeks are flushed with pleasure. Her pussy is a glistening mess, and her eyes are wide as she stares at the ceiling. Her arms are thrown over her head, her palms open to the ceiling, her hair pooling around her in honey-colored curls.

She looks like a filthy Renaissance painting. If I didn't want to fuck her so badly, I'd want to sit down and draw her.

Or paint her with my come.

I'll add that to the list of things I want to do with her.

"I have never in my life come so hard," she says between breaths.

"And we're not done yet," I tell her. "Now get up, because you're going to ride me."

CHAPTER 32
CARSON

t's hard to stand up after the orgasm Dan just gave me. I feel like someone has melted all the bones in my body. My ears are ringing, and my vision is still a little black around the edges. The man is talented with his tongue in ways I did not know were possible. Certainly not ways I've ever experienced before. After the way he just wrung me out, I'm tempted to take to bed like an exhausted Victorian lady.

But the prospect of having him inside me helps me find the strength I need.

I stand barefoot on the linoleum, the evidence of my orgasm running down my inner thigh. Dan takes my place in the chair, his fist still stroking his cock. The three shiny barbells lined up horizontally on the top of his shaft move with each stroke, and the sight sends even more heat to my core. I want to know what they feel like, and I'm about to find out.

Dan reclines in the chair like a Greek god, his muscles flexing.

My knees nearly give out at the sight of him.

"C'mere, baby." He reaches out a hand. I take it, letting him pull me forward. As if I'd go anywhere else. I'd go wherever he led me right now. He helps me climb atop him, my knees astride his hips on the chair. I'm hovering just above him when he hands me the condom.

"You want me—?" I begin, another sliver of anxiety peeking through the haze of desire. I've never put a condom on a man before. The guys I've been with in the past acted like it was akin to flossing your teeth—something best not viewed. They always did it under the covers in the frantic moments before we finally had what always turned out to be disappointing sex.

I don't anticipate that'll be the case this time, but I don't want to mess it up right from the jump.

"Yes, Carson. I want. I want *you*," he says, his eyes boring into me. "I want my beautiful, confident girl to show me what she's got."

In that moment, I have no trouble believing he's talking about me. *I'm* the beautiful girl. *I'm* the confident girl. *I'm* the one he wants, so badly that he can't wait to get me home.

He wants *me*.

And he should.

I pluck the condom from his hand, tearing off the foil and sliding the latex down his length. At my touch, he hisses in a breath through clenched teeth, sending a flood of heat to my core. He fists his cock, positions himself beneath me, then looks up at me.

The fire in his eyes and the pressure at my entrance nearly makes me come again.

As he slides into me, hard and hot, I'm overcome by how much more this is to me than just sex. I feel like for all the ways life has taken me apart, Dan encouraged me to put myself back together. These last two weeks with him have felt like my real life is finally beginning. I'm finally becoming who I'm supposed to be.

Not at his hands, but with his encouragement.

He's been quick to point out that it's all been me.

When he's fully seated inside me, my inner walls flexing around the size of him, my lips part in a sigh.

And something else.

"Dan, this is more...I mean, it's—" I try to find the words, but I can't, even though I know they're there. Even though I know they're so important. Even though I know this is probably not the time to tell him what this means to me—what *he* means to me. But also I just can't not.

"I know," he says, his hips twitching beneath me. His fingers sink into my waist hard enough to leave marks. It's like he's trying to hold on to his control by gripping my body.

"I don't want...I mean, I want you to know..." The feeling of him inside me is driving me to madness, but so is his presence. My brain is glitching out, but it seems important that he knows how I feel. I won't hide from it. I won't pretend.

I'm done hiding.

He's the one who showed me I don't have to.

"I've wanted this for a long time," I confess. "I've wanted you. And as good as you feel and as much I want you, I don't want this to be just sex. Because it's not. Not for me."

My heart is pounding like a bass drum, so loud I worry he can hear it. My body is screaming at me to move, to slide up the length of him. I want to feel that delicious drag, but I can't. Not yet.

"Carson, I want you now, and as many more times as you'll let me for as long as you'll let me," he says. "But this has *never* been about sex for me."

"Are you sure?" I breathe.

"You've got to stop acting like you're not fucking incredible," he says, his gaze softening but the fire in his eyes still burning bright. "You seem to be under the mistaken impression—maybe because of the idiots you've been dating—that you're somehow average. It's the one thing you're consistently wrong about."

My heart stutters, and my hips begin to move. I brace my hands on his chest and rise, feeling the exquisite drag of him, the added friction from his piercings sending electric shocks through my body. When I lower down onto him, the head of him presses against my inner walls, and I can't contain the moan. Soon we're moving together, his hips rising to meet me, his hands controlling the rhythm of my hips. Our gazes are intertwined, our breaths aligning as we move faster, racing toward each other's pleasure.

"Fuck, I'm going to come," Dan groans through gritted teeth, nearing the limit of his control. "I won't come without you."

He reaches for my hand, guiding it down to the place where we're joined. My rhythm stutters as he places both his fingers and mine on my clit to coax out another orgasm. The feel of his hands on me, my hand in his—it's too much. Every one of my senses is a raging inferno, and Dan's touch, his words, the way he looks at me, all of them are fanning the flames. My head tips back, and a sound I've never heard before claws its way up my throat.

"That's it, baby. Fucking come for me," he begs, his control breaking just as my inner walls clench around him. His hand circles my wrist, holding my fingers to the sensitive bundle of nerves sending vibrations through my core as he follows me over the edge. His hips shudder beneath me. I feel the pulsing of his orgasm, the sound of his pleasure trapped deep in his chest.

As we pause, joined and spent, the sound of our breaths filling the quiet room, Dan looks up at me.

"You are perfect, Carson Webber," he breathes, and I hear the words he leaves unsaid.

Perfect for me.

CHAPTER 33
CARSON

Once again, I have a forty-five minute drive back to Cardinal Springs, trailing Dan's taillights while I relive every moment of pleasure at his hands.

It is both incredible and torturous.

But when I tumble out of my car in the driveway, Dan is already striding up the walkway toward me, and I know the tension was worth it. I leap into his arms, his hands cradling my ass as he holds me, then turns and marches straight for the door.

"I believe last time we were here, I made some plans that were rudely interrupted," he growls into my ear.

"Up against the door?" I ask.

"At some point we'll make it to a bed," he says, pulling my keys from my hand, transferring my weight to one arm. His strength is effortless and impressive and makes me all the more excited to get inside this house. I think I might like being thrown around by this man.

"Sleep in mine tonight?" I ask.

He shoulders the door open and pauses, setting me down on the carpet. "What about your mom?"

"I don't care. I'm an adult, and this is my house. And I want to wake up in your arms tomorrow," I tell him.

He grins. "I want you to wake up in your arms too, but can we do my bed? I don't know if we'll both fit in a twin."

I laugh. "Deal. And as soon as my mother is gone, I'm redoing the primary bedroom and moving in. It's time I get a bed big enough for you to do all the things to me that I've been dreaming of."

"Ms. Webber, I look forward to hearing that filthy laundry list," he growls into my ear. "Because I've been making a list of my own."

"Let's start with your plan," I say, stealing a kiss. "Then we'll get to mine."

————

Waking up naked in Dan's arms is as good as I imagined. As promised, we had sex against the front door, then brushed our teeth side by side and tumbled into his bed, where he brought me to orgasm again with his tongue. We fell asleep just as I heard my mother creeping back into the house, only to wake again in the early morning hours for a stolen quiet tryst. By the time I wake up to the sun streaming through the blinds of my mother's old craft room, Dan cradling me from behind, his arms around my waist pulling my ass against his lap, my body is deliciously achy.

"Good morning," he groans into my ear, his hands wandering my skin.

"Same to you." I roll over, and he pulls me in for a kiss that nearly becomes something more, until we hear my mother's door click open, her footsteps in the hallway.

"Think you can sneak out without her noticing?" Dan asks.

I shrug. "Remember how I said I don't care? I meant it."

"You go, girl."

I roll my eyes. "Hilarious. Now, let go of me, I have to brush my teeth."

I slide on the pajama shorts and T-shirt I brought into Dan's room even though I had no intention of wearing them. Before I turn the knob, I brace myself.

Because sure enough, as soon as I step out into the hall, there she is.

"Oh! Carson, there you are." She has a hand to her chest like I've surprised her, even though the door to my bedroom has been open all night, revealing my obviously empty bed.

"Good morning," I say with a bright smile. I know I look freshly fucked, what with the mussed hair, swollen lips, and what I suspect—but haven't yet had a chance to confirm—is a rather large hickey at the juncture of my neck and shoulder. Dan gave that spot quite a bit of attention while he fucked me against my front door. He liked the way it made me scream his name.

"Were you, uh—" She peers over my shoulder, where Dan is stretching, shirtless, in a pair of gray sweatpants. Her eyes go wide when she realizes that what she's seeing isn't a T-shirt but a large collection of tattoos on the man whose bed I obviously just vacated. "Oh my. Carson, are you…well, I mean, I thought, uh— I thought he was just staying here because of a burst pipe."

It takes everything in my power not to grin and reply, *That's what she said.*

"He is. But we're also sort of seeing each other?" I hate the question mark, but while we said a great many things to each other yesterday, the defining-the-relationship conversation hasn't happened just yet.

"We're seeing each other," Dan confirms, his voice firm and sure. Well, I guess that solves that. My heart trips over itself as he bends down and kisses me gently on the cheek, then looks up at my mother. "Good morning, Mrs. Webber."

"Oh my…" is all she can say, her cheeks crimson, her brow furrowed, but when her eyes land on my forearm, they go wide with shock. "Carson Jane, is that a *tattoo*?"

I nearly forgot about the lemon, though now that she's pointed it out, there's a dull ache beneath the ink. It doesn't look great, since the protective wrap Dan applied collected all the ink and plasma that bled out overnight. He told me he'd change it for me today and it'll look much better. Right now it sort of looks like a soy sauce packet.

"I got it yesterday," I say, leaving out the part about how the shirtless man behind me is the one who gave it to me. Though I probably should tell her. She must be imagining all manner of horrific back-alley ways this art could've landed on me.

She tuts loudly, in a state of peak Midwestern discomfort. "I can't believe this, Carson. This isn't like you at all."

I tilt my head. "What do you mean?"

"Well, this kind of behavior." She gestures to Dan and me, then at Dan's rumpled bed. This is as close as my mother has ever gotten to acknowledging the existence of sex to me, and there are basically no words involved. Just a very concerned, Midwestern game of charades. "I thought you were more proper than this."

Dan gives the smallest, quietest snort that almost makes me burst into a wicked case of church giggles. I imagine he's thinking about the way I sat on his face last night and how after he made me come, in my post-orgasm haze, I thanked him. I'm very proper indeed, Mother.

"Mom, I say this with all the love in the world, but this is my house, and what I do in it is my business," I say, making sure my voice stays gentle. While she's more than a little out of line, I've never actually drawn any boundaries like this with her. This is the first time she's hearing it, so I owe it to her to be reasonable and kind. What happens from here is entirely up to her. "I'm happy to have you stay, though I hope you'll give me a little more notice in the future so I can prepare. But it's important to me that you understand that I'm an adult. I make my own choices."

She opens and closes her mouth like a largemouth bass as she grapples with what I've just said. "I just don't know what to say, Carson. We raised you better than this!"

"You raised her to be kind, thoughtful, generous, and hard-working. She's fierce and tough and an incredible friend," Dan says, and I don't know if my mother can hear the tiniest sliver of menace in his voice, but I can. He threads his fingers through mine and gives my hand a squeeze. "You should be proud."

My mother looks like she's not sure how to respond. Her good manners require her to graciously accept the compliment while her Midwestern roots require her to eschew the flattery. In the end, she just nods and huffs out a flustered, "Well, okay, then."

"What time are you headed out?" I ask.

"My Uber is on the way, actually," she says, pulling out her phone and tapping the app.

"Well, I'm sorry we didn't get to spend more time visiting," I say, a polite Midwestern lie. I love my mother, but I'm learning that her visits are like fresh fish—after two days, they start to go bad. I hold my arms out for a hug, and I'm not sure if it's because she's still flustered or because she's decided to take my newly announced adulthood to heart, but she steps into them and embraces me. "Have a safe trip."

"I will, honey," she says, and when I start to pull back, she tugs me in tighter. "I'm sorry, Carson. This is…well, it's a lot. I need to adjust, I think."

She releases me as her phone dings, signaling the arrival of her driver. "It was good seeing you, Daniel," she says, giving him a nod but refusing to meet his eyes.

"You as well, Mrs. Webber."

She waves him off. "Oh, call me Donna," she says, blushing again. "Well, I better scoot. I stripped the bed and put the sheets and towels in the washer. Don't forget to move them to the dryer so they don't mildew. I'll talk to you soon, Carson, dear."

And then she's gone.

"Holy shit, my mother knows I had sex," I mutter. The adrenaline drains away and I lean back against Dan's chest, my heart pounding. I feel good about what just happened, though there is still enough of a church kid in me that there's a little bit of guilt floating around in there.

"She took it well," he says, wrapping his arms around my waist and burying his face in my hair. "Are you okay?"

I nod, then look up at him over my shoulder. "You stood up for me."

He shrugs. "You stood up for yourself."

"It was easy to do with you at my back."

"I'll always have your back, Carson," he says, his lips going to that spot on my neck. "But you did the hard parts yourself."

I want to see myself the way Dan sees me, and I like that in the moments when I don't, he reminds me what I'm capable of.

"Take me back to bed?" I ask.

He groans. "I told Drake I'd open the shop this morning."

"Make sure you clean that chair real good before anyone else sits in it," I giggle.

"You sure you don't want to come in for another?" he asks, nuzzling my neck with his nose. "I could give you a really sexy tramp stamp."

"Yes, please, a butterfly right above my ass," I laugh.

"Whatever you want," he says. "But unfortunately, our extracurriculars will have to wait. The walls of those booths are pretty thin, so eating your pussy in the shop while it's open is probably a bad idea."

"Well, then, we should use whatever time you have before you head in wisely," I say, dragging him back to his bedroom.

CHAPTER 34

CARSON

When Dan finally leaves for the shop after another round, I head straight for my parents' old room, inspired to make a change. And that's only a little bit because the futon mattress in the guest room is deeply uncomfortable. I was only able to get any sleep on it last night thanks to the ten thousand orgasms Dan gave me. I was positively worn out.

The primary bedroom is small and filled with oversize furniture. A queen-size mahogany sleigh bed takes up the majority of the space, and I start by pulling off the plaid comforter, folding it up, and placing it in a trash bag for donation. I take down the heavy velvet curtains on the two small windows, which brightens the room considerably. I check the city bulk pickup schedule on my phone so I know when to pull the mattress onto the curb. Then I take a picture of the bed and post it on Facebook Marketplace, free as long as the receiver picks it up. Same with the large dresser and mirror and matching end tables.

There's nothing I can do about the shabby carpet until the furniture is gone, but I head into the bathroom to see what awaits me. The en suite is small, barely the size of a walk-in closet, and contains only a shower and a small vanity. There is diamond-patterned linoleum, and the shower is yellowing cream fiberglass with a frosted glass door. The whole things is deeply nineties and very not cute. I flop onto the bare bed and search YouTube to see how easy it is to replace drop-in showers and vanities, then scour Pinterest for ideas on updating small bathrooms.

The problem is, none of it looks right to me. I want a bathtub big enough to lie in after derby practice, but there's no way I can fit one in here. There's only one tiny window, making the whole place feel incredibly cave-like.

And even if I could fix all those things, I just…don't want to. I don't want to redo my parents' bathroom. I don't want to move into my parents' bedroom with its two small windows positioned high on the wall so I can't see outside. Not if I don't have to.

And with the gift of this house, I have the assets I need to make my own home.

So I pull up Zillow.

I spend nearly an hour scrolling listings in Bloomington, falling in love with little stone houses with cozy fireplaces and picture book cottages with original built-ins. I imagine what it would be like to live in the house with the pink-tiled bathroom, or the one with the wide front porch, or the dark wood midcentury modern hidden in the trees. I look at houses for sale around Cardinal Springs, trying to see how far my money will go if I sell this house. Not far, it turns out, but my salary is more than enough to rent an apartment near campus while I figure out my next steps. And if I'm close to IU, I could easily work toward my master's in elementary education while I'm teaching, which would mean a raise that would help me eventually buy a house.

Seeing the contours of an actual future, one I'm choosing for myself, makes a tingling excitement start in my chest that surges out to my fingers and toes. I'm practically levitating off the bed with the energy that comes from this daydream.

No, not a daydream.

A plan.

I'm several pages deep in a real estate rabbit hole when my doorbell rings.

"I heard a little something while standing in line at the bakery this morning," Grace says, side-eyeing me as she hands me a bag of muffins from Crimson 'n' Cream.

"What flavor?" I ask as I glance down into the bag, following her toward the kitchen.

"White chocolate raspberry," she says, then pulls out a chair and points at it. "Sit."

I do, plucking off a chunk of muffin and shoving it into my mouth. What with all the sex and real estate research, I've managed to make it to almost noon without feeding myself. I'm absolutely famished and in need of some serious carbs.

Grace takes the chair across me. She leans her elbows on the table, hands clasped, and studies me like an interrogator.

"What?" I ask.

"Why didn't you tell me you were sleeping with my brother?"

"*What?*" I shriek. It's only been, like, twelve hours. How could she possibly know that?

"Apparently Mrs. Eberle saw you two at CVS buying condoms. She says that you said they were for Wyatt and Owen, but Wyatt has an IUD and a big mouth, so I happen to know they weren't for her. And anyway, you've been all moony over Dan for a while."

The muffin turns to sand in my mouth. It takes effort to swallow it. I don't know what to say. This might actually be harder than letting my mother know I'm sleeping with Dan.

I settle for a simple shrug.

"Are you *kidding* me?" Grace cries—the truth must be all over my face. I have never been a very good liar, and Grace knows me better than anybody. Of course she can tell when my hand is in the proverbial cookie jar. "I can't believe this!"

I thought maybe it was guilt I was feeling. Or maybe a little bit of shame. But once I catch my breath, I realize that the sensation roiling in my gut is anger. Anger at my mother for keeping me on such a tight leash, anger at myself for letting her, and now anger at Grace for sitting across from me like a cop, talking to me like I've committed some kind of crime.

I drop the muffin bag on the table.

"Why are you mad at me?" I cry.

Grace blinks like she wasn't expecting that. And maybe she wasn't. My Midwest nice usually manifests in an awful lot of apologies for things I haven't done and graciousness where none is warranted. But I'm good and pissed now, and Midwest nice has left the premises.

"Because you're my best friend," Grace says. "You're my best friend, and I had to hear it from Daphne at the bakery, who heard it from Lizzy at the salon, who heard it directly from Mrs. Eberle. Why didn't I hear it from *you*?"

I cross my arms over my chest. "Because every time Dan comes up, you shut the conversation down."

"I'm trying to protect you! I know my brother. He's moody and secretive, and you're a talkative ray of sunshine. He'll hurt you, Carson. He won't mean to, because he's not an asshole. But you'll wind up hurt nonetheless. Starting something with him is a bad idea. He's bad for you."

All I can think as she rants is, *I don't think you know your brother at all.*

"I'm your best friend," she says. It sounds like a last-ditch effort to get through to me.

It doesn't work.

I shake my head. "Grace, I love you, but right now you're being a real asshole."

She looks at me like I've slapped her. "What?"

I sit back in my chair and cross my arms. "When you were falling in love with Decker, I was nothing but supportive. Did I ever say, 'Hey, isn't he kind of a fuckboy with a garbage reputation who plays a professional sport in another city? Starting something with him seems a little dicey.' I did not!" I shrug. "All I'm asking for is the same support I gave you—the same support I've always given you."

She's quiet for a moment, and I can see her controlling little heart doing battle inside her. I know she means well. I know it. But that doesn't mean that I have to accept it. Maybe we've both been bad friends lately. Her with the judgment, and me for not speaking up. For not telling her how I really feel. For not setting a boundary.

"And what happens if things go badly?" she asks in a whisper.

I let out a laugh tinged with bitterness. "The same thing that happened when they went badly for you! I was there for you, I comforted you, I fed you wine and cake and commiserated, and then when Decker got his shit together, I helped him fix things with you!" At the reminder of all she went through on the way to her own happily ever after, Grace's eyes go watery, and mine do a little too. But I charge on. "If Dan breaks my heart, I expect you to be my friend and let me cry about it and not say 'I told you so.' If Dan breaks my heart, that's going to suck, but you know what will suck more? Walking away from someone who makes me so happy just because there's a possibility it won't work out. I want to put my money on things working out for me. I want to bet on myself. And in this moment, that means betting on Dan."

She nods, but I think it's more for herself than for me. Like she's trying to get herself to catch up to what she knows is right.

"Okay," she says. "If this is what you want, then I'm here for you. For better or for worse."

"As you should be," I say. I can't keep the heat out of my voice, because she still sounds like she doubts me. Like her support is a concession, not an act of friendship.

"But I'm going to tell you the same thing I told Wyatt—no details. I'm glad you're getting dicked down well and good, but I don't want to know anything about it. He's my brother, and ew, no thank you."

I laugh. "Deal," I say. I reach for the muffin bag again, but Grace intercepts my wrist, flipping my arm over.

"What is that?" She's staring wide-eyed at the lemon tattoo on the inside of my arm. It looks much better after Dan redressed it this morning, peeling off the adhesive protectant, cleaning it, and covering it with a fresh clear film.

"It's a tattoo," I tell her.

"Where did you get it?"

I pause. I don't know if Grace knows about Dan's side hustle, and I'm not about to spill his secrets.

"Bloomington," I say, which has the virtue of being the truth.

Grace studies it, her eyes tracing the lines. "It looks really good," she says. "Did it hurt?"

"I mean, yeah," I say, laughing. "But it wasn't unbearable. Mostly just uncomfortable."

She looks up with a knowing smile. "Does this mean you're going to hang your lemon wallpaper?"

I shrug, leaning back in my chair. "I don't know," I confess.

"But you love that wallpaper! You just got a permanent tribute to the wallpaper on your arm. What's stopping you?"

I glance around the kitchen and think of all the work it would take to redo the floors and repaint the dark wood cabinets, and then I'd have to replace the old white appliances, stained and aging. "This house, I think. I'm not sure if I want to stay here."

Grace's eyebrows shoot up to her hairline. "Seriously? Where would you go?"

"I think maybe Bloomington," I say. The first time I articulated this plan aloud—to Dan, naked in the quarry—there was a question mark there. But now it doesn't seem like a question, and that feels good. "I can rent a place while I wait for the house to sell, see if I like it. If I do, then I can save the profits from the house until the right thing comes along for me to buy."

"And you'd leave your job here?"

"Yeah. And if I were in Bloomington, I could apply to get my master's. That would mean a raise." I glance down at the tattoo. "I don't think Cardinal Springs is the right place for me. I think that if I'm going to grow up for real, I need to go."

Grace gives a slight smile, but when she sucks in a breath, she sniffles a little. "I think that sounds like a great plan, Carson."

"You don't think it's insane to give up a free house?"

She shakes her head. "Not if it's not what you want. If someone gives you an ugly sweater, that doesn't mean you have to wear it."

I scoff. "Have you met me? It absolutely does."

Grace laughs. "It seems like maybe that's not true anymore."

And then I'm laughing too. "I don't think it is."

CHAPTER 35
DAN

The next three weeks with Carson are so good, I want to retroactively kick my own ass for hiding my feelings from her for so long.

We spend a few more nights together on the futon in my room while she works to clear out her parents' old bedroom. A woman from a local nonprofit that collects furniture for people starting over after leaving abusive partners comes by and picks up the bedroom set. I help Carson haul the old mattress out to the street. She orders a new one, and when it arrives, she places it in the middle of the room on a standard-issue metal bed frame.

"It's a little frat boy, but I want to take my time buying furniture," she says. She doesn't say that she's thinking about buying furniture for an entirely different house, but I see her scrolling Zillow at all hours of the day.

Unfortunately, we make it only one night in her new bedroom before she declares that it feels like her parents are watching her.

The next morning the woman from the nonprofit returns to pick up the futon, and I move her new mattress into my room.

And every night after that, she curls up in the nook of my shoulder and traces her fingers across my tattoos while I tell her the story of each one—the ones that mean something and the ones that simply mean I wanted another tattoo. When she lets her fingers wander down to play with the metal in my cock—one of her favorite activities—we end up staying up later as I make her scream my name.

But every night, she eventually falls asleep in my arms.

I sleep well for the first time in my life.

Most mornings we wake up with the sun and head to the gym. Her confidence grows right along with her strength. I teach her to squat, and her form is impeccable—as is her ass.

Most days we tumble into bed as soon as we get home.

The pipe in Decker's apartment gets fixed, but neither of acknowledge it. It goes unspoken that I should stay.

Other than the gym and trips out to the quarry (where we have yet to don swimsuits), we keep our romance mostly within the walls of the house. Neither Carson nor I is ready to submit to the watchful eyes of the residents of Cardinal Springs. People have guessed what's going on between us—Mrs. Eberle certainly didn't keep her mouth shut—but my family knows better than to talk to me about it. Carson refers to this period of hibernation as our "long sex weekend." I'm happy to go with that.

"Should I wear the red socks or the black socks?" Carson asks, holding up two pairs of knee-high athletic socks. She's getting ready for her first scrimmage with the other new skaters today. "I'm trying to decide if I want to go all black or if I want a pop of color."

"All black. You'll look extra badass," I say. I'm stirring a pot of high-protein chili for dinner. Between her lifting and her derby practices, she's going to need it. There's a cast-iron pan of corn-bread in the oven to go with it, and I'm going to pick up muffins for dessert.

She leans in and kisses me, then turns and skips over to the kitchen table to put them on. She's already wearing the black shorts that I love peeling off of her so much and her new practice jersey. It's black with the Bloomington Bruisers logo on the front, her name and assigned number on the back. After she gets drafted to a team, she'll get to pick her derby name and her own number. There's a list of names on the fridge that we've been adding to for a couple of weeks. The current frontrunner is Gluteus Maxximus, Maxx for short—my suggestion.

"We have track setup at ten, and then we're doing a freshie class lunch. We're supposed to be back at four for final setup and warm-ups. Doors open at five, scrimmage starts at six," she says, running through her mental schedule.

"I know, babe, you've told me six or seven times, and the schedule is on the fridge," I say, laughing.

"I can't help it. I'm nervous! I get hyper-organized when I'm nervous."

I go over and plant a kiss on the tip of her nose. "How about doing a little swipe of eye black for the scrimmage? That'll look tough as shit."

She grins with delight, her nose wrinkling. "I love it," she says.

I love you, I don't say. I've been thinking it for weeks, and the words have been on the tip of my tongue for days. But she's been so busy preparing for the scrimmage, so busy making plans for her future, that I don't want to put anything else on her. I want her to focus on *her*.

"I'll be there around five thirty. I've got a tattoo appointment at four. Someone requested a nightshade tattoo from my weeds flash, but I don't think it'll go long," I assure her. "I can't wait to see you kick ass."

She's practically vibrating as she jumps out of the chair and does a spin. She looks incredible in her scrimmage uniform. Like the feisty little fighter I know she is.

"Okay, I'm going to head out," she says, but she doesn't move. She looks like her feet are glued to the floor, and I can tell that the nerves are taking over. I take her shoulders in my hands and give her a little shake.

"Hey. Look at me," I say, and wait until she gazes up from beneath her long lashes. "You've worked really hard and come really far. You're going to crush it today, and I'm going to be on the sidelines cheering louder than anybody."

She laughs. "I'll believe that when I see it," she scoffs.

"Hey, for you I'd cover my shirtless body in paint like those weirdos at IU basketball games," I tell her, then plant another kiss on the top of her head. "Now go get 'em, killer. I'll see you tonight."

She takes a deep breath and blows it out before she nods and pivots. Before she makes it out of the kitchen, I land a slap on her ass that echoes with a satisfying crack. She squeals and bolts. After some rustling in the entryway that I know means she's wrestling with her giant gear bag, the door slams.

Fuck, I love that girl.

I'm dipping a spoon into the bubbling chili to test the seasoning when my phone rings. I flip it over and see Marcel's name.

"What's up?" I ask.

He laughs on the other end of the line. "An actual greeting! My how far we've come. That girl is a good influence on you."

Oh yeah, and I told Marcel and Jameson. What can I say? Carson has made me chatty.

"Shut up," I grunt, adding some smoked paprika to the chili.

"As much as I'd like to grill you about your romantic life, I have news," Marcel says, and I immediately drop the spoon. Marcel wanting to get down to business? This must be something big. "I hate to tell you this, but I think you're about to be indicted. You need to come to New York. The SEC is requesting a meeting with you prior to the grand jury being impaneled."

"That's weird. They want to see me *before* the grand jury?"

"I know. I tried talking to my contact at the SEC, but they haven't gotten back to me. It's weird."

"You think I'm going to be arrested?"

"I don't know. They're not being particularly quiet about their intent to charge you, but something feels off about it. I think you need to come prepared, though."

"So I'm coming to New York to go to prison?"

"I mean, there will be a hearing, and I doubt they'll remand you. They'll definitely release you on bail. But yeah, this could be it."

I turn off the burner and pull the chili from the stove, then scrub my hand over my face. This is real. This is happening.

"Tomorrow morning?" I ask.

"Yeah."

Fuck.

"I looked at flights," Marcel says. "You can fly out of Indianapolis at two thirty this afternoon. Can you get up there that quickly?"

I look at my watch. It's not a question of whether I can make the flight. It's what I'll miss if I do.

"I'm not being subpoenaed?" I ask.

"No."

"And they haven't indicted me yet?"

"Not yet, no. I'm telling you, something is weird—"

"So what happens if I don't come?"

There's a long silence.

"Dan, I wouldn't advise screwing around with—"

"What happens if I don't come?"

"Well, if the grand jury does in fact indict you tomorrow morning, then a warrant will be issued for your arrest. Field agents from Indianapolis will probably head down and pick you up in Cardinal Springs. Handcuffs and all."

The kitchen suddenly feels very hot, and it's like the walls are pressing in on me. It was bad enough when investigators showed up here in front of my friends and family last fall, looking to question me. The way people talked, I felt like a fucking criminal back then. But actually being stuffed into the back of a car, my hands cuffed behind me, some federal agent's hand on the top of my head as I duck inside?

Carson would see that.

And fuck *me*—everyone would talk about *her*.

I can't do that to her.

"I can make the flight," I say, determination in my voice but a pit in my stomach.

"Sounds good. Take a cab to our place when you get here. Jameson is going to make dinner," Marcel says.

"Last supper?" I ask.

Marcel laughs, but there's no humor in it. "Let's try to stay positive."

"Right. Positive," I mutter. "Because that's worked so well for me in the past."

"When have you ever been positive?" Marcel cracks weakly.

For the last three fucking weeks.

I end the call and lean back on the counter, my head in my hands. I feel like I'm going to be sick. In the two years I've been living under this threat, I've thought a lot about what it might feel like for all my testimony and evidence to mean nothing up against the force of a multimillionaire's lawyers. What it would mean to actually face a prison sentence.

None of those images live up to the terror I'm feeling right now about all the bad things that are about to happen. To me. To my family.

To Carson.

The front door crashes open, and Carson's feet pound the floor as she sprints back into the kitchen. Her eyes are wild, her pigtails flying out behind her. "Forgot my water bottle!" she cries, snatching it off the counter. She's already halfway out of the kitchen again when I grab her wrist and yank her back in, covering her lips with mine. I kiss her and wonder if this is the last time. Because if it turns out that I am going to be tried, I'm not going to make her stick around and wait for me. I won't put her through that. Not when she's finally getting her own life together. Not when she's made so much progress.

And so I kiss her like I might never get another chance. Like I'll need to remember this one for the rest of my life.

It won't be hard.

She sinks into me, her hands pressed against my chest as she whimpers into my mouth. Her tongue tangles with mine, and I devour every sound, every sigh. I sketch them all onto my brain, permanent little tattoos disguised as memories.

She pulls back too soon, but then again, there will never be enough time with her.

"What was that for?" she asks with a grin.

"Just a little extra good luck for today," I tell her, because I'm not going to unload on her, not when she's about to do this thing she's worked so hard for. I won't fuck that up for her.

Her smile is wide as a sunrise over a cornfield. "Thank you," she says, then steps out of my arms. I feel her absence like it has weight. "I gotta run. See you tonight?"

And then I do the worst thing I can possibly imagine.

I lie to her.

CHAPTER 36

DAN

The flight to New York is uneventful, unless you count the baby who cries from takeoff to landing. I think they call that foreshadowing.

I'm too miserable to care.

I land in New York at five and sit in traffic for an hour, trying to get from LaGuardia to Greenpoint. I'm nearly to Jameson and Marcel's apartment when I tell the Uber driver to pull over.

The shop looks the same as it did when I left two years ago. Eamon gave me a compass on the inside of my biceps for the road. Funny that it brought me back here.

The sidewalk is somewhat crowded for a Sunday evening, people doing their last errands before the new week begins or squeezing in a meal at one of the bistros that line the trendy street. Everywhere I look there are faces, and none of them are looking at me.

I used to love the anonymity of New York. It felt big and crowded and free. I reveled in it, the invisibility. But all I feel right now is the itch to be seen by the one person who may never look at me again.

"Dude!" Eamon says as he shuffles out of the back. He looks the same, though I'm sure he's gotten at least a dozen new tattoos since the last time I saw him. He's still got plenty of real estate, though designs are starting to creep up his neck and down his knuckles. He pulls me in for a back-slapping hug. "Long time! How goes it? How's Drake and the shop?"

I glance at my watch. Her scrimmage is starting right now. I know she's in the first lineup. She's proud to have earned the spot. I should be sitting in the bleachers of the rec center cheering her on. I should be watching the love of my life do what she loves.

I should have known better than to encourage her feelings for me. I've been poison for her from the beginning, and knowing that I'm hurting her *right fucking now*? That she's scanning the crowd for me and that she won't find me? It causes an ache deep in my chest that I don't think anything will ever ease.

All I can do is distract myself from that pain with something else.

"I don't actually have a whole lot of time," I say. I texted Marcel that I had to make a stop, but I've probably only bought myself an hour at the most before they're expecting me for dinner. "Can you get me in? I need you to do a quick piece for me."

"Of course," Eamon says, leading me back to his booth. "What have you got in mind?"

When I sit down in the chair, ready to feel every single press of the needle, I crack and pull out my phone. The scrimmage is well underway now. There's no chance a message from me could distract her, so tap out a text. I can't tell if sending it makes me more or less of a coward.

Then I put my phone down and suppress the urge to ask Eamon to press harder.

CHAPTER 37
CARSON

He's not here.

I take my position on the pivot line at the back of the pack. Jax is beside me looking fierce, Mercedes in front of them. A vet named Spitfire is playing pivot at the front of the pack, rounding out the blocking lineup for our team. Madelyn is our jammer.

I make eye contact with each of them as we wait for the whistle to blow. I should be going over strategy and rules. I should be sizing up the opposing blockers, my fellow freshies and future teammates.

Instead, all I can think about is the fact that he's not here.

I looked for him during warm-ups and when Violet, playing the role of announcer, introduced us to the crowd of our families and friends. Grace and Wyatt are both here, wearing brand-new Bloomington Brawlers T-shirts. Decker and Owen are with them, and Felix too, though I think he's mostly here to check out the other skaters. He was eyeing Mercedes during warm-ups.

At first I figured Dan was just running late. That maybe his tattoo appointment ran over. But there weren't any messages on my phone. I broke down and asked Grace if she'd heard anything from him, and the look on her face when she said no made me want to cry.

I'm half mad, half terrified that something awful has happened to him. Maybe he got in a car wreck or there was a carbon monoxide leak at the house. Maybe he was mugged, or maybe he's just stuck in traffic.

A million possibilities fill my mind, ranging from mundane to horrifying, and I fixate on each one.

TWEEEEEEEET.

The whistle blows, and my body reacts, even if my brain doesn't. Maude Forbid, blocking for the white team, can sense my distraction and immediately cracks me in the sternum with her shoulder.

I got down in a heap.

Shit. I need to get my head in the game.

I jump up onto my skates and take off, trying to catch up to the pack, just barely in front of the approaching jammers. It's embarrassing to be behind already, but when I glance over my shoulder, I realize that I'm in a perfect position to let Mercedes draft off me. I catch her eye and give her a nod, then race forward, closing in on Maude from the outside. Just like Violet taught me, I bend my knees and lead with my hip, popping up when I make contact to shove her to the inside of the track.

She goes down, and Mercedes sprints by, finding a hole in the front of the pack. The ref points at her and blows the whistle, awarding her lead jammer.

Unfortunately J'Nisha, the white team jammer, sneaks out of the pack right behind her, and it's a foot race to get around the track and approach the back of the pack. I hustle to get to the front, because if J'Nisha manages to get her hips past mine, her team gets a point off of me.

Mercedes darts into the pack, tapping her hips to call off the jam.

The opening score is 1–0, black team.

I hit the team bench, my chest heaving. Violet is bench

coaching for my team. She hustles over. "Maude woke you up right off the bat there," she says, handing me my water bottle. "You recovered well. Keep your eyes open out there, okay?"

"Yup," I say, and force myself not to look out into the stands.

"You okay?" Violet asks, knees bent so we're eye-to-eye.

"Yup," I say, hoping she'll believe me.

I don't think she does, but she knows better than to get into it now. Instead, she taps me on top of my helmet and moves down the line to send other skaters out onto the track.

I go back out in the fourth lineup, Jax by my side again. I'm starting to block out Dan's absence and really get into the game. This time the two of us decide to try some partner blocking. When Tilly, who's jamming for the white team, hits the back of the pack, Jax and I form a wall of ass, holding her back while Mercedes, jamming for us again, whips around the outside with a helping hand from Jax. We manage to hold Tilly back for almost a full lap, giving Mercedes the opportunity to score five points.

As we approach the half, everyone's adrenaline is up. I can hear Wyatt and Grace's screams and Decker's loud whistles, and they fuel me. Despite my rough start, I'm in it now. Violet keeps sending Jax and me out together; our wall of ass is becoming a signature move. My hips have come alive, and I've started taking down opposing jammers, smiling as I send them out of bounds.

I'm sweating and aching and smiling and having the time of my fucking life.

Almost.

There are just under two minutes left in the half when Violet sends me back out on the track. I line up against Maude again. She's tried to take me down twice more, but each time I've shaken off her attacks.

I think I'm ready for her.

I don't even see Madelyn coming.

She's skinny but sharp. When her shoulder collides with mine, the pain is instantaneous. I make the tragic mistake of standing straight up in shock.

And that's when Maude swoops in.

Her knees are bent, her ass low, but this time her hip doesn't connect with mine. Instead she slides in front of me, tossing her shoulder back. It connects with my sternum, sending me backward just as Mercedes hits the pack. I try to catch myself, but it's no use.

I go down.

Hard.

Mercedes tries to jump over me, a tangle of arms and legs on the floor, but she can't get enough height and trips, her skate landing directly on my ankle.

I scream.

CHAPTER 38
DAN

"Dan, you've got to eat something," Jameson says.

We're gathered around the kitchen table in their small but well-appointed apartment. Jameson has cooked chicken parmesan using pasta he made from scratch. It smells incredible, but I feel like my stomach is full of lead.

"Leave him alone," Marcel gently chides, then refills my wine glass. *That* I have an appetite for. I'm not drunk, but I'm two glasses in and appreciate the low-level numbness that has taking over my body. Marcel reaches over and places a hand on my arm. "I'm still not totally sure what all's going on. Like I said, the call from the lead investigator was very odd. I think there's something strange happening with this case."

"Yeah, like the fact that the wrong guy is going to prison," Jameson snaps. He raises his glass in a snarky toast. "Eat the rich."

"I was rich," I say, sliding my eyes toward Jameson.

"Oh, please. Compared to Anders Holt, you were practically Little Orphan Annie. That motherfucker was rich and he *still* stole. From elderly people! It's only our corrupt capitalist system that has you fearing for your future right now."

"Sweetheart, you went to Princeton," Marcel gently reminds his husband.

"I majored in art history!" Jameson cries. He's also had a couple glasses of wine.

I shift in my chair, the ache on my thigh from the new tattoo a welcome reprieve from the ever-growing headache at the base of my skull. To say nothing of the way my heart feels like it's cracking open. I feel like an absolute motherfucker for leaving Carson like I did. I check my phone again, but there's no reply. Just the message I sent two hours ago.

DAN

> I had to go to New York. I'm sorry. I hope you crush it.

It was a pathetic attempt that I only made because I'm a selfish asshole. I probably should have made a clean break.

I deserve whatever I get tomorrow.

I check the time on my phone and see that it's only eight p.m. I have a feeling I won't be sleeping much tonight.

And then my phone vibrates in my hand. I nearly drop it trying to swipe it open, my heart in my throat, hoping for a text from Carson. Even a simple *fuck you* would be better than radio silence. I'd rather she fight with me than disappear.

But it's not Carson. It's my sister.

GRACE

> I don't know where you are, but Carson got hurt at the scrimmage. I'm at the ER with her. They think it's a broken ankle. No surgery, but I thought you should know

Her ankle isn't the only thing that's hurt, Dan

Fix it

"Shit," I mutter, fumbling with the phone as I try to type a response.

"Is everything okay?" Jameson asks.

"It's Carson. She's hurt," I say. My fingers hover over the screen, but I don't know what to say. Should I her I'm sorry? Tell her I love her? Tell her I'm probably going to prison tomorrow and that's the only thing that could keep me from her? None of it feels like enough. I should have told her everything when she raced back into the kitchen to grab her water bottle. I'm a fucking coward for running away.

Because tomorrow my entire life may be over, but tomorrow isn't today.

I stand so fast my chair nearly tips over.

"I need a flight," I say before I even know what I'm doing. My suitcase is still by the door, and I grab it.

"Dan, what?" Jameson cries.

"I have to go back. She's hurt and she's in the hospital and I just *left* her," I say, my voice driven to the point of madness. "I fucking left her, and I need to go back."

Marcel stands and comes around the table, approaching me like I'm a lion and he's the tamer. "Dan, I know you're freaking out. That's natural. But tomorrow we're going to figure this out. Even if you get indicted, that doesn't mean you're going to prison. There will still be a trial. All the evidence you saved? We can use that for your defense. A jury will believe you. I will *make* a jury believe you. But you need to stay here and face this."

"Face *what*? If they're going to arrest me, they can do it in Indiana just as well as in New York," I tell him. I'm already on the

Delta website, searching for the earliest available flight. There's one at ten thirty that I can make if I hurry.

"Dan, this isn't—"

"Fuck this!" I roar. "I've spent two years in Indiana waiting to find out if my life was over, and while I was waiting, I found a new one. I made a new life that was good and…and…*happy*. I was happy in a way I never thought I could be, and it was only a temporary bout of madness that made me walk away from it."

I shrug on my suit jacket and reach for my suitcase.

"If they want me, they know where to find me."

CHAPTER 39
CARSON

"I brought you a Coke," Grace says, creeping into the little curtained area in the Bloomington emergency room where I've been for the last six hours. It's almost midnight, and I'm exhausted, and I'm sticky from dried sweat and smelly and my ankle hurts and my heart is broken.

DAN

I had to go to New York. I'm sorry. I hope you crush it.

For the ten thousandth time, I stare down at the text and let out a bitter laugh. Crush it? I *got* crushed, Dan.

In so many ways.

I keep replaying the moment before I left the house, when he pulled me in for that knee-melting kiss. I was distracted and nervous and didn't pay attention, but looking back, something was definitely up. He had a desperate look in his eye that I chalked up to lust, but it was obviously more than that. What happened that made him board a flight without saying a word to me?

After I hit the ground during the scrimmage, there was a cacophony of whistles. Violet came racing out along with the medic. My ankle was already swelling, so they eased off my skate and helped me to the sideline. Grace sprang into action, running to the locker room to gather my stuff while Owen looked at my ankle. I talked everyone out of calling an ambulance, and Owen agreed that Grace could give me a ride to the emergency room.

It wasn't until I'd settled into a curtained-off bed for my interminable wait that I pulled out my phone and learned that Dan had left the state.

Grace hasn't said a word about her brother's absence.

"Thanks," I tell her, reaching for the Styrofoam cup.

A doctor in a white coat who looks like he's about twelve breezes into the space, his eyes never leaving the iPad in his hands. "Okay, looks like you have a Weber A fracture—hey, Carson Webber! That's appropriate!" He looks up at me like I'm going to laugh at the coincidence. Instead I burst into tears. His eyes go wide as dinner plates. "Hey, it's okay! Of all the ankle fractures to get, this is probably the best one. Just six weeks in a boot, and you should be good to go. It'll look like a Picasso for a few days until the swelling goes down and the bruising starts to fade, but it should feel better in a week or so. And once you're done with the boot, you shouldn't have any other complications."

He flips the iPad around so I can see the X-ray, but the image is blurry through my tears. It's the first time I've cried since Mercedes landed on my leg, and it doesn't have a thing to do with the injury.

"I think she's just a little overwhelmed and tired," Grace says, smiling as she ushers the doctor away from me.

"I'll just put in the order for the boot," he says, looking slightly traumatized. This kid is going to need to toughen up if he plans to work in an emergency department. The eye black running down my cheeks cannot be the most horrifying thing this man has ever seen.

"Yup, we'll be here," Grace says, whisking the curtain shut behind him. She turns and rolls her eyes. "I cannot believe society thinks men are stronger than women."

I chuckle through my tears.

"Oh, honey, I'm so sorry this is happening," Grace says, pulling the flimsy plastic chair beside the bed closer. She drops down into it. "But it sounds like you're going to be back on your feet in no time, and you were so incredible out there today. I bet you won't lose a step."

"I was pretty good, wasn't it?" I say between sniffles.

"You were better than good," she says. "I just wish you could have enjoyed it."

I wait for her to say something else, maybe remind me that she warned me about Dan. That I'm sunshine and he's rain, that he doesn't know how to open up, that I shouldn't be surprised that he's left me without a word.

She doesn't.

"He wasn't there," I say, the tears coming faster now.

"I know," she says, taking my hand in hers and stroking her thumb across my skin. "But if he had to go to New York, I'm sure it was for something really—"

The curtain flies open, and his frame fills the small space. He's wearing a dark navy suit, his white dress shirt rumpled, his collar open and his gray tie loose. His eyes are dark and wild, like he hasn't slept in days, and his chest is heaving like he sprinted all the way here from New York.

"Are you okay?" he asks, his voice a deep rasp, like its clawing its way out of his throat.

"No, she's not okay," Grace snaps. "She has a fractured fibula, and you weren't there."

"I know, I—"

"No," Grace says, jumping up from her chair. She approaches her brother, puts a hand on his chest, and gives him a gentle shove. "Dan, you're my brother and I love you, but *no*. You don't get to come crashing in here looking all tortured and expect her to listen to your excuses. The time for explanations was *before* you jumped on a plane and left Carson wondering where the hell you went."

But Dan plants his feet into the shiny white floor of the hospital, his eyes never leaving mine.

"I know. I know I hurt you, Carson, and I'm so fucking sorry. Please just let me explain."

Grace, my best friend and personal hospital bouncer, looks at me over her shoulder, her eyebrows raised.

I give her a nod, and she turns back to Dan. Based on the way he takes the tiniest step back, she must be giving him a hell of a glare.

"I'll be right outside," she says, and I don't know if that's meant to reassure me or threaten him.

He stands there, feet planted wide, his hand scrubbing the back of his head, looking absolutely tortured.

And I let him.

For a bit, anyway.

"You left," I say finally, the words coming out as a watery whisper.

Dan looks like I've driven a knife between his ribs.

"Yeah," he croaks.

"And what's worse, you left without talking to me," I say. "You're supposed to talk to me. That's what we did. We talked."

He hangs his head. "I know."

I sigh. "I thought...I don't know. It's just, I thought maybe this all meant more—"

His gaze snaps back up. He takes two long steps toward me but stops short of the bed. "It does," he says, his voice desperate. "It means so much more. *You* mean so much more. Fuck, Carson, you mean everything."

I shake my head. "But when it came down to it, you left."

He closes his eyes, breathing in like he's trying to endure physical pain. "I made a mistake. I'm so, *so* sorry."

I don't know what to say. I want to reflexively accept his apology. To toss off an *it's fine*. To brush it all away. That's what I do. It's a hazard of being a generally positive person.

But it's not fine. I'm not okay.

"You hurt me," is what I finally say.

Dan drops to his knees, leaning on the bed like he's going to pray for my forgiveness. "I know. I fucked it all up. Marcel called and told me I was probably being indicted, that I needed to come or they'd arrest me here, in front of you. And I just couldn't bear it, Carson. I couldn't do that to you."

"What you did was worse."

"I know that now. And I'll regret it forever," he says. "You've spent this summer becoming the fiercest, most independent version of you. Tonight I was going to get to see you prove it. See you be out loud the person you've always been inside, and I fucked it up. I ruined that moment for you, and I'll never forgive myself."

I'm crying again, silent tears streaking down my face. It's all too much. My ankle hurts, it's sinking in that I won't be able to play roller derby for a while, and this man who wrecked my heart, really raked it over the coals, is on his knees at my bedside, apologizing.

And he's here.

He flew to New York, then turned around and came back.

For me.

"Wait, did you say you're getting arrested?" I ask.

"Yeah."

My mouth drops open. "Dan, that's a big deal. What are you *doing* here?"

"I don't know. I just knew that I couldn't live with myself for treating you like that. I get it if you can't trust me anymore. I've certainly given you every reason to think you aren't important to me. But please, let me make it up to you. If you give me another chance, I'll spend as long as I have proving how much I love you. I'll be at every derby game. I'll buy you that wallpaper and hang it wherever you want. I'll follow you wherever you want to go. Please, just let me back in. I'll be the luckiest motherfucker on the planet if you let me bask in your sunshine a little longer."

He takes my hands in his and gazes up at me, his eyes filled with desperation. "I love you, Carson. I'm a coward and an asshole for not telling you that earlier. But please, let me tell you now. Let me tell you forever. I love you, my sunshine girl."

"Fuck, Dan," I say, laughing through tears as I realize, the combination of the emotions letting me know that I'm going to be okay. That *we're* going to be okay. "I love you too, goddammit."

He lets out a breath like he's been yanked back from a ledge. Then a smile begins to spread across his face. "There's that dirty mouth."

He stands, leaning over the bed, and gives me a look that says, *may I?*

I reach for his tie, wrap it around my fist, and pull him down until he's kissing me, his lips repeating every beautiful thing he said to me. He groans into my mouth, his knee landing on the bed beside me as he moves to cover my body with his.

"I was so good today, Dan," I say against his lips. "I killed it."

I feel his smile against my mouth. "I have no doubt, baby."

Someone clears their throat nearby, and I look up to see the teenage doctor holding his iPad and the boot I've been sentenced to.

"Sorry to, uh, interrupt," he says, his cheeks red. "We ready for this?"

———

The boot, as Nancy Sinatra so famously sang, is made for walking.

But apparently not for a week or so.

My ankle throbs when I put any weight on it, so the hospital issues me a pair of crutches to go with it. It takes another two hours to get discharged, during which Grace and Dan get my car from the rec center. Grace gives her brother a stern look before leaving me with him.

By the time Dan and I pull up to the house, I'm nearly wild with exhaustion and emotional overload. I feel like my eyes are spinning in two different directions, so it's good when Dan comes around to the passenger side and dumps my crutches in the grass, scooping me out of the car and into his arms like a damsel in distress.

"Do you want to try to take a shower?" he asks, and while I definitely need one, I think I'm too exhausted.

"In the morning," I say through a yawn. "I think just bed."

Dan places me gently on the bed in the guest room.

"Arms up," he says, reaching for the hem of my shirt.

"I can do it," I retort, but he gives me a stern look.

"Let me help," he growls, all authoritative in that dangerously tailored suit. Yeah, I'm definitely going to let this happen.

He peels off my shirt and sports bra, planting gentle kisses on my bare breasts before helping me lift my hips and sliding down the black spandex shorts. When he sees that I'm wearing nothing beneath them, as usual, he lets out a growl that sounds like a caged tiger.

"I think I'll just sleep like this," I say, giving him a smirk as I recline naked on the bed. I gesture to that sexy suit of his. "You next."

Now it's his turn to smirk.

He steps back, loosening his tie and pulling it off, looking like a real live suit daddy ready to level me with a sexy, stern look. He winds the tie around his hand like a boxer wrapping his knuckles, then places it on the bedside table. He shrugs off his suit jacket and makes slow work of the buttons on his shirt, revealing his bare skin and ink in torturous increments.

"I feel like I should be slipping dollar bills into your belt," I say hungrily.

"I think I'm at least worth fives," he says with a raised brow.

His belt clinks, and I squeeze my thighs together, the sound deliciously sexy.

But everything changes when he lowers those impeccably tailored suit pants. His muscular thigh, formerly bare, now features fresh ink.

"I got it today," he says, glancing down at the art. "I stopped by my old shop when I got to Brooklyn."

"It's a lemon," I say, my eyes widening as I take it in. It's just like mine. Only—

"It's the other half," he says. And I see it immediately. My bisected lemon fits together with his to make a whole. "I hope it's okay."

"Dan…" I whisper, at a loss for words. All I can do is beckon him closer. He drops his boxers and comes toward me, crawling onto the bed and propping himself over me.

"I love you, Carson," he says. He plants a gentle kiss on my lips.

"I love you, Dan," I whisper, and run my hands up his muscular back. I arch into him, chasing the sensation of his hard length against my soft skin. I reach down, grip him in my fist, and give him a long, slow stroke that makes his chest rumble, the metal in his cock digging into my palm. "Now, my ankle hurts a little bit. Do you think you could do something to distract me from the pain?"

"I have one other surprise for you," he says with a devious grin.

"Tramp stamp?" I ask, smiling wide.

He laughs, then reaches for the bedside table, pulling open the little drawer. He takes out a sheet of paper. "I did this before I went and epically fucked up. It was going to be your post-scrimmage gift."

I open the folded sheet to find a lab report.

"I got tested. All clear," he says.

My eyes widen, and I look up at him. "Wait, so we can—"

He nods. "If you want to. I'm absolutely fine with using

condoms for as long as you want, but you said you were curious about the added sensation of the barbells, and...well, you can feel them better bare, so—"

"*Yes*," I hiss, bringing a thigh up over his hip, opening myself to him. "Oh my god, this is the best, most filthy surprise I've ever received."

"Let me," he says, his fingers trailing down until they reach my slick heat. "Jesus, Carson. You're soaked."

"Between that tattoo and the news that I get to feel you inside me bare, this is turning out to be one of the best nights of my life," I say. "And that's *with* the broken ankle."

"High praise," he says, dragging the head of his cock up my slit, pausing at my clit until my eyes nearly roll back with need. Then he glides back down, slipping inside me up to the first barbell. I feel the chill of the metal and hiss, pressing into him. "Gentle," he chides.

"I don't want gentle," I whine, rolling my hips. "I want it all."

"Greedy girl," he whispers into my neck as his tongue laves my skin in gentle strokes. Then he snaps his hips, his cock stretching me, filling me, and I cry out. He presses a palm down into my lower belly, dragging himself out, and fuck, I feel every ridge of him, natural and augmented. The friction of the barbells sends little zips of pressure and pleasure racing through my body.

"More," I cry, writhing on his cock, desperate for the sensation of him moving inside me.

"You feel so fucking good, baby," he grits out as his hips pull back once again. When he presses in, I arch my back to meet him. He drops his lips to my nipple, laving the dusky pebbled peak with the flat of his tongue. "So fucking good."

Then he drops his fingers to my clit, rubbing messy, frantic circles as his thrusts grow deeper, harder, and I rise to meet them. I whine and beg, the edges of my vision crowded with stars as I chase my orgasm.

"I want you to come," Dan pants, his muscles bunched as he

works to pull me over the edge. "I want you to come, and then I want to come on you."

"*Yessss*," I hiss, the request hitting me right as I feel myself tip over the peak, tumbling down into an abyss of stars and sensation. I scream his name, clutching his shoulders as my body spasms with pleasure. "Fuck, Dan, come! Now!"

He pulls out, grasping his cock in his fist, his eyes hooded as he watches the aftershocks shake my core, my chest heaving as I work to catch my breath. I reach up and press my breasts together, my fingers dancing over my nipples as I beg, "Come on me, Dan. I want it."

He loses control with a shout, painting me with warm ropes of pleasure.

When he's wrung out and folded over, his hand pressing into the bed beside my cheek, he locks eyes with me.

"You are going to be the death of me," he whispers. "And I cannot wait."

CHAPTER 40
DAN

"We have to talk about the fact that your STI test came from a pediatrician's office," Carson says from her perch on the couch, her ankle propped up on a stack of pillows with an ice pack on top.

I set the tray of snacks down on the coffee table beside her. "I don't have health insurance right now, so Owen was my only option. Indiana isn't exactly rolling in free clinics."

"Ugh, sad but true," she groans. She hands me the ice pack and reaches for her boot. "God, I look like such a wreck."

"More like an adorable fender bender," I say. "How's it feeling?"

"It's fine as long as I don't move it," she says.

"Luckily there are plenty of ways for me to make you come that don't involve your ankle."

"Yes, I'll just starfish in the middle of the bed and you can go to work. Very sexy," she laughs.

"Don't threaten me with a good time."

The doorbell shatters the mood.

I have no regrets about fleeing New York and my potential prosecution. Even if I get only twenty-four happy hours with Carson before my life turns upside down, it'll be worth it. But the fear of what could be coming for me is like a high-pitched noise that's been squealing quietly beneath everything else since we woke up this morning. I tried calling Marcel but had no luck. I googled to see if there were any press releases, but there was nothing.

So now I'm just waiting for police officers to show up on the doorstep and lead me away.

And it feels like maybe that's about to happen now.

From the way Carson tenses, her eyes filling with worry, I can tell she's thinking it too. I filled her in on everything last night.

"I've got it," I say, crossing the floor and pulling open the door.

"Surprise!" Jameson says from the stoop, a rolling suitcase at his feet. He thrusts a paper bag into my hands. "These muffins are *excellent*. I don't know why you're always complaining about this town."

"It's quite charming," Marcel says, following his husband through the door. "Though I wouldn't last more than three days here before I required a real slice of pizza and a Broadway show."

"To say nothing of the corn. Popular culture really undersells the sheer number of cornfields. How much corn could you people possibly be eating?" Jameson sticks out his hand to Carson, the same wide and welcoming grin on his face that he gave me way back in freshman year. "I'm Jameson Lewis, your boyfriend's college roommate. Pleased to meet you. So sorry to hear about your ankle."

Carson shakes his hand, returning his smile. "Carson Webber. And thank you. You can express your sympathy by telling me all about this one in college." She points at me, waggling her eyebrows. "I'm dying to hear about the lost years of Dan McBride."

"The jeans were so skinny," Jameson says. "I'll start looking for pictures on my phone."

"Please, no," I groan. "What are you two doing here? Do you have an update?"

"Boy, do I," Marcel says, sinking into the gingham armchair in the corner of the living room. "I took the meeting without you. I'm charging you double for that."

"And I'm still mad you didn't eat my chicken parm. It was *excellent*," Jameson adds.

"Someday I hope to be able to actually pay you," I say to Marcel. Since my savings ran out several months ago, he's been working basically pro bono.

"That day might come sooner than you think." He pulls a thick file out of his bag. "Anders was indicted this morning. The court saw him as a considerable flight risk, so they confiscated his passport. His bail is eye-wateringly high."

I blink, trying to make sense of the words. "Wait, *Anders* was indicted?"

Marcel nods. "Remember how I said the meeting invite was strange? That it was unusual to be called to surrender before a grand jury was even impaneled?"

"Michigan Law is so proud that he figured that out," Jameson says, stroking his husband's cheek as he grins.

Marcel brushes him off with an eye roll. "Apparently the feds have been focusing on Anders for months, but in an effort to keep him from fleeing the jurisdiction, they kept up the fiction that it was *you* they were interested in. Anders has had private investigators keeping tabs on you, so the feds figured calling you in would be a clever ruse to keep him from hopping on a private plane on Monday before they could arrest him."

My mouth drops open. "You've got to be kidding."

"I'm not. They actually did want to meet with you, though," he says, shaking the file. "Turns out your evidence led directly to Anders's arrest. Which makes you, my friend, a whistleblower."

My mouth drops open.

"Oh shit, does this mean you have to go into witness protection?" Carson asks from the couch.

I shake my head. "Is this real?"

"It is. The Securities and Exchange Commission has determined that your information is worth twelve percent," he says, a smile spreading across his face.

"Twelve percent of what?" Carson asks.

Marcel turns to her. "According to SEC whistleblower laws, anyone who provides information that leads to a conviction receives a percentage of the money that's recovered by the investigation. The percentage is based on level of information. How useful it is in the investigation." Marcel looks at me, a brow raised. "You, sir, were docked for not going to the authorities the moment you discovered the discrepancy. Instead, you tipped off Anders by bringing it to him. So they're offering you twelve percent instead of the maximum thirty."

"Twelve percent of *what*?" Carson asks again.

"Fourteen million dollars," Marcel says, and my heart does several somersaults in my chest.

Carson gasps. "So that's—"

"More than one point six million dollars," I finish, doing the math faster. "You're fucking kidding me."

"I'm not," Marcel says. "You will, of course, be paying a percentage of that to me."

"Are you kidding? Take as much as you want," I say, pulling him in for a hug. "You saved my life."

"Did you hear that, honey? He said it in front of witnesses. As much as you want!" Jameson laughs, throwing me a wink.

"So it's really over?"

"Well, you won't get the money until after the conviction, but from what I hear, Anders's high-powered lawyers are already trying to cut a deal that would involve a guilty plea. So it's only a matter of time," Marcel says. He sits, crossing his leg over his knee and leaning back in his chair with a satisfied grin. "So yes, it's over."

"Dan, I just want you to know that if I didn't have this broken ankle, I would be leaping into your arms right now," Carson says.

"I've got it," I say, crossing the floor. I pick her up, and as her arms go around my neck and her thighs hook over my hips, I kiss her. I kiss her like it's the first time, not like it's going to be the last. The first of so many more to come.

"Can't believe I bagged me a millionaire," she giggles against my lips.

"How would you feel about letting me buy us a house?" I ask.

EPILOGUE

CARSON

The afternoon sun is streaming into the kitchen through the red and yellow leaves of the enormous elm tree in the backyard. The dappled autumn light makes the lemon wallpaper glow.

We closed on the house just after Labor Day, a charming two-story colonial near campus. Built in 1928, we could afford it because the last family hadn't updated it since the late eighties. The bathrooms have a lot of teal tile, there's a black toilet in the powder room, and the wallpaper borders are atrocious.

But I don't care. I can't wait to renovate it, room by room, with Dan at my side.

We started with the kitchen, and I was right about that lemon wallpaper. It's going to be bright even on the cloudiest of days.

I love this house so much that I frequently joke that I'm going to die here. Each time, Dan replies, "Not soon, I hope," before kissing me.

At the end of the summer, I started teaching at an elementary school a mile from our house. On nice days, I can ride my bike there. On really nice days, I walk.

I decided to wait to apply to the Master of Arts in Teaching program and instead spend this year getting used to my new life, the one I worked so hard to build for myself. I also wanted to see what a full season of roller derby felt like before adding a graduate course load to my schedule. So far I'm loving my rhythm of school, practice, and coming home to make dinner with Dan in our sunny yellow kitchen.

My parents are coming to visit us for Thanksgiving, a trip they arranged with plenty of notice. They were a little freaked out at first when I told them Dan and I were buying a house together. The speed with which we made the decision didn't bother them; it was more about the order of operations. To them, the proper order is to get engaged, then married, *then* move in together. The living in sin thing was quite the adjustment.

They're coming around.

And when they express opinions I don't agree with about how I should live my life, I'm learning how to gently set boundaries with them.

I even got a text from my Mom this morning:

MOM

Kick butt today, honey! Send us pictures!

"How do I look?" I ask Dan, holding my arms out to the sides.

Today the Bloomington Brawlers are playing the Cincinnati Attack Pack, and I'm playing my first ever game with the travel team in my new red-and-white jersey. I turn so Dan can read the name, GLUTEUS MAXXIMUS, and my number—four, in honor of my quads. I've got stripes of eye black on my cheeks, my hair in long pigtails down my shoulders.

"You look like you're going to ruin some girl's life today," Dan says, his eyes molten as they rove over my body.

I grin. "I'll do my best."

I have to be at the rec center in an hour for track setup, and I'm practically vibrating with nerves. Partly because last time I did this, I broke my ankle, and partly because this is my first real game. We sold tickets to this one—sold it out, in fact. The crowd is going to be large and loud, and Cincinnati is a tough team.

And I want to win.

"Okay, Felix says he's setting up the tailgate an hour before doors open. Your entire family is going to be there. Sorry I can't be a buffer, but we have warm-ups," I say, rattling off the schedule.

"I will be there," Dan says. "I promise."

"Good." I gather up my gear bag and double-check the lid on my water bottle.

"Before you go, I need you to approve my outfit," he says, rushing out of the kitchen, as giddy as I am. Since the investigation wrapped and Dan settled into life in Bloomington, deciding to use his freedom and his award money to commit to tattooing full-time, his personal storm clouds seem to have cleared. He's still quiet and I can tell when my man would prefer to Irish goodbye a room. I'm the first person to help him pull it off. But he doesn't seem to have any trouble talking to me.

"I hope it's that sexy suit," I call, even though most of his suits didn't make it to the house. He kept a few for special occasions (i.e. when I want him to put one on so I can take it off of him), but making his living as a tattoo artist means he doesn't need quite so many Italian suits.

It's fine—I prefer him in a T-shirt. Especially now that his tattoos have started migrating down his arms. I didn't think his corded forearms could get much sexier, but then the ink started appearing. Respectable? No thank you. I like him dirty.

Dan returns to the kitchen in a red Bloomington Brawlers T-shirt that stretches dangerously across his pecs and over his shoulders. Then he turns.

Stretched across his broad shoulders, the shirt reads MR. MAXX.

"You asshole!" I cry.

He turns, stricken. "What?"

"I can't believe you showed me that when I don't have time to fuck you!" I stomp my foot on the floor for effect.

He grins and grabs me, pulling me in for a knee-melting kiss. "I have one more thing to show you before you go."

"Oh yeah?" I hook my finger into his waistband, peering down into his jeans. "More metal?"

He swats my hand away. "If you want more, I'll do it for you, but only if you're willing to forgo sex for several months while it heals."

I shake my head, my nose wrinkling. "No deal."

"Well, then, I guess this is all the metal I've got to offer," he says, then sinks to his knee on the floor of our perfect kitchen. Clutched in his large fingers is a dainty gold band, a single round diamond set in the center.

I gasp, my fingers flying to my mouth.

"Carson Jane Webber, I didn't really figure out who I was until I saw myself through your eyes. Now I'm not myself without you by my side. Please tell me you'll marry me and let me spend the rest of my life warm in your sunshine."

I drop to my knees with him, grasping his face in my hands while I kiss him.

"Yes," I cry, laughing as I press my forehead to his. "Of course! Yes please oh my god I can't wait!"

He grins and takes my left hand, then slides the ring onto my finger. I hold it up to catch that perfect October sunlight.

Then I burst into tears.

"Oh no, baby," he says, pulling me in. "Are these happy tears?"

"Yes, but also…" I hiccup, gazing at the ring, which sparkles in the warm sunlight. "I'm going to have to take this off to play so I don't lose it! But I don't want to take it off! It's so pretty!"

Dan laughs. "I'll get there early and come back to the locker room to take it from you. Then you can be free to skate like the bruiser you are. I'll slip it back on you after the game."

"Really? You promise not to lose it?" I ask, laughing through tears.

"Carson, I've had this ring since right after Marcel and Jameson came to tell me I was free. That was the day my life began again, and I knew I wanted to spend it with you. I've just been carrying it around, waiting for the right time."

I glare at him. "You've had this for more than three months? And I didn't know?"

"Well, now I use my broody, mysterious powers for good." He winks, then kisses me again, and it feels like another new beginning. We keep finding those together, Dan and I. When the case ended. When we found this house. The day we moved in together. When we hung the lemon wallpaper. We're going to have a whole lifetime of new beginnings.

I can't wait to see what comes next.

ACKNOWLEDGMENTS

I wrote this book while opening a bookstore, and it was the craziest, best decision I ever made. Thank you to Rayanne Streeter, the founder and co-owner of Good Girl Books, for being my biggest cheerleader in the romance community. Thank you for all the TikToks and fountain cokes. The community you've built in Knoxville in such a short time is INCREDIBLE! Thank you also to our store manager Katie Hopper for all the butt pats and hugs. You are the engine that runs this very pink truck, and I'm pretty sure I'd be in shambles without you! And thank you to every Good Girl (and Good Boy and Good Pal!) who's shopped at GGB and bought my books there. You guys are the reason I do this.

Thank you to my fabulous agent Kate Testerman, who is the reason you can listen to the Cardinal Springs series! I've never felt more supported in my career than when I got Kate in my corner.

Thank you to Tiffany Schmidt, who read this book when it was a disaster draft, who encouraged me to write when I didn't want to, and who unlocked a major character arc/chemistry beat that changed this whole book. I don't know if it's possible for me to write a book without you!

Thank you to Hannah Slaughter, who texted me frequently to tell me she wanted to read about Dan skinny dipping. I would be lost without our bestie breakfast. Thank you for manifesting our friendship and bringing all the color to it!

Thanks to my boys, (please don't ever read this). Thank you to Poptart for snoozing underneath my desk while I wrote.

Finally, thank you to Adam, my real life book boyfriend. I don't ever want to do a minute of this without you.

ABOUT THE AUTHOR

Lauren Morrill is the author of spicy adult and sweet YA romance. Active on social media, Mashable called her "one of those rare authors who tweets more about others' books than her own." Her publicist would like her to tweet a little bit more about her own books. She's working on it. Lauren grew up in Maryville, Tennessee, graduated with two degrees from Indiana University, spent four years playing roller derby in Boston, and now lives in Knoxville, Tennessee with her husband, two sons, and Poptart the pup. She is the co-owner of Good Girl Books, a romance bookstore in Knoxville.

ALSO BY LAUREN MORRILL

Cardinal Springs

More Than A Feeling

Caught Up In You

Just What I Needed

Heat of the Moment (coming soon!)

Sister of the Bride